THE
WANING
AGE

THE WANING AGE

by

S. E. GROVE

VIKING

VIKING

An imprint of Penguin Random House LLC
375 Hudson Street
New York, New York 10014

First published in the United States of America by Viking,
an imprint of Penguin Random House LLC, 2019

LIBRARY OF CONGRESS CATALOGING-IN-PUBLICATION DATA IS AVAILABLE.
ISBN 9780451479853

Printed in the U.S.A.

1   3   5   7   9   10   8   6   4   2

FOR MY BROTHER, OLIVER

"THE ALL-IMPORTANT EMOTION OF SYMPATHY IS DISTINCT FROM THAT OF LOVE. A mother may passionately love her sleeping and passive infant, but she can then hardly be said to feel sympathy for it. . . . Adam Smith formerly argued, as has Mr. Bain recently, that the basis of sympathy lies in our strong retentiveness of former states of pain or pleasure. Hence, 'the sight of another person enduring hunger, cold, fatigue, revives in us some recollection of these states, which are painful even in idea.' We are thus impelled to relieve the sufferings of another, in order that our own painful feelings may be at the same time relieved. . . . But I cannot see how this view explains the fact that sympathy is excited in an immeasurably stronger degree by a beloved than by an indifferent person. . . . Sympathy may at first have originated in the manner above suggested; but it seems now to have become an instinct, which is especially directed towards beloved objects. . . . In however complex a manner this feeling may have originated, as it is one of high importance to all those animals which aid and defend each other, it will have been increased, through natural selection; for those communities, which included the greatest number of the most sympathetic members, would flourish best and rear the greatest number of offspring."

—Charles Darwin, *The Descent of Man* (1871)

THE
WANING
AGE

NATALIA

The Landmark Hotel on Third Street off Market has four glass doors speckled with mercury and the portico is high-relief painted gold. The entrance gives the impression of a gilt mirror rescued from a duchess's castle. Inside, the walls are white marble, the lobby chairs are rose damask, and the carpet looks like the polar bear population of the Arctic, scythed and steamrolled. In the atrium the marble spills from walls to floor, making a cold white bowl beneath the crystal lid of the ceiling. Hotel guests and tony San Franciscans come to the atrium for lunch or tea, to hear the lone cellist who sits beside the potted palms on most afternoons to play Beethoven or, if the weather's foul, Schubert.

I almost never go to the atrium, because I clean rooms on floors seven to ten. Even if I could afford the macarons, the spiced chocolate, the flowered tea, and the sugared almonds, I wouldn't eat there. I don't like the company.

Case in point, the epic meltdown I'd been called down for. He was huddled on the floor of the men's room off the atrium: tanned, broad-shouldered, and only a few years older than me by the look of him. He wore a navy linen jacket and cream-colored pants in summer wool. The shoes, ocher suede, had a quatrefoil on the leather sole. I recognized the brand. One shoe would have cost me two months' wages. His knuckles were bleeding from where he'd pounded ineffectually at the marble. He was turned toward the wall, but I had caught a glimpse of his face when he flung it over his shoulder to shriek at us. Even brows, dark brown like the wavy hair; shadow on the jaw and dimpled chin; red, red eyes, wild as a hunted animal's, bulging and stricken. Taken all together, he was an allegory of vanity on a precipice. Then again, terror distorts faces. There was no telling what he might have looked like had he been calm and quiet.

I took a step forward to see if I could find out.

"Are you sure, Nat?" Olsen asked me. "I could just call the police." Olsen is one of the security guards. He's solid but he's new. He hasn't had to deal with too many of these yet.

"Nat can handle it," Marta said confidently, shooing him away with wide hands. She has too much faith in me, but it's true that I have practice.

"I'll give it a shot." I raised my eyebrows at Marta. "Better if we can spare him the trip to San Quentin."

At this the kid turned around and screamed, "Put me in San Quentin! Put me in San Quentin if it will keep them away from me!"

"Hey," I said, taking another step forward. I knelt down on the cold floor a yard from his feet.

"Stay away from me!" he screamed, throwing a terrified

glance over his shoulder. He was trembling, his bones rattling against the marble.

"My name is Nat," I continued. "You don't know me. You've never met me before. What's your name?"

He stared at me, eyes wide. He didn't say anything.

"See? I'm asking your name because we've never met. If you knew me, you would know my name, and I would know yours, right? What is it?"

"Troy," he said, turning away, his voice abruptly two octaves lower. It had a grated sound from all the screaming.

"Ah, Troy," I said. "Like the city, right? Hector and Achilles. Horses. Long speeches." He didn't budge. "You're right," I decided, changing tack. "Way too literary for the moment. Troy, let's talk about what's in this room." I looked around like I was taking inventory of a freight car. "There's two bathroom stalls, two urinals, two sinks, two mirrors. Two people on the floor—you and me. Two people standing— Marta and Olsen. Hm. Lots of twos." He followed my commentary, his eyes darting warily around the room. "Very hard floors, which you know already, and rather dim lights. We used to have brighter lights but the men complained about what it did to their complexions." I opened my eyes wide as if asking a three-year-old a question. "Do you know where we are?"

Troy blinked his red eyes. He looked at me suspiciously. "A hotel?"

"Yup." I nodded. "We're in the men's room on the ground floor of the Landmark. The atrium is right past that door. Were you having lunch there?"

"Ye-es?" The first part was a statement, and the second was a question.

"Were you by yourself or were you with someone?"

Troy crumpled. It always happens at some point, when the fear begins to ebb. His shaking grew more violent, but his eyes were soft. He wrapped his arms around himself. "My mom," he whispered.

"What's her name?"

"Frances Peters," he said.

I had to lean forward to hear it. "Great. Frances. And what is she wearing, do you remember, so we can find her more easily? We don't have a loudspeaker in the atrium, worse luck."

"She has brown hair," he said helpfully.

"Okay, Troy." I nodded to Olsen, who gave me a pair of raised eyebrows before heading out the door. "Can I put this on your shoulders?" I showed him the hotel blanket I was holding. He nodded. "Olsen is going to get her," I said, to keep talking as I hung the blanket over him. "She's the only other person who's coming through that door. No one else. Just you and me, Marta and Olsen, and your mom."

He nodded dumbly. His teeth were chattering, so I put my arm around him and tried to rub some warmth into his shoulders. He leaned against me. His cologne had citrus and cedar in it, and his hair was damp from the sweat. He felt as fragile as a bird.

"One time a couple months ago," I went on conversationally, "someone dropped a cuff link in the left-hand sink. Remember, Marta?"

Marta rolled her eyes. "Do I ever."

"They took the entire sink apart. Faucet, bowl, pipes. This place was a mess. You should have seen the contents of the pipes. Jewelry. Buttons. *Money*."

"Two bullets," Marta added.

"Yup. Even bullets. People do some strange things at the bathroom sink."

He shifted slightly so he could look at me sideways. His lower lip was trembling with cold. "Why are you being nice to me?" He forced the words out in a whisper.

It was a good question. The easy answer—because I work here and I clean up messes—was only partly true. And wouldn't help to distract him. "I have a kid brother," I said, "and he makes me practice being nice, like exercise for ogres. Ten-year-olds can be very demanding."

The door had opened when I started speaking, admitting Mrs. Frances Peters. She wore a raw silk suit and tasseled loafers. All the surgery made her face look slightly mis-assembled, like an experiment with spare parts. Ultra white. But she had the same dark eyebrows as Troy and the same long jaw. She studied her trembling son impassively. She looked as maternal as a rusty table saw.

"I know all about demanding ten-year-olds." Her voice was cold metal. "Get up," she said to Troy.

I stood and helped Troy to his feet. "He's going to need an arm on the way out," I said to Spare Parts.

"He can have your arm," she replied. "Troy earned this." She frowned, and her dark eyebrows strained together like leeches caught in concrete.

I looked at her. Troy beside me didn't even flinch. He was used to this. I debated for a moment and then wrapped my arm around Troy's waist. "Let's go," I said. "Put your arm on my shoulders."

He draped his arm shakily over me; then, as we started moving, he clung to me like a lifeboat. We followed the imperious backside of Mrs. Frances Peters out into the atrium and into the shiny lobby and through the glass doors to the curb, where Olsen had a cab waiting. I folded Troy into the backseat.

"Hey, dulce," I said to him quietly, leaning down into the cab. "I'm going to need the blanket back." He was staring straight ahead, still shivering like a man caught in a blizzard. "Troy," I said.

He looked up at me. "What?" he whispered. His pupils were still dilated with fear, but the light in them had changed. Through the flurry of the blizzard I could see a flicker of warmth.

"Aw, shucks," I said. "Just keep it." I stepped back and Olsen closed the door.

"Hey," I said to Spare Parts. She stopped near the trunk of the car. I stepped closer so that I wouldn't have to shout over the traffic. "If he's too much trouble, you could always sell him. I hear the prisons pay top dollar for boys under twenty."

She stared at me, the contempt gathering in the lines of her face. "You insolent tart."

I stepped closer. I felt Olsen's hand on my arm and I shook it off. "Tell me more. I still got lots to learn about insolence."

Olsen took my arm again and tugged. "Skip it this time," he said quickly.

"What is your name?" Troy's mother asked coldly.

"Natalia Peña. What are you going to do, Mrs. Frances Peters? Report to my boss that I peeled your son off the bathroom floor after his spectacular and completely avoidable crash? I'm sure she'll be horrified. Just maybe not at me."

She looked hard at me for another moment, and then her eyes filled with lazy amusement. She chuckled. She rounded the car and got in, and the cab took off.

2

NATALIA

Olsen had a point. Sometimes I do throw spitballs at the Landmark guests. Maybe even a little north of sometimes. But believe me, they always deserve it. And my supervisor never gets wind of it, because no one ever seems to care. When you're well and truly moneyed, insults from a hotel cleaner brush off you like confetti.

I figured Peters would ignore me in the manner of her predecessors, and Troy would be the same as all the other crash cases: splattered everywhere like raw egg, then cleaned up and gone for good.

I was wrong on both counts.

The next day there was a box and a bouquet waiting for me in the supply room. Marta was waiting for me, too. "You will not believe this," she said.

I dropped my bag on the Formica table and looked at the flowers. They were pretty. Chrysanthemums, tuberoses, and irises. Marta handed me a piece of ivory card stock embossed in gold with the letters TP.

"You read the card?" I looked at her. "Who does that?"

She shrugged. "Maybe I thought it was for me."

I snorted. The writing was in a light, uncertain hand. *Dear Natalia, Thank you for helping me yesterday. I will never forget your kindness. I am sorry to have been so much trouble. Yours, Troy.*

"Huh," I said.

"He was handsome," Marta announced.

"Not really. His eyes were crazy bloodshot."

"You have very high standards."

I rolled my eyes. "Marta, I'm not interested in some rich brat."

"I didn't think he was a brat."

"What's in the box?" I asked, to distract her. I opened it. The blanket had been laundered with something that smelled of bergamot. Wrapped in tissue paper on top of it was a copy of Homer's *Iliad* with another handwritten note. *Dear Natalia, Hector—always Hector over Achilles. What do you think of Penthesilea? Yours, Troy.* Beneath the signature was a phone number. The book looked expensive. It wasn't in Greek or anything, but it was old. "Huh," I said again, just to be original.

"What?" Marta asked.

"Guess he remembers what we talked about in the men's room."

Marta looked at her watch and stood up. "When he comes to the hotel, you should say yes."

"Yes to what, exactly? Yes, I'd be happy to scrape you off the floor again?"

Marta gave me a long look. "This one is different, Natita."

She was right, but not in the way she thought.

———

Until three p.m. I washed sheets, I made beds with perfect corners, I picked up and threw out all manner of indescribable discarded things on bathroom floors, I scrubbed toilets and sinks and tubs, I rearranged flowers, and I kept my nose down. Just like I do every day. Then I said my good-byes to Marta and the other cleaners and walked three blocks to the BART, avoiding a pair of hopped-up crazies who were fighting on the corner of Mission Street over the carcass of a cat. Two men, their faces wild, stretched into contortions of rage and terror. From six feet away, I could smell the mildew and urine and the lingering cloud of fear they'd taken—bitter, sharp, rancid. As I passed them, two cops moved in, taking them apart with no more trouble than trash collectors tossing bags in a truck.

Fear is cheap. The Landmark crowd can buy better, though it amazes me how often they slum it. But for most people, fear is all they can afford. I get it: sometimes it's better to feel something, even something bad, rather than nothing at all. It's supposed to feel like a nervous flutter, a thickening of the senses, a thrum of anxious anticipation. It's supposed to feel a little scary and a little exciting. It's supposed to feel familiar.

I've tried it a couple times. The first time, I saw a six-foot spider eating the contents of the refrigerator, and the second time, I was convinced that Cal—kid brother, almost eleven—had fallen from the upper-story window. There was no third time. When the drops are good, they're not supposed to make you afraid of made-up things, but, obviously, the drops I could afford were not good.

When Mom was alive she used to buy us some good times on birthdays. Seven hundred dollars an ounce, last I checked. At the back of the medicine chest she saved some top-quality peace of mind for emergencies (five hundred an ounce). But that's all gone now, along with her. Maybe nothing's changed. Happiness and tranquility weren't cheap five hundred years ago, either. Bought with the blood and sweat of serfs, with the bondage of entire peoples, with the darkness of mines and the poison of mercury. Different form of payment now, same high cost. And what do you know, orphanhood doesn't make them any cheaper. As my pal Raymond Chandler says, "Dead men are heavier than broken hearts." An accurate misuse of the line, since Mom's death did pretty much sink my chances of feeling anything. I couldn't even afford to be glum for the funeral.

Not that I'm complaining. That's how 99 percent of humanity lives. But the other 1 percent? They can afford to feel whatever they like.

As I waited for the train to Oakland, I stared at one of the ten-by-ten-foot screen decals on the BART platform. The screens stand at forty-five-degree angles to the rails every twenty feet and play an eight-second clip on a loop. First a beautiful house, coming closer until you're on the doorstep. The door opens. A beautiful blonde woman. For just a moment, long enough for you to imagine incorrectly that you and she have something in common, her face is blank. Then, suddenly, she's gasping with surprise. A moment later, sadness. The bittersweet kind, with tears running down her face as she tries to smile. Maybe you're the husband she thought was dead. Maybe you're a long-lost sister. Maybe you're her favorite child. She's wiping away tears, and the joy is overtaking her face until she's smiling, beaming, laughing. Then the words appear just below her chin. White italics: *Real Feeling*. The *Real* fades, only to reappear on the other side: *Feeling Real*. I've seen the RealCorp ad a thousand times, and I still can't look away. Nor could any of the other suckers, by the looks of it. We all stood there crammed together, staring at the beautiful face of the 1 percent going through the costly cascade of emotions over and over again until the train arrived.

I got a seat and let my back sink into the flattened cushions. Even soiled upholstery feels good when you've been on your feet for eight hours. The woman next to me, eyes sleepy, was reading headlines on her decal about an earthquake and a deployment of Marines. Nothing new there. In front of us, a pack of girls, likely third-graders, huddled together around a pole, giggling, eyes darting, clothes sparkling, smelling of strawberry shampoo and gum. I let myself watch them, the way their laughter moved through them like an electric current, making even the quiet one who clung too tight to the pole drop her guard and light up.

That's what real emotion looks like.

That's how Cal laughs. He's jolted. It's involuntary and inelegant, like sneezing.

With Mom gone, it's Cal who keeps us afloat. I might be

the one who pays the bills, but he's the only one who gives us a reason to. He still feels everything—I mean everything. It's constant fireworks with Cal: one minute he's wailing the whole building down, and the next he's laughing so hard he might puke. I love him to death. And before you say I can't really love him because love is beyond unaffordable, let me tell you that I do, and I'm not going to belabor it or fight you on it. I just do. I can't explain why. But I know I do because when I think of a world without Cal, it is an entirely pointless world.

He's almost eleven, so the fading should start any day now. He's overdue. But he hasn't started waning at all. If anything, it seems as though he's feeling more than ever. Almost all of his classmates are looking the way I did at that age, dull and kind of mystified, like they can't figure out who stole all the Halloween candy. Lo siento, kids—it's gone. Gone for good. And unless your parents can afford top-shelf synaffs, which in our neighborhood no one can, it's not coming back.

Every day I tell myself, "It could start today, so prepare yourself." Then Cal blows up because of some story on the radio about children working in a rug factory or comes home mooning over the most beautiful old Ford and I think, "Okay. Not today. But it could start tomorrow." Each time I'm glad—glad in the way you don't pay for, where it's not a high but you have the satisfaction of seeing a plus sign appear in the right column of your brain.

Except for when that plus sign gets converted into a big, big minus.

I didn't see it coming.

I walked home around the lake from the BART station, just to make my feet extra sore, and dragged them, two cement blocks, up the stairs. From the hallway, I could hear the radiators clanging, even though it was nearly eighty degrees out. I rolled my eyes as I unlocked the door. Our building is made from remnants of the 1915 Panama-Pacific International Exposition, which means we are surrounded by fussy decorative elements that were meant to last about a year. Most parts of the building have never been renovated—the claw-foot tubs, the Pullman beds, the wood floors. The radiators have minds of their own. The kitchen is run by an army of ants. And Cal's bedroom has so much water damage on the ceiling that it will crumple like tissue paper next time there's an earthquake. Cheap is the only thing going for it.

I walked through the rooms and tightened all the radiator valves, and on the kitchen counter I found Cal's note: *With C, T, and J.* It's an old note that we keep in the cabinet; Cal is over there a lot. After taking my shoes off and changing out of my day clothes, I trekked across the hall. Joey, same age as me, is my best friend and has been since we were four. His parents, Cass (Cassandra) and Tabby (Tabitha), have been our foster parents since Mom died last year. I was only sixteen, so someone else had to take on the task of defending us from the adult world, with all its straightforward sordidness. Cass is an artist turned sign-maker, mostly for dingy half-stocked stores in Oakland, and Tabby is an actress, when she can get the work. Her day job is retail at the Good Ole Days, the block-long vintage shop in downtown Oakland. When she's not selling leather bomber jackets and cravats and antique surfboards, she's taking care of the stray half-children in her life. For Cass and Tabby to collect the benefit, we are all supposed to live in the same residence, and they have two beds at the ready in case anyone from social services decides to visit in a fit of governmental conscience. But Cass and Tabby know I can take care of Cal myself, so really they just check in on us once a day and invite us over for meals a lot. Also I get many of Tabby's hand-me-down clothes, which is fine by me because she has the best vintage wardrobe in all of Oakland.

I knocked and opened the unlocked door. "Hello?"

"Kitchen," Cass called. I walked through and found her standing by the oven while Cal, Joey, and Tabby sat around the petite dining room table. They all looked up at me expectantly, their movements suspended.

I am good at doing two things. Cleaning rooms and reading faces.

What do you know, they have a few things in common. They both have to be learned. They require that you pay attention to minutiae. They are hard to do well and easy to take for granted. And they are both things I would rather not have to do. Because, let's face it, cleaning that sticky seam between the floor and the toilet is a major drag. And so is having to study the angle of a person's nostril to figure out what they're feeling. But neither one has yet become redundant and so far they seem to be my only life skills. So I'm hanging on to them.

At the moment I was reading Cal's face, and it was a complicated story. Eyebrows crinkled and raised. Mouth tensed, one side quirked slightly upward. Eyes unable to stay still.

Slightly contracted pupils. I saw distress, anxiety, nervousness, and some guilt. A tiny sliver of relief in the midst of it all, probably because I was home. Even if I'd been unable to read all of this, I would have known that something was wrong because Cal was clutching a glass of chocolate milk, and Cass was making madeleines, and these two things in combination are, on very rare occasions, the only way to make Cal feel better.

In case my descriptions have not made this clear, Cal is a sensitive boy. He cries at least once a day. Most days, it's more like five times. I wouldn't have it any other way. He is the world's most generous ten-year-old. He notices everything. Four times out of five, he's crying for somebody else, not for himself. He has messy brown hair and a dainty nose and big eyes that look at you with old, old humor—like there's an ancient soul inside him that is finding this whole tragic-orphan-trying-to-make-it story deeply amusing. Right then the old soul's humorous side was a little dampened.

"What's wrong?" I asked.

Joey pushed his glasses up his nose and silently—a lot of what Joey does is silent—handed me a sheet of paper folded in thirds. It was from Cal's school. It read:

To the parents of Calvino Peña:

We are writing to request your attendance at a consultation with Dr. Elizabeth Baylor, school physician. Cal has exhibited acute affect signaling for longer than expected, and it is recommended by

Dr. Baylor that he undergo testing. Please indicate your availability to attend a testing session and a meeting on October 8 at 3:00 p.m.

Sincerely,
Charles Freeman,
Principal

"What?" I said eloquently.

Cass closed the oven and put her hands on her hips. "Don't worry, we'll go with you," she said. She is tall, with square shoulders and a square jaw and curly blonde hair that I have never seen loose. She pulls it back with rubber bands like the hair is her enemy and she is going to win at all costs. In fact, that is her stance toward a lot of things. Pale blue eyes, solid nose, and straight teeth that make it out often because she laughs a lot. She doesn't believe in jewelry, other than her wedding band.

"I'm not worried about who's going," I replied.

"She's worried about why they want to do testing," Tabby explained helpfully.

"I realize that." Cass rolled her eyes. "I'm just saying, Natalia, you don't have to deal with this alone."

Nobody but Cass calls me Natalia.

"That is true," Tabby agreed. She stood up and put her arm around my shoulders. Tabby is barely as tall as I am— five foot five—and about the same weight. But she is curvier, and in general she is softer than me and Cass combined— soft round face, soft brown eyes, soft brown hair, soft gentle hands. She does everything gently, which I have reflected more than once is hard to do when you don't have feelings.

"Did your teacher say anything else to you about this, Cal?" I asked.

Cal shook his head. "She only said that the principal wanted to see me, and when I went to the principal, he gave me that letter." His voice was watery. "It was addressed to my parents, so I gave it to Cass and Tabby."

He looked at me pleadingly. I could see what I needed to do, but I had that familiar sense that he was calling out to me over a chasm, and that I had to strain to hear what he was saying. I sat down in Tabby's empty chair and took his hand. It was kind of grubby from the chocolate milk and who knows what else. He squeezed my hand tightly. "We don't have to do this testing if you don't want to," I said.

There was silence in the kitchen. I could feel Cass's skepticism and Tabby's acceptance and Joey's silent encouragement, because Joey can be counted on to back up any scheme, crazy or not.

Cal looked at me earnestly. "Really?" he whispered.

"Really. There are very few things you have to do, and this is not one of them. If you want, I will tell them you won't get tested."

"What if they say I have to?"

"Then we'll fight them on it. We'll move you to another school. We'll go somewhere else."

I had never heard of someone getting a letter like this one, but I knew what it could mean, just as everyone in the room old enough to get it—everyone other than Cal—knew what it could mean.

Over the years, many a huckster has tried to claim renewed feeling, like medieval blind men restored to sight by the touch of a saintly relic. It's always a scam. Synaffs, good acting, or self-delusion. Every once in a while, there are real cases of partial, usually dysfunctional, restoration. A woman who feels genuine euphoria, and never anything else. A man who flies into fits of real fury. Another who suffers from bona fide, unshakable depression. These are freaks of nature, splashed on the tabloids and then, no doubt, sequestered in a lab for neurological tinkering.

And every once in a while you hear of children who somehow, unpredictably and defying any kind of pattern, fade late. At age eleven. Or twelve. Fourteen is the latest I've heard of. They always fade eventually, but they linger. When a child fades late, it means there's something different about him. That he feels emotion for longer. And if he feels emotion for longer, that means maybe something about his brain is resisting the fade. And if he's resisting the fade, that means he might keep resisting. Maybe he'll get to fifteen. Or sixteen. Maybe he won't fade at all. And that . . . Well, that would be a game changer.

Cal squeezed my hand again. His brow softened. His tensed lips relaxed. Then he sighed, and I saw that old soul in there perk up, looking not cheery, exactly, but at least peaceful in a way that could be cheery again soon. That was good. If Cal was okay, then for me, everything was okay. "It's just a test, right?" he asked me. "We can just do the test and see what it says."

"That's true," I agreed. "It's just a test."

There are times when it can be an advantage not to feel things. This was one of them. I couldn't conjure up the feeling of dread, because it was lost to me along with everything else, but as I made rapid calculations—odds, distances, nickels and dimes—I got the definite impression that Cal and I were standing at the mouth of a tunnel. And my calculations told me that at the end of that tunnel there might be a guillotine, or maybe a six-foot spider, or maybe something worse—something I had no power to imagine.

3

CALVINO

oct-11

11:07 a.m.

calvinopio:

Essay: <u>What are emotions?</u> By Calvino Peña

Over many centuries there has been much debate over what emotions are. Long ago people believed they were placed in our souls by God or by the gods. Then philosophers believed that they were created in our bodies by thoughts but others still believed it was God. Then scientists argued that emotions were caused by chemicals in the brain.

For as long as there have been emotions, which is forever, there has been debate over what they are. For example today we do not believe that it is possible to die of rage but people in the past believed that. Today we believe that emotions are reactions that happen in the brain and that affect the whole body.

We know this because it is possible to watch these

reactions with special scientific equipment. And after age ten most people do not have most of the reactions that we call emotions. They have other reactions still like responding to pain and hunger but not the ones we have mostly considered emotions like fear, anger, sadness, happiness, or all the related ones.

[Note: Scientists haven't realized that even if you do not have equipment you can see these reactions. Adults cannot see them without equipment but children can. Children are able to see emotions that adults cannot. They can see that even after waning, adults still have some emotions. This has not been discovered by science but it is true.]

hglt: Thanks for this essay, Calvino. By the way, do you go by Cal, Calvino, or Calvinopio?

calvinopio: No, I just chose this username because it was my mom's nickname for me but no one calls me that. I go by Cal or Calvino.

hglt: Great—got it, Cal! Your note at the bottom presents a fascinating idea. What makes you think adults still have emotions?

calvinopio: I can see them. They are invisible emotions, which means that they are invisible to the people who have them but not to children. Only children are able to see them.

hglt: If they are invisible to adults, that explains why I haven't seen them! What do they look like?

calvinopio: That is hard to answer. Sometimes people conceal emotions on purpose, but they know they are there. Sometimes people conceal emotions so much they don't even realize they are there. But you can still see them.

hglt: I think I know what you mean. You're describing what we call "repressed" emotions. A person might be really angry or really sad and lock that feeling away so tightly that they actually don't realize it exists. Nevertheless, the emotion has an effect upon them. And an outsider might be able to detect that anger or sadness.

calvinopio: That's kind of what I mean.

Are we done now? Can I come out?

4

NATALIA

October 8

Moses Elementary is a mid-twentieth-century effort—executed in concrete and paint—to ignore all of the natural inclinations of children. Ignore and extinguish, I guess, since most of those inclinations were considered a nuisance when the school was built. The dining hall is a row of picnic tables chained to concrete posts, and there are far fewer seats than students. In my day, I mostly ate my lunch standing next to the chain-link fence. The screen decals, flurries of movement and color, are attached to the desks. The desks are attached to the chairs, and the chairs are screwed into the floors. You get the idea. Limit mobility. Ensure attentiveness. Get them all in line. Once upon a time the place used to make me want to run screaming, but now it just seems like a joke in poor taste. A school for children run by adults? It's like summer camp for bunnies run by wolves.

Cass and Tabby and I walked in along the chipped wall of the open corridor, past the "library" with its mucky keyboards and its paltry offering of decaying books and its more generous offering of mildewed wall-to-wall carpeting. As we passed the tall windows, covered with smudged handprints, I caught a glimpse of myself then and before. There was a reflection of Nat, the solid-looking individual in a pinstripe skirt suit, a peach blouse, and a pillbox hat. And looking out through her reflection was small Natalia Peña: heavy bangs, sullen expression, wide and wary eyes, a lively sense of mischief wrapped in a livelier sense of insecurity. The sight of her was a numbers problem I couldn't solve. I knew who she was, and I knew in theory I should miss her and feel some fondness for her, but mostly she struck me as a stranger: that bundle of raw emotions, hurting all the time and always wanting things she couldn't have. A canopy bed. A puppy. A trip to the beach. A father.

Why did I want a canopy bed? Beats me.

We made a formidable team, I thought, as we strode down the peeling corridor. Cass in her gray suit and derby hat, Tabby in her violet sheath dress and serious pumps, me in my intense scowl. The principal's office had clearly been renovated recently, unlike the rest of Moses. There was nothing left of the dowdy Mrs. Sarah Lambert, whom I remembered as a perfumed cloud of friendly inefficiency. Mr. Charles Freeman had his own style. It was striking, to say the least.

Tabby's theory is that everyone wants vintage now not just because vintage reminds us of the "time before," the time when everything was still pretty much working the way it was supposed to and we could all feel things. She thinks that those old objects—all objects—absorbed the sentiments of the people who used them, and that we crave old things because we can sense through them, like distant echoes, those long-ago emotions. Maybe. I guess it is true that the objects I like most do seem *more than* in a way I can't pinpoint.

But what isn't debatable is that there's vintage and then there's *vintage.* Maybe working summers with Tabby at the Good Ole Days had made me a snob, but still. You might not care about the difference between herringbone and houndstooth like I do, and you might think Arts and Crafts is something you do with construction paper and crayons. But everyone knows the difference between people who make the residues of the past come together into something beautiful versus people like Mr. Freeman.

He clearly had a soft spot for the nineteenth century, and that was probably part of the problem, because that stuff is *old.* How much of it, do you really think, has absolutely no mold on it? I'd say not much. Mr. Freeman had Persian carpets, gilt frames, silk flowers in a massive Chinese vase, a wooden desk that looked about double the weight of our refrigerator, multiple religious paintings featuring blood in large quantities, and velvet curtains so plush you could easily suffocate a couple children in them and no one would be the wiser. All this in a building made of concrete block.

I was a little taken aback. Were we at a funeral parlor or an elementary school? Mr. Freeman himself did not offer helpful clues. He wore a black three-piece suit, a heavy mustache, round-rimmed glasses, and an expression of listless unconcern that struck me as ominous. Cal was already there, sitting on a straight-backed wooden chair and looking, understandably, terrified. Eyes wide, pupils shrunken, hands clenching the straps of his backpack. I went over to him right away, before even greeting Mr. Freeman, and put my arm around him. He sank into me.

"Mr. Freeman," Cass was saying, extending her hand over the mountainous desk. "I am Cassandra Lawson, this is Tabitha Lawson. We are Natalia and Calvino's foster parents."

"Nat," I said, shaking hands with him after Tabby did. I'd taken off my gloves to shake his hand and now wished I hadn't; it was clammy and strangely cold, as if he'd spent the last fifteen minutes clutching an ice cream carton.

"Thank you for being here. This is Dr. Elizabeth Baylor." He gestured to an open door that I hadn't noticed because it was obscured by the profusion of silk flowers.

Dr. Baylor had white-blonde hair pulled back into a pony-tail. She wore a lab coat and slacks and burgundy clogs. Her hands were tucked into the pockets, like she was entirely at ease. "Hi, bienvenidas," she said, giving us a big smile with lots of teeth that was meant to convince us how friendly and safe she was. It didn't work. The smile did nothing to conceal a brain that was cool, remote, clinical. She looked about as safe as a razor blade on a bed of lettuce.

Dr. Baylor didn't offer to shake hands. She motioned us into the adjoining room and we tromped in behind her. Thankfully, this room had not been decorated by Mr. Free-man. Cement block had never looked so good. Screen decals ran in a line down one wall, and a cart of medical equipment stood waiting by a reclining chair. A standing desk perched like a podium below the high windows. There were no other seats besides the reclining chair. Dr. Baylor made a big show of turning down the lights to a muted yellow, closing the curtains, and tapping off all the personal screen decals on her desk: six streams of activity blinked off one after the other. "Have a seat in the important chair, Calvino," she said, still smiling sunshine.

"Before we start, Dr. Baylor," Cass said politely, putting a hand on Cal's shoulder, "we wanted to understand more fully why this testing is being done now and what the potential outcomes are."

This had been my idea. Cal wasn't due for testing, and I wanted to know: whence the damn test?

Dr. Baylor beamed a little brighter. "Of course. As you know, students go through standard testing once a year. They are also assessed regularly—even daily, in this crucial year—by their teachers. In-class assignments and activities provide the basis for assessment."

"So this was recommended by Cal's teacher?" I cut in. Her verbiage was starting to wear on me.

"Nope." Dr. Baylor smiled at me. "Teachers don't make those kinds of decisions. But they do gather information which they share with me, and I, in turn, share the information with my supervisor."

"You mean Mr. Freeman?" Tabby asked.

Dr. Baylor actually laughed at this absurd notion. "I work on-site at the school, but I am employed by RealCorp, the company that manages and implements all student testing.

In this case, there was probably some material in Cal's file that suggested to my supervisor that we should take a little peek."

She opened her eyes wide and made a tiny lifting motion with her hand, like she was opening a magical music box. Nonetheless, what she'd just described was more spy story than fairy tale. Basically, Cal was surrounded by traitors and someone had ratted on him; now he would be interrogated. Nothing she said answered the important question: why now?

I did my best to rearrange my features so Cal wouldn't see what I was thinking, but it's hard to get anything by him. He looked worried.

"As for outcomes . . ." Dr. Baylor looked sunnily at Cal. "That depends on you, Calvino." She shifted back to her script. "Just to remind you of what we're doing here, we'll be testing to see how your brain responds to affect stimulus, which is another way of saying we want to see your range of emotions. As you've learned in school, your brain is like a city, with lots of different neighborhoods. One of those neighborhoods is where all the emotions live. Sound familiar?"

Cal nodded. "Yes."

"In children, it's really easy to get to that neighborhood, no matter where you are in the city. But once affective waning occurs, the neighborhood is harder and harder to get to. It's still there. Every adult still has that neighborhood. But by the time they have fully waned, the neighborhood is closed off. No one can get in or out."

"But the emotions still live there," Cal said quietly.

"What's that?" Dr. Baylor asked, grinning fiercely.

"The emotions are still there in the closed-off neighborhood."

Dr. Baylor's grin faded a little. "Hm, interesting theory! We don't really know what's going on in that neighborhood in grown-ups. But we do know that we can measure where you are by seeing how many roads go in and out of the neighborhood. That's what we're going to check for now. Okay?"

"Okay."

"Ready to climb on into the important chair?"

Cal shot me a look and then smiled briefly at the tiny roll of the eyes that I gave him. He climbed up into the plastic reclining chair. He leaned back but followed Dr. Baylor with his eyes. Cass, Tabby, and I stood in a line near the chair, facing the screen decals and waiting for the magic show to start. Mr. Freeman hovered by the door to his office.

"Well, Calvino. Let's begin, shall we?" Dr. Baylor asked Cal brightly.

"Okay," he said.

Dr. Baylor opened the cart and pulled up a panel that had dozens of thin wires with clear suction cups. "This won't hurt a bit," she said, putting her full row of upper teeth into a wide grin.

With children, reading faces is pretty easy. They feel what they feel, and they hide it badly. With adults, it's more complicated. There's synthetic affects, which are pretty obvious, and then there's sheer fakery. Everyone fakes it a little. I try not to, but sometimes I do. Mostly it slips into what I say, not how I act. *I'm sorry. I'm not worried. You surprise me. That freaks me out!*

Yeah, I'm posturing. It's no different than choosing the plastic bag that looks like real leather or the knockoff pumps that look designer. Faking it makes you seem like you can afford to feel. And who doesn't want that? Every person you look at, you have to wonder, did that come from the pharmacy or the fake-factory? My shortcut—look at the clothes. If they've paid for actual leather, they've paid for actual drops.

Dr. Baylor was something of a puzzle. As an employee of RealCorp, there was no doubt she could afford the actual drops. The clogs were scuffed, but they were Scandinavian. Yet the sunny disposition was clearly fake. Her eyes were overly wide; she had to strain to keep them open. Her lips kept sliding into a slight protrusion of contempt, no matter how hard she tried to preserve the big grin. So Dr. Baylor's expensive drops were there to offer other emotions, emotions she had hidden behind the fake smile. I didn't much like the effect.

She plopped suction cups all over Cal's arms and head. "There we are!" she pronounced, stepping back and flipping a switch. The big screen decals on the wall came to life. One had a list of words on it: emotions. The rest had pulsing circles, each a different color. "Now," Dr. Baylor chirped. "Cal, this will be similar to the tests you've done in the past at the start of every school year, but the equipment I have in this instance is looking more closely at what's going on in your brain and your body overall."

"Okay," Cal agreed.

"I'm going to prompt you to think about certain things, and you follow my lead. If one of the things I mention makes you think about a memory or a person or anything other than what I've mentioned, let me know. And as we go along, I'd like you to try to name the emotion you're feeling. You can use the list on the screen, or come up with a different word if one comes to mind."

"Okay," Cal said again.

I gave him an encouraging nod when he looked at me.

"Let's begin." As she concentrated on the script before her, Dr. Baylor's false cheeriness vanished. Her voice was flat. It could not have been flatter as she said, "Think about your deceased mother."

Cal's face tensed, but he didn't say anything.

"Which emotions are you feeling?" Dr. Baylor asked.

The circles on the screen decals dissolved into amorphous blobs, each of them expanding or contracting and pulsing or shuddering as they shaped and reshaped themselves. Digital fireworks. Cal took a breath. "Anxiety. Sadness. Fear."

"Which of those would you say is greatest?"

Cal swallowed. "Anxiety."

"Good. Now imagine you are traveling with your sister. You are going somewhere that was special to all three of you—you, your sister, and your mom. You are at the airport. You go to the restroom, and when you return to your gate, your sister is gone. You cannot find her anywhere."

Cal and I could hardly afford to take the train to Sacramento, let alone fly anywhere, but he seemed to find the situation plausible enough. "Anxiety," he said, his voice strained.

"Anything else?"

Cal's eyes searched the list. "Guilt," he added.

"Interesting," Dr. Baylor murmured. "Imagine you have located your sister. She has boarded the flight. You watch through the windows as the plane leaves without you. As it prepares for takeoff, the plane malfunctions. It explodes and goes up in flames."

The colors on the screen decals were bursting away, and I glanced at the others to see what they thought of Dr. Baylor's cute fantasy. Mr. Freeman looked like he was planning ahead to whether he should have Thai or Chinese for dinner. Cass was watching Dr. Baylor with that familiar expression indicating that she had found a new enemy, which was excellent news. Tabby was pointedly ignoring everyone but Cal. She was looking straight at him, her face open and encouraging but not falsely reassuring. Good old Tabby.

"Which emotions?" Dr. Baylor prompted.

"Anxiety," Cal whispered. "And fear."

"Now you are standing at the window watching the plane, and you feel a hand on your shoulder. It is your sister. She never boarded the plane."

Cal blinked with relief. "Happiness."

I could dimly remember what it was like to have that ability—the imaginative faculty. The power to conjure a thing and make it real around you until, poof, you decided it wasn't real anymore. That ability had vanished around age ten as well, come to think of it, but no one seemed to lament its loss or even remark upon it. As far as I know, people have always outgrown the ability to make the imagined real, long before waning entered our world. Isn't that the point of Peter Pan?

I could still recall my first failed attempt. I was standing in the patch of weeds that grew beside our building, and that patch of weeds could be many things—a desert, a cold tundra, a mountain, a forest. On that day it was supposed to be a city of skyscrapers. I looked around me and found that I was surrounded, to my surprise, by weeds. Wild carrot and clover and crabgrass. I tried again. Nothing. It was like opening your wings and finding they'd been shredded down to the bones.

Cal still had wings. I could see that the things Dr. Baylor was describing were real to him.

"You cancel your trip and head home. When you get there, you find that your house has been transformed into a mansion. There's a pool and fancy cars." Dr. Baylor stopped. "Hm." She turned away from the monitors and peered at Cal. "What is it?"

Cal looked sad. "If we live in a mansion it will be harder to see Cass and Tabby and Joey. I like where we live now."

You can see why I love him to death.

Dr. Baylor seemed stumped. "Okay," she improvised. "You find your apartment just as you left it, but when you get upstairs you find a winning lottery ticket on your kitchen table."

Cal looked uncomfortable.

"Which emotions?"

"Um . . . I guess . . . there isn't a word on there that fits."

Dr. Baylor turned the honey on and smiled at him. "What are you thinking about?"

"I'm thinking about what to do with the lottery money."

"You can do whatever you want with it."

"I've been to the hotel where my sister works," Cal said. I could tell he was trying hard to be polite. "I don't think being rich is for me."

I wanted to laugh but I thought that might make Cal look bad, so I pretended to sneeze into my glove.

"Well," Dr. Baylor said. "Imagine you come home and find the thing you want most in the world to find." She paused. "Got it?"

Cal nodded. He closed his eyes. I watched his hands, stiff at his sides, drift unconsciously toward each other. He clasped them. "Sadness," he said quietly, his eyes still closed. Then his chin wobbled a little, and a tear slid sideways down his cheek toward his ear. I knew what he was thinking about, and it was no surprise his thoughts would drift there, helplessly carried along like a paper boat in a storm gutter, careening toward the drain. This was the cost of having too much imagination, of having too much sentiment, of having too many painful, unanswerable questions. Of being Cal.

"What are you thinking about?" Dr. Baylor asked, her treacly voice heavy in the quiet room.

I spared him the necessity of trying to talk as though he weren't crying. That was something I could do for him, at least. "He's imagining coming home to find our mother," I said, and my voice was just as flat as Dr. Baylor's. As flat as an ocean horizon, viewed from a shore you know you'll never leave. "Is that your last question?"

She blinked rapidly. "Yes. The test is over."

I crossed the room and put my hand out to Cal. He gripped it hard and pulled himself up out of the chair, and I observed the dignity with which he wiped his eyes. He didn't apologize for crying.

5

NATALIA

Plausibility. It's one of the many reasons I'm indebted to Raymond Chandler. Yes, the author. Early twentieth-century noir, located on the fiction shelf right between "abundant alcoholism" and "misguided masculinity." His detective, Philip Marlowe, comes as close as I've seen to our emotionless future. Maybe Chandler had a nightmare, and Marlowe's world was in it, or maybe, prophet-like, he could see the slow decline approaching in the cold hearts and callous faces of 1930s Los Angeles. However it happened, his Marlowe does it—even in a world still premised on the availability and influence of emotion, Marlowe moves through it, calm and unflappable, making it seem plausible that one might survive in a hard, sordid, unfair world without the soaring ecstasies and raptures of triumph and true loves that seem to carry every other character ever written.

I know he's not actually emotionless. Sometimes his face gets red. Sometimes he even gets mad. And yes, Chandler sees all the people who are not white men with the eyes of a 1930s white man, and he uses some nasty names in the process. Nevertheless, Marlowe has been a good guide to me. My mom was not tough. Her approach to the world could be summed up with the oft-misused, typically Californian term "easygoing," which is a nice way of saying that she was like a kite in a windstorm. I knew, watching her, that easygoing was not for me. But most of the truly tough people I've known are tough without integrity, and that doesn't seem right, either. With Marlowe, I've got tough and principled with the occasional condescension to underhanded when the game is rigged and the stakes are against you. That's an approach I can live with.

One of the reasons Joey and I are best friends is that he sees it this way, too. Sometimes his idea of toughness differs from mine, but we always agree on the big picture. Unbeknownst to me, Joey had taken the day off from his job at the pharmacy on the day Cal had his testing done. When we got home close to five, Cal's favorite music (Dolly Parton) was blaring through the apartment windows. On the kitchen table was a cake that looked like a fortune in chocolate and butter with the crooked words TEST RESULTS: AWESOME! written in purple frosting.

"Wow!" Cal said, staring at the cake and beaming. "Wow!"

I gave Joey a hug. "You are actually awesome," I said to him quietly.

Joey hooked his arm around me. "No problem," he said. "Hope it tastes good." He didn't ask, didn't even sniff in the direction of the test. He just took plates out of the cupboard and told Cal that it was his job to cut pieces.

The other thing about Joey is that he has Tabby's acting gene. Most stage actors do synaffs to simulate emotion, but Tabby is one of the purists who thinks it's about remembering emotion and cultivating that memory, then channeling it when you act. Maybe that's why she often is out of work. Regardless, she is very convincing at feigning emotion when she wants to, and Joey is the same. Neither one of them uses it in the show-off way, to pretend they can afford synaffs. Joey uses it very sparingly, and with Cal he almost never uses it at all. He sees it as a kind of manipulation, because for children the emotions are real, and to show children false emotion that seems real is . . . well, deceitful. At my mom's funeral he feigned grief, and I could see that he was doing it so that Cal would not feel alone or strange in his misery. It worked—Cal held his hand and mine the whole time, and as Joey cried I could see Cal thinking, *This is okay. This is okay, to fall apart.*

Right now Joey wasn't acting, but he was sending a subtle, celebratory vibe into the room, throwing the napkins, wrestling Cass into an apron—subtle enough that Cal was laughing and loosening without realizing why. I looked around at them—Cal exclaiming over the cake, Joey and Cass horsing around, Tabby kicking off her heels—and I thought Cal was really right about not wanting a mansion.

———

Dr. Baylor hadn't given us any test results. She had recorded the entire session with her magical cart and promised to look at it closely, along with her supervisor at RealCorp.

"Can we have a copy of the test, even if you don't have results yet?" I pressed.

"The testing equipment is owned by the Realism Corporation," she said cheerily, "so technically anything produced by the equipment is also owned by RealCorp."

This flummoxed me, and I could tell Cass and Tabby weren't too pleased by the logic, either. But it made sense, in a messed-up way. The Realism Corporation is one of the four largest pharmaceutical companies that produce synaffs and I wouldn't expect it to give away anything for free, not even the time of day.

"How is it any different from a blood test?" I asked. "The test might be yours, but the blood is Cal's."

"Actually, that's the wrong analogy," Dr. Baylor persisted pleasantly. "Think of it more as a drawing that Cal made on really, really special RealCorp paper using RealCorp pencils."

I frowned, but I didn't keep arguing with her because Cal was already uncomfortable. I did ask her for a time frame and she said a week. Fine. That meant we had a week to sit and stew and think about what it all meant.

All afternoon and into the evening, I did just that. What did it all mean? What did it mean for Cal? What could I do to help him that I wasn't already doing? What was I missing?

Cal was asleep in his room, and I was sitting in bed with only the reading light on. It cast a circle of light on the quilted bedspread, and I turned the light so it shone away from me. The living room came into view: on one side, the tweedy sofa and oval coffee table; on the other side, my bureau between two bookshelves. Above the sofa was a canvas painted by Cass, all surreal figures and dripping landscapes. The thin curtains covering the casement windows shifted a little in the breeze.

There were a few things I had never told Cal during any of our conversations about growing up. Hadn't told anyone. Memories I didn't mind leaving packed in the attic.

I couldn't remember the feeling of fear, but I could remember the fact of the fear. Constant—ebbing and flowing, but always there. There was a long, lingering sense that something was wrong. It was like forgetting something and not being sure what you'd forgotten. Mostly it came into sharp relief when I was with other children, because then the stages were starkly evident. The older ones who had already faded inspired mixed terror and envy—they seemed cool, unapproachable, faintly menacing in their transformed state. We were like a troop of monkeys beside them, and they were an army of ice princesses. But the moments of incremental change could be horrifying.

There was Coral. Yes. Coral was definitely one of the worst moments, but not the only one. She had been friends with us, me and Joey. For a time, we were inseparable. I remember all of us falling asleep in a tent made of bedsheets, waking up to see Coral's wispy, pale hair stuck to her face. I remember our easy flights of fantasy and making a spell book to ward off the change we knew was coming. Wing of crow and drop of wax. A coil of paper burned to ashes. Murmured rituals with words that tasted old, like prayers. The spells didn't work, of course. First me and Joey, almost at the same time, began to fade. But Coral was slow. During that year when most of us were fading, she waited—like Cal, she was hanging on to every ounce of feeling she had.

I didn't know how far I'd faded until Coral showed me. We were at school, at the end of the day. I was sitting on the grass, doing nothing, when I heard screaming. Someone was calling my name. The other kids were clumped around a chained-up picnic table, and I drifted over. *Nat! Joey!* I understood that it was Coral crying, but the sound of her screams didn't do anything to me. I was intrigued. I pushed the other kids aside to see what was under the table. I laughed. The sight was funny. She was naked, and she had something smeared on her back that smelled *really* bad. I couldn't be sure what it was, but it was hilarious. The other kids were laughing. I was laughing. Coral's face was red and puffy from crying. She looked me straight in the eye. "Nat, please," she said, her voice shaking. "Please help me."

I blinked. "What's wrong?" I asked.

Then a boy in our class who hadn't faded much yet, Derek, crept in under the table. He didn't say anything, he just crawled in with Coral and handed her a rain jacket that had probably been moldering in the lost and found for a few years. She snatched it and pulled it on, hiccuping through her tears. Then Derek put his hand out. I remember thinking, *What is he doing?*

I had the sense that I was forgetting something really, really important. I had to think of it. I had to think of it before it went away completely. *What was it? What was it?*

Coral took his hand and squeezed it. She was trembling.

Then I remembered. Cruelty. Shame. Fear. Compassion.

They hit my stomach like a load of bricks, and I turned away from the pack of demons that were my classmates. I ran and ran and ran, but there was nowhere to go. Only the chain-link fence at the edge of the school playground and my own deadened brain, fading fast.

———

The first month of high school was aimed at that. At them. At me. All those deadened brains. It was pure carrot and stick. Carrot being lunch in three different sizes—tiny, adequate, and generous. Stick being cages. Also in three different sizes. In the biggest you had space to rant against the steel bars, if you were so inclined. In the smallest you couldn't even turn your head. Once we'd figured out the basics of rewards and punishment, it was on to the real lessons.

The objective? Stay human. Don't become a Fish. As in Cold Fish, as in the creeps who troll around wrecking things for the sake of it. The Fish are the reason Los Angeles and a dozen other smaller cities are ghost towns now: depopulated, urban jungles, slowly being swallowed by the water and the sand, the vegetation and the mold.

The Fish have all the senseless destructiveness of ten-year-olds, like the ones who reduced Coral to a stinking, naked mess. They sink into the void and stay there. No synaffs to remind them of how things used to feel. No fear to stop them from anything. You can't even call them sadists, because there's no pleasure to be gained.

The worst part of Coral's waning wasn't even that she waned late. The worst part was that once she waned, she turned Fish. Her and a few others in high school. Not Derek, who disappeared beforehand, probably whisked away to private school. She found new friends more like her. The carrot and stick didn't work on them. They hurt people the way gardeners hurt slugs: rationally, easily, with a practical goal in mind. *The slugs are ruining my garden, so I will pour salt on them. The boy is in my seat, so I will stab his ear with a pencil.*

I threw the covers off and walked silently to Cal's room. The glow-in-the-dark stars on the ceiling were bright, the constellations so close that it felt like the heavens were sagging. Cal was a small shape beneath the covers, slender as a branch. He was snoring a little. His clothes for the next day were draped over his chair: a tidy small shirt, a tidy set of folded pants, a tidy sweater, a pair of worn shoes. The books on his desk were neatly stacked. I stood beside his bed like a creepy sandman, watching him sleep. Sometimes I do that. Mostly because I'm trying to figure out how everything I've learned about the emotions I don't have can possibly explain how I feel about Cal.

Maybe I don't actually feel anything. Maybe the rules drilled into my bones about defending the innocence of childhood and protecting the weak and committing to kin have messed with my brain so badly that I just *think* I love Cal.

Maybe the rules really work. Much as I loathed the assault on my sensibilities known as high school, I have to admit that it's the only thing keeping all of us from becoming Fish. Six years of brutal training, hammering into you over and over the seemingly senseless rules by which society is governed. The fact that you can no longer count on your emotions to navigate the world. You have to rely on your brain. And the rules. A thousand dictums on matters great and small. A complex code, to be memorized and practiced and practiced again. You follow traffic signals. You respect personal space. You acknowledge effort and discomfort with thanks and apologies. You recognize the limitations of youth and old age, and you provide assistance. You do not touch people if they do not want to be touched. You only use weapons in self-defense. You do not set fire to buildings. You do not stab pencils into people's ears. You do not pull dresses off girls.

Know what harm is. And cause no harm. Know what need is. And help those in need. Know what the law is. And follow the law.

By the end, the rules aren't senseless. By the end, they seem like the only things that actually make sense.

I don't envy them, the cops who taught us, and I envy even less the people who had to come up with this survival raft of a strategy to begin with. What could they do? On one side, you have a sandy shore overpopulated with people hopped up on synaffs, so desperate to feel again they'll pay anything and feel anything. A crazy beach party gone haywire. On the other side, you have a sea full of sharp-toothed Fish, happy to wreck the little raft you've made out of timber and tar and earnest, nostalgic, unrealistic rules.

What are you going to do? It's not lonely on the raft, because you don't feel lonely. You don't feel anything. But nevertheless, you know you're lost.

I padded back into the living room and lifted the handset of the old rotary phone. Then, for no reason adhering to logic, other than one conjured from the memory of Coral, the sight of Cal, and the prospect of my raft, I pulled the rectangle of cream-colored card stock out of my work bag and slowly dialed Troy's number.

As I waited, listening to the ringing sound, it occurred to me that it was probably late. I was about to hang up when he answered.

"Hello?"

I paused only a fraction of a second. "Hi. This is Nat. Natalia Peña."

His pause was longer. No doubt he had forgotten about the cleaner from the Landmark, as was to be expected. "Hi," he breathed, a smile of surprise in his voice. "I'm so glad you called me. I really didn't think you would." I heard the sound of screen decals in the background being silenced.

"I didn't think I would, either." No sense denying it.

He laughed.

When I can't see a face, it's a little harder to read emotions. I listened to the tenor of his laugh: not rapid or mechanical; relaxed and spontaneous, like a hiccup. The effect was warm and easy, unoffended and untroubled. He asked: "What made my luck change?"

"I wanted to thank you. For the book and the flowers.

People are rarely kind enough to do something like that. Actually, never kind enough. I can't remember the last time anyone sent me a book and flowers."

"You probably just get the flowers." He played dejected, as if dismayed at all the competition. "What, like, every other day, maybe?"

"Nope. Surprisingly, I don't get flowers more than once a week."

He laughed again, then sobered. "I'm actually relieved. I didn't know how you would take it. I was such a mess, there isn't really any gift to make up for what you did. Seriously—thank you. And then I was positive you wouldn't call, because as far as first impressions go, you could not get much worse. I'm not really like that, but you'd have no reason to believe me. Still, I had to at least try—" He paused, stopping himself.

It sounded earnest. It sounded genuine. Even though I knew it wasn't genuine, couldn't possibly be genuine; it could only be synaffs. Well, what was I expecting? Wasn't that why I'd called, for the feeling of something genuine that I knew not to be? Just like every other idiot adult, I was dialing random numbers into the void, looking for the nonexistent real article.

I still hadn't said anything, and he was embarrassed. "Long speeches," he said sheepishly.

That made me laugh. "You must be totally sick of all things Homer by this point in your life."

"No, actually, the opposite. When you said Hector and Achilles, it was like something clicked in my head. That copy is from the Cloak and Dagger; it's one of my favorite bookstores."

I knew the place. It had an espionage theme, carried to a logical and almost counterproductive extreme. No signage outside; secret knocks and passwords to get in; subterranean rooms with hidden doors behind bookshelves. "I've been there. Not for ages, though. Do they still have the one-way mirror?"

"Yeah," he said fondly. "They still have it. What's new is the torture chamber. Have you seen it?"

"That doesn't ring a bell."

"Just a small room with two armchairs and two kinds of books. Russian novels and German philosophy."

I chuckled.

"We should go," he said lightly.

"Sure," I replied, matching his tone.

He paused. "Great!" He seemed surprised. "I'm out of town for a few days, but when I get back?"

"Sounds good. I'll call you in a week or so." The rotary wasn't traceable, and he was smart enough not to ask for my number.

"Thanks, Natalia," he said, sounding suddenly wistful. "Thanks for calling."

"Good night, Troy."

6

CALVINO

oct-11

2:38 p.m.

calvinopio:

Essay: <u>What is waning and where does it come from?</u>

By Calvino Peña

Waning is what happens to children as they get older. Beginning at age nine and ending at age ten children begin to go through a huge change called waning. During waning scientists say children lose the ability to feel emotion and they become adults. Scientists say adults do not feel emotions at all. They feel only instincts and they still have reason.

Scientists don't know where waning comes from. They know that it has occurred for several decades and that everyone experiences it. As far as is known there is no one who has not waned. The explanation that is taught is that adults many decades ago began to lose their emotional intelligence, because emotion is a form of intelligence. But it isn't known what they did to lose their emotional intelligence since other kinds of intelligence remained the same.

What scientists agree on is that the change is all over the world so it must be something that affected everyone. It could be a disease like smallpox, it could be a type of pollution or something in the water, it could be something completely outside of us like a change in the atmosphere. (The atmosphere did not cause waning, but something outside of us like that.)

(Note: What scientists do not know is that waning doesn't affect everyone the same way. Scientists think that everyone changes exactly the same, but this is not true.)

hglt: Thanks for this response, Calvino. I learned a lot from your essay. Scientists seem to get a lot of things wrong! What do you mean when you say that waning doesn't affect everyone in the same way?

calvinopio: It has to do with the invisible emotions I was talking about. I was taught that the brain is like a city and that emotions live in one neighborhood then after waning the neighborhood is cut off.

hglt: Yes, that metaphor is an effective teaching metaphor, though it isn't _exactly_ what happens in the brain.

calvinopio: So what I mean is that adults have different emotional neighborhoods even if they are cut off. That is very obvious.

hglt: Can you give me an example?

calvinopio: Yes. For example my mom. I can't prove that her neighborhood wasn't cut off but I know that she was not like other adults.

hglt: In what way?

calvinopio: She was bothered by things. You would probably say that it was her reason but I don't think so. Often times she really seemed hurt.

hglt: That's interesting. How could you tell that she was hurt?

calvinopio: I can't explain it I just know she was.

hglt: Could it have been your imagination? Sometimes we do something called "projection." We project our feelings onto others. So in this example, it might have been that you were feeling hurt and you imagined that feeling coming from your mother, not yourself.

calvinopio: No. I wasn't imagining it. It was real.

hglt: I'm just saying that it's a possibility.

calvinopio: It's not a possibility. You don't understand. She was really hurt.

Was that the end of the test?

hglt: Not quite. You're doing a great job.

7

NATALIA

Three days after Dr. Baylor introduced us to her idea of a good time, I was at work when my phone rang. I consider it tacky to have a phone visible, let alone on, but I always keep it within reach because of Cal. The translucent decal is tucked inside a slim, leather-bound translation of *De rerum natura*, which I know makes me something of a luddite, but the phone is too flimsy and expensive to keep it anywhere else. Book pages make excellent padding.

In this case the timing worked for me, because I was in the middle of trying to extricate myself from a sticky situation. It happens, not that often but maybe once a month, that one of the Landmark guests, male or female, gets it into his or her head that the cleaning staff are all available for the use of guests, much like the towels and the free shampoo. This is not the case, or I wouldn't be working there. Usually it starts with an unwelcome look in the hall. Then a spurious request for a clean bathrobe or a new pillow. Then, once you're in the room, they tend to get more creative.

After I got the handbook in high school explaining about

the five instincts, I turned to Mom for more explanation. Reproductivity?? Mom did her best to explain how lust and love are two different things. (Explaining sex stuff falls neatly under "easygoing," which is one thing I can say for the adjective.) "Love," Mom said to me, "is like building a ship, Talia. Do you know how to build a ship? Because I don't. Planks and masts and ropes and sails? Way, way too complicated. Lust, on the other hand, is like an ocean. Calm and soothing or crazy and wild or stormy and scary. Sometimes good and sometimes bad, but not terribly complicated. The first you have pretty much no chance of figuring how to do on your own, ever. And the second requires no figuring out at all."

I found this unsatisfying, coming from Mom, as an explanation for why my dad and Cal's dad never pictured in our lives, but I found it very satisfying as an explanation for the unpredictable, irrational, and often self-destructive behavior of many adults of my acquaintance.

Officer Gao, the cop who taught our high school D&D class (Discipline and Defense, for those of you lucky enough to have forgotten it) taught me all I would need to know about rendering one of these unwelcome advances impossible and likely painful for its protagonist, should it ever come to that, but usually it wasn't necessary. Usually a very firm and clearly worded "I'm not interested and the cleaning staff aren't here for that" does the trick. I try my best to keep it polite.

The dim bulb who was giving me a hard time that morning was a bit more persistent than usual. Very white, short blond hair, invisible eyebrows, predatory blue eyes, and one of those misguided workout bodies where the shoulders, arms, and chest are huge while the legs are little spindles. I knew that because he was wearing a towel around his waist and socks on his feet—nothing else. Even without speaking he'd gotten on the wrong side of me by having a live Fish stream on his decal, pasted up on the wall right next to the gold-plated light fixture. The Fish was using brass knuckles on someone's ribs, and the sound of it made terrible background music.

I could see by the strewn clothes that Spindle Legs had money—lots of it—which all the Landmark guests do, but they usually handle it with more discretion. In addition to some possibly shaved pectorals and veiny biceps, I could also see that this one, being on the young side, still had some discretion left to acquire.

"Come on," he was saying, with a lazy smile. It wasn't fake. He was taking one of those fancy calibrated regimens where you get a nice cocktail of synaffs once a day and most of the emotions you might want to feel release at the right moment. It's like having a programmed juice maker in your head. Very handy. Never mind that doctors are woefully corrupt, and I've seen them prepare some pretty suspect juice recipes, with about 95 percent hedonistic joy and 5 percent relaxed serenity. This guy was on something that was probably more like 70 percent of the latter. I wasn't worried, but I did want to avoid having to damage his lazy smile and then explain it to my supervisor.

"There's a place right down the street," I said informationally. "It's open twenty-four hours. The guys and gals are very friendly. And I'm really not. As you can see."

"But I want to have a good time with *you*."

"Sorry. We don't do that here."

A flicker of frustration, probably more about sex than synaffs, made its way into his eyes. His nostrils flared a half millimeter. Contempt. "Are you sure you can afford this? Being all uppity costs money, dulce."

What did I tell you? They always deserve it.

"Lucky for me I'm an heiress. I just work here because I love rubber gloves." I snapped mine on with deliberation, making him blink.

That's when my phone rang, saving me from doing further damage.

"Excuse me," I said, turning around quickly and pulling *De rerum natura* out of my apron pocket. As I was opening the book I was also listening, trying to hear whether his steps were following mine on the polar bear rug. They weren't. The serenity had kicked back in, drowning out his brief bullishness. I reached the room door, opened it, and shut it quickly behind me, turning my full attention to the phone. It was a number I didn't recognize in Oakland. I answered anyway.

"Hello?"

"Hello, Miss Peña?"

"Yes."

"This is Mr. Freeman. The principal at Moses."

"Yes," I said again. I stopped myself from asking what was wrong.

"I'm calling to let you know that Cal's test was very informative, and we'd like to do more tests with him."

I didn't understand what that meant. It seemed like two statements that didn't belong together, or maybe three that did but the middle one was missing. I put that thought into more coherent words. "If the test was informative, what is your intended purpose with doing further testing?"

Mr. Freeman fell momentarily silent. "Dr. Baylor is in charge of the testing," he said, apparently in response to some other question, because it didn't say a thing about mine. "Could you come to the school now? Cal requested your presence."

That was a problem. There were many problems, actually, and I tried to see them all at once as I answered Mr. Freeman. The main problem was that they wanted to do more tests at all. Then there was the problem of Mr. Freeman not being entirely forthcoming about why, which appeared to contain other problems I couldn't guess at. And there was the problem of my leaving work. I had taken my last sick day for Cal's previous test. One more sick day and I'd lose my job. "That would be difficult," I said, going for understated and decisive. "Let's schedule the test for another day."

"No, we can't. Dr. Baylor would like to do the tests now."

"That may be, but today is impossible. We'll need to re-schedule."

There was a pause on the other end of the line. "Dr. Baylor has already started the test."

I stopped for a moment. "She does not have permission to do additional testing."

"I'm letting you know that she's already begun."

This conversation was going nowhere. The time for getting the upper hand had clearly passed, and I wasn't sure if I'd missed it or just hadn't been given the opportunity in the first place. I recalculated. Cass and Tabby were in Richmond installing a sign. Joey was at work with his tyrannical boss. There was no one else who could go, and I wanted to be there anyway. "I am leaving San Francisco immediately. I will be there within an hour. Dr. Baylor should know that we will not be cooperating further with her demands for testing."

"I'll tell Dr. Baylor," Mr. Freeman agreed.

I hung up, dropped *De rerum natura* into my apron, and pushed my little cart as fast as the tiny little wheels would go through the ridiculous carpet. Marta was at the other end of the hallway. I practically threw my cart at her. "What's wrong?" she asked me, eyes alert.

"They are testing Cal again. Without permission. Now. And I have no more sick days." Marta knows all about Cal— I'd explained the whole thing to her.

"Go," she said at once, pointing down the corridor like she was an oracle of the ancient world, gesturing the way toward my doom. Marta, what a gem. I'd spotted for her once or twice, and I knew she'd cover me as best she could.

"Thank you, you beautiful thing."

"Hurry," she commanded, still pointing.

I hurried. I grabbed my bag from the supply closet but didn't change, so I was still wearing my black-and-white uniform as I left the hotel—back entrance, naturally. My work shoes were good for this. I scooted to the BART, half running, half power walking. I waited four minutes for a train and sent Cal a message saying I was on my way. Twenty minutes later I was leaving the station in Oakland, walking as fast as I could but knowing I wouldn't make it if I tried to run. Forty-three minutes after Dr. Freeman had called me, I knocked on his open door.

His room was still overly odorous and funereal. Sweat was running down my neck, and I could tell my hat was wonky from the look he gave me. "Miss Peña," he said tonelessly.

"I'm here. Where's Cal?"

"I believe Dr. Baylor has already taken him to the lab for additional testing."

"I told you on the phone that I was coming in from San Francisco."

"I did pass that on to her."

I looked at him hard, trying to figure out whether to dress him down or ask another question. "What do you mean she's 'taken' him?"

"She said it would be necessary to take Cal to RealCorp to conduct the additional testing."

"She doesn't have permission to do that."

Mr. Freeman paused. He opened the desk drawer to his left, flipped through some files, and pulled out a piece of paper. "The Lawsons signed this on the eighth. It gives Dr. Baylor permission to do additional testing, either on the school premises or at RealCorp."

I remembered them signing the paper, but I'd had no idea there was a hand grenade in the fine print. "Could you give me Dr. Baylor's phone number?"

Mr. Freeman blinked. "I don't have it."

"You don't have it," I repeated, disbelieving.

"I've never had occasion to call her."

I didn't feel much of anything as the words rolled out from under Mr. Freeman's mustache, and yet I had this sense that I was suddenly seeing some rooms in my head that I hadn't seen for a long, long time. They were empty now, but in the past there were ugly things there: a dark, shapeless stain of uncertainty; the nasty, soiled furniture of terror; a hunched figure screaming with ceaseless, high-pitched panic. Even in the empty room, I could still hear the echo.

I turned my back on Principal Freeman's hideous office and headed back out into the sunlight.

8

NATALIA

On the train back to San Francisco, I sent Joey a message telling him what was happening. He replied within seconds, *Should I join?* which was swell of him, but I told him that no, I would keep him posted.

I got off at Embarcadero, where I used one of the public restrooms to change out of my uniform and back into my street clothes: khaki skirt, cotton blouse, navy raincoat, and low heels. It was one thing to show up dressed as a maid at Cal's school, but it was another to show up like that at Real-Corp, where they would be happy to find any reason to put me out on the curb.

All the big pharmaceuticals in SF are by the water, including RealCorp. I got on the southbound trolley. The fog had moved in during my truncated trip to Oakland, and now it lay thick on the streets, making it seem as though the whole city was struggling under the weight of a persistent, unwanted ghost. I sat and watched the fog swallow the buildings along the pier until I noticed the man standing next to me on the trolley. He was gripping the pole inches from my face, and his arms and hands were covered with dried blood. I could see it had been there awhile because it was flaking, leaving his hairy arms bare in patches.

Without moving my head, I shifted my gaze upward to look at his face. He didn't look like a Fish, but I guess they come in all shapes and sizes. He had long hair pulled back in a band, an unkempt beard, and a lost, vacant expression in his eyes. Maybe he had forgotten about the blood. Maybe he hadn't noticed it. Maybe he was a butcher, I thought optimistically, although the velour shirt with rolled-up sleeves seemed to argue otherwise. He was considering the fog, too, looking at it with a pensive air as if trying to remember where he'd seen fog like that before. I didn't want to be around when he lost interest in the question.

I got off at the next stop, ducking around him carefully. No sense adding my blood to the stuff he already had, I figured. I walked ten minutes more and arrived at RealCorp.

It drifted toward me out of the fog like a ship made of steel and glass. Translucent screen decals were affixed to the windows, each square forming one tiny piece of a massive whole. The eight-second loop with the beautiful blonde woman was playing, her surprise and tears and joy shimmering across the RealCorp tower. Her mascaraed eyes were ten feet wide.

I took the revolving door with a steady step and clipped over the marble floor in my low heels. The entrance was a long, oversized nave filled with indoor trees and empty little islands made of linen sofas. They looked cozy, with magazines and throw blankets, like maybe it wouldn't be so bad to be shipwrecked there.

At the long marble counter stood four women who must have been kin to the advertising blonde. Different haircuts and colors did nothing to hide the copycat makeup, the uniform of muted cashmere and silk, and a set of synaffs that made their faces variations on a single theme: happy, welcoming, relaxed. I walked up to one of them who was already beaming at me, a brunette with pearl-colored eye shadow and perfect teeth. Leave it to RealCorp to staff their offices with models.

"Hi there," I said.

The brunette's smile widened. "Hi! Bienvenida. I'm Lucy. How can I help you today? Are you here to try one of our free twenty-four-hour synthetic affect regimens?"

"Nope." Her smile stayed put regardless. "I'm here to find my brother, Calvino Peña, who was brought by a Dr. Elizabeth Baylor for testing."

Lucy blinked a couple times in quick succession. "Testing?" she said, with mild distaste, as if I'd said "regurgitating."

"That's right. My brother Calvino is a ten-year-old student at Moses Elementary, and Dr. Baylor, employed by RealCorp, brought him over to use the equipment."

Lucy's smile had dimmed somewhat. "Hm. Lo siento. I don't believe we do any testing in this building, Miss . . . ?"

"Peña. Nat."

"Miss Peña, I certainly haven't seen anyone like that

come in here." She tilted her chin a little sideways. "Our clients come principally to meet with in-house consultants and determine their synaff regimens." Her smile brightened. "Would you like to do that?"

I bit back the retort. "Lucy, could you please find someone for me that will be able to locate Dr. Elizabeth Baylor?"

Lucy looked briefly crestfallen, and then she gave me a reassuring smile. "Of course, I'll do everything I can to help."

She picked up the handle of a new-retro phone, black, modeled in the manner of the mid-twentieth century. Her eyes glanced upward and sideways, holding a line of vision, and I realized she was looking into a camera. After dialing three numbers she spoke into the receiver. "Could you send Kathy to the lobby?" she asked cheerfully. She listened and hung up. "Someone will be here in just a moment," she said to me brightly. "In the meantime, please take a brochure." She handed me a glossy pamphlet with a cropped photo of the familiar blonde. "If you'd like to wait . . ." She gestured to one of the cozy linen islands.

"Thank you."

I didn't sit. I glanced through enough of the brochure to see that (1) there were no prices listed and (2) you could feel pretty much anything you wanted to feel if you were the kind of person who didn't need to see prices listed. The synaff regimens, illustrated with photographs of models, had names like spa packages: Natural Indulgence, Easy Balance, Cool Contemplation. The latter promised to put you "in a frame of mind that observes the world with thoughtfulness and consideration. You pick up on the finer points, because that's who you are."

Right. I tossed the brochure onto the shining surface of a lacquered coffee table, and I stood in front of a potted palm with my arms crossed, watching the models gab and giggle with one another. Lucy had already forgotten about my existence.

Within minutes, a woman in her mid-fifties emerged from a hallway at the far end of the marble counter and gave me a friendly wave. She wore the same makeup and cashmere, but her age and her air of efficiency marked her as a different pay grade. I was guessing in-house lawyer.

"Miss Peña?" she asked, extending a cool hand. I shook it. "I'm Kathy Moore." She smiled and gestured to the hallway she'd come from. "Please follow me."

I followed her to the hallway and into a small room off it, an even cozier version of the lobby islands. The linen sofas had embroidered throw pillows; abstract prints in warm pastels hung like prospective sunsets on the walls. Kathy motioned me onto a sofa, and as I sat down, one of the Lucys came in carrying a tray with tea. "Thank you," Kathy said without looking at her. She poured me a cup from the white china teapot and handed the steaming cup across. It smelled nice. Something flowery and maybe licorice. It tasted nice, too.

Holding my tea, I perched on the edge of the sofa and watched as Kathy leaned back, running a hand comfortably through her hair, crossing her legs. Her smile was confident. "I understand you're looking for someone."

"My brother, Calvino Peña, is a student at Moses Elementary in Oakland. The on-site physician there, Dr. Elizabeth Baylor, is employed by RealCorp. Today she brought Calvino here for testing to use RealCorp equipment, and I'm trying to find him."

Kathy had been nodding thoughtfully, as if I'd presented her with a real puzzle. "What makes you think he was brought here?"

"The principal at Moses told me so."

"Hm." Kathy shook her head slightly. "Dr. Baylor does work here, but we have no record of anything like what you describe."

"Could I talk to Dr. Baylor?"

"I already have. She remembers testing your brother at his school recently, but that's all." Kathy leaned forward and met my eyes, her expression earnest. "Sorry I can't tell you more."

I felt something in my head unspooling, a ribbon of thought that was normally tight and logical but that now seemed on the verge of unraveling completely. "Are you saying that the principal at my brother's school lied?"

Kathy's eyebrows shifted to concerned. "That would be strange, I agree."

I took a breath. "Look, Mr. Freeman is many things, but he's not imaginative. He doesn't care enough to lie about this." Even as I spoke the words, I was trying to figure out some reason, any possible reason, for Mr. Freeman to go bananas and make up some story about Dr. Baylor and Cal.

Maybe he wanted a junior assistant at his funeral parlor. Maybe he needed someone to help hold cold cartons of ice cream. It was unlikely, but it was the only thing I could think of if Cal wasn't at RealCorp.

"There must be some explanation," Kathy said, still looking concerned. There was something else there, besides the false concern. Eyes and mouth relaxed: confidence. And patience.

As I watched her face, I realized that something had changed. The hard questions at the front of my brain began softening. It was hard to remember what they were, exactly. I sat back against the embroidered pillows. Incredibly, I felt relaxed. More than that—I felt *good*. Content, at ease. I couldn't remember the last time I'd felt this way.

Even as I thought about kicking off my shoes, I understood that something was wrong. I knew, rationally, that I should not want to chat with Kathy for a little while longer and then take a nap on the sofa. I looked at her. "Did you put synaffs in this tea?"

She smiled. "It's just a little pick-me-up that I like to drink during the day."

That seemed like an understatement. I took a deep breath and put down my tea. I struggled against the enveloping, persuasive feeling that everything was okay. Everything was *not* okay.

Then Kathy made a mistake. She reached out and put a hand over mine. "Miss Peña, I can see that you are a very conscientious sister. But I'm sure that Cal will turn up on his own. In the meantime, I'd be happy to help with a longer-term synaff regimen that can take the edge off. On the house." She smiled.

For a moment I looked at her. The smile was fixed, unchanging. Her eyelids had come down a millimeter, intending to convey relaxation, and thereby reassurance. Instead they conveyed avarice.

It didn't bother me. What I felt was pleased—pleased at the prospect of more synaffs, and pleased that Kathy was so nice. I forced myself to say the words I knew I should say: "I want to see Calvino."

Kathy regarded me. "Why don't you sit here and make yourself comfortable? You look like you could use a rest. I'll be back in a little while."

"No." I pushed myself to my feet. It was excruciating. I had to get out of that room. I had to get away from this woman. From that tea.

"Miss Peña," Kathy objected. She stood up as well.

I pulled myself over to the door and opened it. Outside, a discreet five feet away, stood two men in loose blazers who would never make it as models. They held themselves with the encumbered weight of bulky muscles and concealed weapons.

Even the two thugs didn't dim my sense of sleepy well-being. I felt the tug of the room behind me, the warm light, the soft cushions. The tea. I forced myself forward. As I wheeled out into the hallway, the guards didn't move. I walked away from them as quickly as my mushy brain would allow. When I glanced over my shoulder, Kathy was watching me leave, her expression calculating.

Mr. Freeman hadn't lied to me. Not by a long shot. Cal was somewhere inside RealCorp, and they weren't going to give him back. He'd been snapped up into the steel and glass trap as surely as a little bird in a cage, and I was going to have to break it if I wanted to see him again.

As I scurried out I did not look up at the cameras that I knew were there. My heels clattered against the lobby floor and I stepped out into the fog. It had thickened. I couldn't even see the sidewalk under my feet.

9

CALVINO

oct-11

4:15 p.m.

calvinopio:

Essay: <u>What is the difference between instincts and emotion?</u> By Calvino Peña

Scientists say that emotions and instincts are different because adults still feel instincts. The five instincts they feel are hunger, exhaustion, shock, self-preservation, reproductivity. They say these instincts still exist because they keep people alive, unlike sadness and happiness. Adults still get hungry and eat, get tired and rest, getting shocked is like the body's way of saying it is overwhelmed, self-preservation is when you run out of the way when a car is coming, reproductivity is about human beings reproducing.

Instincts are very important. Children have them too. Adults have them and they use reason and instincts because they do not have emotions. Reason is something you can use when emotions are no longer kicking in. For example if you come home and find the door to your house open, a child would feel afraid but an adult would not. But an adult can use reason to think that someone must have broken into the house and then call the police.

There are some reactions like surprise and curiosity and suspicion that children can have as emotions but adults can have through reason. They are thoughts rather than emotions, for example with the open door I was describing that would make an adult suspicious but not afraid. There are also some reactions like discomfort or disgust that children would have as emotions but adults would have as instincts. It would be uncomfortable for an adult to sleep with a rock as a pillow, that is the body responding with an instinct. But for a child it would be uncomfortable for everyone to be staring at you. An adult wouldn't feel that.

Another one is humor. Humor is not an emotion. Humor is achieved by the intellect, which is part of reason. If you laugh at a joke it is not the same as laughing because you are happy. Just as crying because you are sad is not the same as crying because someone broke your leg. Both adults and children can laugh and cry. But children laugh and cry with emotion.

(Note: There are also emotions that can't be explained by reason or instinct that adults still have. For example it is true that liking something can be rational, such as liking money is rational because money allows you to survive. But liking a person is not rational.)

hglt: Thanks for this response, Calvino! Don't you think it could be rational to like companionship? There's a lot of evidence demonstrating that people do well—they thrive—when they are part of social units, like couples or families.

calvinopio: Maybe but I can't think of a rational reason for wanting children around and yet people do it. They just take a lot of work.

hglt: Are you thinking of your own situation?

calvinopio: Partly. There is no rational reason for my sister to want me to live with her, but she does.

hglt: Well, your sister has been through high school and has learned the value of social bonds. She's probably an excellent rule follower.

calvinopio: I really don't think so.

hglt: Then what do you think it is?

calvinopio: I have told you that there are invisible emotions. You may not believe that my sister can feel love but she does. You are going to say that it's projection again.

hglt: You know me so well!

calvinopio: Not really because all we have done is type. I know nothing about you.

hglt: What I mean is that you're very quick at picking up concepts.

calvinopio: Why isn't my sister here?

hglt: I'm afraid she can't be here right now.

calvinopio: You're afraid? Really? I thought you weren't capable of being afraid? Or are you on synaffs?

hglt: It's a figure of speech, of course.

calvinopio: How do I know if you are feeling afraid or not? How do I even know you are one person or many? Or a person at all? When are you going to let me out?

10

NATALIA

October 11—midday

The fog was my friend at the moment. Even RealCorp cameras couldn't see through the San Francisco fog. I walked down the block to the corner, crossed the street, and ducked into the trolley stop that was waiting for me, invisible, in the mist. There was an old man sitting there with a folded shopping cart and he gave me a quick look as I leaned back against the wall of the shelter, but he didn't say anything. I took deep breaths, willing the air into my lungs. I didn't know what I would do if the RealCorp thugs came after me. It took all my willpower just to focus on what I needed to do next. My whole body wanted to rest.

The trolley came and picked up the old man and deposited two passengers on the curb. I sat, and sat, and kept working against the synaffs.

Finally, after about an hour, they started to wear off. The contentment faded, and I was back in a familiar landscape. Now the sharp edges of my problem started to reappear out of the fog, even harder and more unyielding than they'd been earlier.

I changed into my crepe soles while I sat in the shelter. Then I walked back out toward RealCorp. Instead of following the main street toward the entrance I made a long detour that took me around to the side. I figured the back of the building facing the water would have all the fancy offices with views, so the loading dock and pleb entrance had to be on one of the sides. That was the case. On the north-facing side I found that the glass and steel frame hung suspended over a narrow alley. The fog allowed a view of an exceptionally well-lit loading dock and a set of steps that led to a double-door entrance.

I cuddled up with the building on the other side of the alley, an old-fashioned brick behemoth that might have been a prison for all the windows it had. There wasn't much in the way of hiding spots, so I looked at my watch and decided I would only stay as long as the fog.

I was lucky. In the thirty-five minutes I spent watching, I saw one shift leaving and another starting. Seventeen cleaning staff went in, seventeen cleaning staff went out. Two floors per person, roughly. Given the time of day, that meant they probably had three shifts. Six in the morning to two in the afternoon, two to ten in the evening, ten to six again. The uniforms were standard gray-and-white janitorial—easy enough to pick up at any rental place—but predictably the staff all carried identification cards in plastic holders clipped to their hips. I noticed that the people starting the two p.m. shift didn't use their cards for access—that was something. They just filed in through the open door past two seated security guards who barely spared them a glance. I had to hope it would be the same at ten.

I padded back the way I'd come and went back to the trolley stop. I checked *De rerum* again, just in case, but there was nothing from Cal. Only a question mark from Joey, which I answered with a brief explanation while I waited for the trolley. Joey texted back with more question marks and a few expletives while I was looking for a uniform rental place. I found one downtown in the Financial District, so I made for that one.

The city seemed cheery now that the fog was rolling back, as if happily surprised to find there were still a few hours of sunlight left to burn. There was no one wearing dried blood on the trolley, which I counted as a benefit. Only a man with a dramatically broken nose and a bouquet of stitches around his left eye. Two schoolkids with matching high-tops cast silent, woeful looks his way. When he was gone they whispered feverishly, their eyes wide with horror. They talked each other through the spectacle, murmuring theories and consolations. I watched them and tried not to think about what Cal was doing at that moment.

I spent more money than I meant to at the uniform place because they didn't have rental plans for single uniforms. That meant I had to buy the piece of polyester junk. *Go ahead, take my money,* I thought. *It's still cheap if it gets me in to Cal.* It was almost four by the time I got back on the BART to head to the Mission. I had one more stop, and it involved a place near Sixteenth that made credible fake identification badges. I was hoping I wasn't the first fool to contemplate breaking into RealCorp and that they had something like a template, because I didn't have a thing.

Probably because I was distracted sending more explanations to Joey by phone, I didn't think about why the train car I stepped into was almost empty. When I closed *De rerum* and put it back in my bag, I discovered the reason. There were three Fish hanging out together in the middle of the train.

Almost all Fish who know what they are embrace the term, and they wear something to signal membership in the decidedly not organized organization to which they belong. This makes them easy to spot, and I'm sure they consider the sidelong glances a benefit. Most settle for a fish pin on the lapel, but I've seen more extravagant gestures. Once, a narwhal costume, which seemed more cumbersome than it was worth. And another time a full-body tattoo of scales on every inch of visible skin, which . . . Well, you couldn't question his commitment, I guess.

These three were going for Roaring Twenties with flair, wearing tuxedo coats adorned with shark fins. They stood on the seats and looked around the car with an air of placid expectance, trying to figure out what to do with themselves. There were only two other people in the car. An older woman who was sitting near-ish to them, her back straight, her hands clasped firmly around a shopping bag, an expression of doggedness on her worn face.

And me.

The Fish looked in unison from her to me and back again. It didn't take much imagination to figure out that one of us was about to become Fish bait.

11

NATALIA

The three Fish were what I think of as prep school Fish. There is another choice besides the penitentiary, excuse me, school system that people like me go to. If your parents have a lot of money in the bank, you can go to one of the private high schools where they teach less discipline and more Shakespeare. I can see the appeal, but having met a few graduates I can say with conviction that it doesn't work out well. It probably worked swell back in the old days, but nowadays serving up Shakespeare to a bunch of untrained adolescents is like handing a serial killer a pack of gum. Yeah, thanks for that tasty diversion. Now let me get down to the business of carving your fingers off.

Two men—boys, really—in their early twenties. One girl a little older. All three with short, slicked-down hair and bright, curious eyes. Their eyes settled on the old woman. I could see their appetites getting whetted.

Fine, I thought. *Change of plan.* The whole identification card thing was a long shot anyway.

I had lost track of which station we were at, but we must have passed the downtown stations because the roaring train wasn't slowing down. Maybe three minutes, I estimated. I walked toward the old woman just as the Fish were jumping down from their seats. They looked at her speculatively, like they were trying to decide which appendage to remove first.

Still, she was staring at them with naked condescension. She was a tough old bird. Tough, but silly.

I stood next to her and she glanced up at me. "You should go stand by one of the doors," I said to her. She stared at me. "Really," I said.

The Fish were hovering around us in a semicircle, their eyes gleaming. The girl, who wore bright lipstick that looked bad with her complexion, pulled a switchblade from her pocket. She held it comfortably at her side; they were old friends, the girl and the switchblade, I could tell. But I could also tell that she didn't know how to balance her weight well, and the two boys even less so. Right now they were slipping on brass knuckles and watching the girl for guidance.

One of the many things my bone-crushing public school has over prep school? Officer Gao. I could hear his voice in my ear as I took out my expandable baton.

"Only fight in self-defense," Gao barked.

I snapped the baton open. The Fish looked at me, their glassy eyes bright. The girl held the switchblade to the side like she was going to toss a Frisbee. Then she swung toward us, aiming to hit me and the seated old lady with a single swipe. I blocked her arm with my hand and used the baton on her exposed ribs. She crumpled a little, and her face made a twisted mask.

"Always aim to disable."

The two boys, surprised, took a moment to jump in. They had already forgotten about the old lady, and despite having done this many times together, they seemed to have no instinct for coordination. One of them raised his fist to my face, and the other lunged forward with no clear objective.

"Never cause more injury than you have to."

I brought the baton down on the tensed neck muscles of the first boy and popped open the can of mace that had found its way from my bag into my other hand. I sprayed the lunger in the face.

"Find the weakest spot that will yield the most effective non-fatal damage."

The old lady was hunched down in her seat, but she was watching us with wide eyes. Bad Lipstick dove toward me with the switchblade out in front of her. I dodged sideways, bumping the boy who was wailing about the mace. Then I brought the baton down on the girl's back as she was trying to stop herself from falling against the empty seats.

The train started slowing down.

"You are always stronger defending than attacking."

That might be so, Officer Gao, but I needed another twenty seconds for the train doors to open. Before the boy who was still standing could try to get in another swing, I closed my fist around the little mace can and punched him in the stomach.

"Come on," I said to the old lady, hurriedly dumping mace and baton into my bag. I took her by the arm and she scurried along with me to the doors.

The two Fish who didn't have mace in their eyes were recovering. I figured they would have no problem following us. The train stopped. After an interminable wait, the doors opened. We spilled out onto the platform and I gave the old lady a gentle push. "Go tell the transit police. Be quick."

"Thank you," she said, her voice strained, and she stumbled off toward the window of the transit police office.

I waited a moment longer to see what the Fish were doing. They had put themselves back together, sort of, and they were careening toward the open BART doors. I pulled the strap of my bag tight against my shoulder and started running.

As I took the steps up to the overpass I thanked myself silently for the crepe-soled shoes. But the bag was annoying. It swung out even with the strap pulled tight, so I hugged it close like a little pillow and kept running. I passed over to the other side of the tracks, where a train heading back downtown was approaching. That was lucky. Waiting around on the platform for a train would have been awkward. I didn't have that much mace. The alarm in the station went off as I hit the platform. So the old bird had actually gone to the transit police. That was very decent of her.

The train pulled in and I shot toward the nearest car. I glanced up to see how far behind me the Fish were, wondering if they would catch the same train. They would. I turned away and jogged through the car. "Fish," I called out, in case the passengers hadn't heard the station alarm. It was only fair to warn them. "Three Fish coming your way." A few people managed to dive out of the car doors before they closed. The rest plastered themselves into their chairs, leaving the aisle free.

I slid out the rear end of the car and through the gangway into the next one as the train started moving. I could see through the grimy window that the three Fish were aboard and, surprisingly, they were not getting distracted by all the cowering people around them. They were looking for me. And they were being very thorough. Was I under a seat or curled up under that big hat? Better check.

I kept going and didn't issue any more warnings, since the Fish seemed so focused in their pursuit. We pulled into the Civic Center. A handful of people climbed in and out. I thought to myself wryly that some help from the Landmark guest with the spindle legs would have been really, really useful right then. It's always about timing. I zeroed in on a guy who looked similar, not that he physically resembled Spindle Legs, because he had black hair and scruff and delicate eyebrows, but he was taking similar synaffs and dropping his eyes at me in a similar lazy-but-interested way. Letting a big, fake smile of the kind I can't stand expand over my face, I walked over to him. He looked startled and pleased. I leaned in close and got up on my tiptoes to whisper in his ear. "Would you help me change my clothes?" I smiled up at him like this was an amazing and fun idea.

He blinked. "Sure."

I took off my raincoat and held it up. "Make a little screen for me?"

He smiled, starting to see what the game was about, and held it up a bit above my shoulders. As he did, we reached Powell Street.

With a sly wink, I pulled on the gray janitorial pants, bunching my dress up at my waist in the process. A little exposure was unavoidable, but I had no intention of giving this guy a free show. I pulled the dress up over my head in a single motion and stuffed it in my bag. To his regret, I was wearing a very sensible camisole. Cream-colored. Not an inch of lace. I pulled on the white-and-gray janitorial shirt, wonderfully loose with no buttons, and put my hands out in a big "Ta-da!" of success. He looked disappointed, and I didn't blame him. He'd seen less of me than he would have at the beach. "Thank you so much!" I said with another big smile. I took the raincoat from him.

"Let's do this again," he said hopefully as I closed my overstuffed bag.

"Sure," I said, but not in an overly encouraging way. Being all saucy like that requires way too much energy.

We had reached Montgomery, and I could see that the three Fish had also just about reached my car. It would have to be Montgomery, then. The doors opened and I stepped out. Two doors down, the Fish burst out onto the platform after me. There was a lot more running ahead of us. I really had to hope that their good-for-nothing prep school had at least prepped them for a little track-and-field.

I launched out of the station onto Market Street and almost right away turned left onto Sansome. I made a staircase on the map heading northeast, stepping into traffic often and earning myself a few spirited hand gestures in the process. As I glanced back, I could see that the Fish were struggling to keep up, Mace Boy especially. But they were still on my tail.

A few minutes later I crossed the trolley tracks and saw RealCorp up ahead. I slowed down a little bit. The Fish were within shouting distance, and they took advantage of it, using up all their air to hurl some keen and very imaginative possibilities about my future toward me. As they closed the distance, I picked up my speed. We'd reached the corner of RealCorp and it was time to sprint. I dashed toward the brightly lit loading dock, where the same two security guards were sitting in almost exactly the same posture. "Help!" I shouted, waving my hands. That made it very hard to run. I put my hands down. "Help," I said again. "Fish! Three of them!" They came into view as they charged after me toward the loading dock, and the two security guards got to their feet. I could see that the two of them together could not have bested a third-grader in a game of checkers, but thankfully they had enough wattage to see my uniform and see three Fish in pursuit and put one and three together. That was all I needed. They reached for their holsters just as I scrambled up the iron steps. "The girl has a knife," I gasped.

"Go," the guard closest to me said, waving me into

the building. "We'll take care of them." He turned a big scowl of concentration on the approaching Fish. His buddy did the same, but he had already pulled his gun from its holster.

Aw, I thought. *So sweet. Two such big guys protecting little old me.* I didn't feel an ounce of regret for the Fish, but it would have been nice to watch them make the acquaintance of the two guards.

I know, I know—Officer Gao would definitely not have approved.

12

NATALIA
October 11—afternoon

I was inside RealCorp. I had tried to find floor plans or interior shots, but the building was a black box—no one knew a thing about it. So I was starting from scratch.

There were four cleaning carts in the corridor, identically tidy and parked diagonally. Four cleaning carts, just for me? It was like a handwritten invitation. I took the farthest one and gave it an appreciative pat on the side. Then I ambled down the corridor, doing my best to slow my breathing. I did not have a hat because none of the janitorial staff had been wearing one, and I knew that anyone looking for someone suspicious on the security cameras would not have to look far.

I took the elevator up to the third floor. From the height of the ceiling in the front foyer, I figured there wouldn't be much on floor two. The elevators opened on 3 and I poked my head out. Cubicles. Lowly administrative, I figured, from their size and the hive-like murmuring of workers who had not earned the privilege of privacy. I ducked back into the elevator and tried 4. It looked identical to 3.

The fifth floor had closed offices. I did a quick loop through the corridors and found that while these employees were lucky enough to count on doors and walls, they were not lucky enough to close those doors. And the walls facing the corridors were made of glass. So even an abbreviated tour gave me a flawless glimpse into the life of RealCorp middle management. Lots of spacing out in front of screen decals. Some listless phone calling. The occasional game of solitaire.

Not until the tenth floor did I hit labs, and there I had to skip a floor because someone with a cleaning cart spotted me from fifty meters away down the corridor. She gave me a confused look and I responded with a little wave. Then I pressed 11.

The lab equipment, apparently, was more deserving of privacy than all the RealCorp employees put together, because there wasn't a pane of glass on the entire floor. Long cement corridors. Smooth cement walls. Very locked doors. I had a little trouble mapping the floor in my head because the corridors were so similar.

I wasn't giving up yet, but I had to admit as I rolled back into the elevator and pressed 12 that I wasn't going to get very far if all the labs were like 11. I pushed the thought aside and determined to look at every floor before deciding on the next step.

Twelve was like a combination of 11 and 5. Glass offices interspersed with very locked labs. The offices here were larger and designed for group work. Counter-height desks. Many more screens. Many more gadgets that I had never seen before. I expected lab coats like Dr. Baylor's, but the scientists seemed to favor late twentieth-century grunge. There were a lot of baggy sweatshirts and crazed hair and thick spectacles.

I was wheeling the cart past one of the long glass offices when an unseen occupant spoke through the open door. "Natalia Peña," the voice said, sounding pleased.

I stopped the cart. I turned around slowly and looked into the office. The voice came from an old man with a gleaming scalp. He was grinning at me, a skeletal grin with thinning gums. His skin was a sheet of damp paper draped over his skull, as colorless as if he hadn't left the offices of RealCorp for thirty-five years. Judging by his fingernails, it had been roughly that long since his last serious attempt at grooming, too. "Do I know you?" I asked.

The old man chuckled with some secret mirth. "Nope." He held out his hand. "Hugh Glout."

Now I was wishing that I'd pulled on some rubber gloves from the cart. Too late for it. I gave him the loosest handshake I possibly could.

"I'm impressed you got up here so quickly," he said, still grinning. "I've been watching on the cameras. Actually, I sort of told security not to bother you." He glanced modestly at the floor and then up at me, eyebrows lifted.

What did he want, a thank-you card? I looked at him noncommittally. "Why?"

"You're looking for your brother, Calvino," he announced.

Well, I thought. *Either my winning streak is over for the day, or I've just hit the jackpot.* I couldn't tell by the look of him. His smile was clearly synthetic, but there was something behind it that was unusual. It seemed more grounded, less one-dimensional than most synthetic smiles. There was a twinge in his eyebrow expressive of an underlying condition—a slight but chronic pain. Melancholy. His head was at a slight tilt, suggesting hopefulness or deference, but he also held his shoulders crooked, so maybe he just had wonky posture.

Old people are complicated. The more years they had before fading, the more emotional luggage they carry. Sometimes that luggage makes it into their faces. Glout had lived with more years of real smiles, and those somehow still lingered in the fake ones. I had to admit that he was difficult to read.

"Yes, I am," I said. I left it at that to see what else he would offer.

"Although it's strange that you've persisted. You're either taking an especially strong dose of attachment, which doesn't seem to be the case." He squinted at me. "Or you are a dedicated rule follower where family ties are concerned." He tried to puzzle it out as I stared at him in silence. "I thought Kathy was very persuasive."

That made some sense as an observation, but it had nothing to do with me, so I waited.

"You must be very proud of your brother," he finally said, like he was testing a theory. "He's a very special kid."

I didn't like that. "Special" has an unpleasant ring to it when it's surrounded by science experiments. But it did at least tell me one thing. He knew Cal. Which meant Glout was worth talking to. "I can't afford that kind of sentiment," I said drily.

He laughed like that was a great gag. "Sure, sure," he said. He waved at the room in a general way. "I told security to let you up because I wanted you to understand the work I do in this lab. Would you like to know what I do here?"

I had my suspicions about the verb "understand," but my suspicions wouldn't get far on their own. "Why not?" I said. I'd already scoped out the room and could glean little from its contents. Despite his neglected personal appearance, Glout was tidier than most of his colleagues and he seemed to favor uncluttered surfaces. There were a lot of screen decals and a lot of polished steel counters. An old-school monitor embedded in the wall was dark and still, like a sleeping portal onto another decade. Glout had a keyboard from last century, beige and with most of the letters worn off, wired to a mainframe the size of a sink cabinet. On the desk before him was an open spiral-bound notebook covered in spidery blue ink.

"Much of RealCorp is devoted to the manufacture of synthetic affects, as I'm sure you know," Glout began. "But like any company, RealCorp puts most of its unseen energy into research and development. Which I am chief of," he added, as an afterthought. "And the matter of most enduring interest to us in R&D is understanding why people wane. We want to understand the source of affect decline and, if possible, stall, reverse, or even eliminate it."

That much I could have guessed. "Really? I thought RealCorp was more interested in promoting affect decline so it could profit from the consumption of synaffs."

Glout laughed generously. He didn't sting easily—bad sign. He was either very used to ridicule or very confident, and it didn't look to me like Glout got out enough to be ridiculed. "RealCorp does profit from synaffs," he conceded. "And it would profit just as much, if not more, if it had the ability to reverse affect decline." He raised his hands, palms up. "Isn't that what everyone wants? The holy grail? The fountain of youth? The ability to feel things again?"

I shrugged. "As far as I can tell, people mostly want money. They can always buy feelings."

He considered my reply in silence for a moment. Then he changed his tack. "What do you think caused affect decline? I mean originally—years ago when people started to wane so slowly that it wasn't immediately apparent?"

"Something about emotional intelligence. You should know better than I do."

Glout frowned. "Yes, I should. But I don't know. No one knows. As you say, we describe it as a problem of emotional intelligence. But what caused the problem? There are all kinds of theories. Theories about brain degeneration. Theories about an infectious disease that permanently damaged transmitters and somehow became heritable. Theories about natural selection. And those are just the saner ones. But that's not the theory I believe." He gave me a wacky smile. "Want to take a guess at my theory?"

"Not really."

"I'll give you a hint," he went on, enthusiasm still at full sail. "It has to do with how we relate to one another."

I gave him a blank look and waited.

"My theory is about empathy. The ability to comprehend and share the emotions of other people. Lazy thinkers have characterized it as outward driven; something fundamentally relational, about interacting with others. That might be so, but empathy is also like a mirror. In seeing terror in others, our hearts start pounding. Seeing people cry, we feel grief ourselves. Do you remember watching Calvino when he was a baby? That was pre-wane for you, so you had emotions, too. And I bet Cal learned about emotions largely from watching you. You'd laugh, and then he'd laugh."

I saw a flaw in his logic. "What about kids who live only with adults?"

"Aha!" Glout said, raising one bony finger in triumph. "Exactly. What about those kids? They still have emotions, we know that, but could it be that waning began in a situation like the one you describe? Children watching parents with no affect."

"Why would parents back then have no affect? It must have started somewhere. You're getting chicken-and-egg-y."

"That's what's so interesting." Glout beamed. "For many years before waning began, there was a measurable decline in levels of empathy. People felt things, for sure. But they felt less and less *for others*."

"Why?"

"We don't know," Glout said triumphantly. "Each generation just seemed to be less empathic than the last, even though according to reason they should have been more empathic. Thanks to successive innovations, they were more in touch with one another, more exposed to different kinds of people in different parts of the world, more informed and more networked. It defied reason. Researchers thought of it as an isolated problem." Glout peered at me grimly. "And it seemed they might be right, because at first nothing else happened. Just waning empathy. People kept feeling the usual emotions even though they empathized less and less with the emotions of others. But eventually, the brain starts to ossify, get stuck in a rut. It forgets about connections it doesn't use. Observing and feeling the emotions of others is critical to unlocking our own emotions. And I think without empathy, we lost the ability to feel not just others' emotions, but also our own."

"Huh," I said.

"This is one of the reasons I've focused so much of my research budget on studying people with acute affect disorders. The people you know as 'Fish.' Most researchers think they are 'poor reasoners'—that is, they are too simpleminded to follow society's guidelines—and I've seen a dozen studies claiming to prove it: that they don't perform as well on IQ tests; that they don't respond rationally to stressors; that their brains, postmortem, are different from normal brains in ways that indicate a shrunken intellect. I disagree. I think their extreme behavior has something to do with empathy. While their behavior *seems* radically un-empathic, I think when they hurt people over and over again, these are actually desperate attempts—desperate *biological* attempts—to feel empathy. To feel what the other person feels."

I was interested, damn him. And I was already several steps ahead. I knew where he was going with this. Yes, Cal was a special kid. Yes, he was very empathic. He was so empathic I had to argue with him not to give his lunch away.

He was so empathic he got teary at the sight of lobsters in a lobster tank. He was so empathic he spent most of his energy wondering and thinking and worrying about other people— not just me and Cass and Tabby and Joey, but every single person we knew and every single person we glimpsed on the street. He was like an ever-burning, everlasting lightbulb of empathy.

I frowned. "Okay," I said. "That sounds plausible. I buy it."

"You see where I'm going. What if the solution lay in the problem?" Glout asked eagerly. "What if empathy was not just the doorway to affect decline, but also the doorway to affect recovery?"

"Could be."

"Then the problem would be this: if we understand empathy to mean the ability to feel what someone else is feeling, how do we provoke empathy in people who cannot feel?"

Abruptly, I realized that I didn't care about this. I didn't care about fixing the problem or reversing affect decline. This was not my problem. I was having a conversation with a loony old skeleton who probably had Cal locked in a room, jabbed full of needles. Glout was giving me the runaround. I took a shortcut.

"You think Cal is not fading because he is so empathic. I get it. But I'm not a freshman in neuropsych at Caltech, so you can skip the rest of the lecture."

"Actually, I teach at Stanford."

Typical. "Whatever. I'm not really interested. And Cal is not a rat from the sewer or a chunk of algae. You don't get to experiment on him just because you have a fantasy about saving the world. I want to know if he's here and if he's okay. And I want to know why he's here."

Glout nodded, a little deflated that I'd derailed his lesson plan. He studied me. "I can't tell you where Calvino is, but I can confirm that he's okay."

"What about a little proof of life or something, pal? Can I see him? Can I talk to him?"

Glout's eyes went sad, and I couldn't tell if it was real. "Lo siento, Natalia. No."

"Can you tell me why he's here? Were his test results with Dr. Baylor off the charts or something?"

Glout pondered for a moment. "All I can tell you is that the directive I received on this came from the very top."

He made it sound like Cal had been awarded a medal. "I'm impressed," I said, not sounding it. "Regardless of how he got here, he's my brother. Whatever form we signed at school, I'm sure it doesn't give RealCorp permission to keep Cal forever. I'm going to ask nicely. Please hand him over."

Glout deliberated for a while. He let out a long, low exhalation. "I was afraid of this."

"Afraid of what?"

"That you wouldn't know." He sighed again. "I do have permission."

I blinked. "Show me the form Cass and Tabby signed."

Glout shook his head. "The form isn't the issue. For reasons all of you understand better than I do, the Lawsons did not actually adopt Cal when your mother died last year."

That chilled me. How did he know all this? Where was this going?

He didn't seem to relish the pause. He was just working his way up to the next part. "A foster parent is not the same as an adoptive parent. And Cal was adopted two days ago. By RealCorp."

I felt the floor tip. My hand swung out for the counter nearest me, and as Glout reached toward me, quicker than I would have thought his skeleton arms were capable of, something flashed through his face that I hadn't seen in an adult face for ages, if ever. But I saw it often enough in Cal's face. Eyebrow heads raised, upper eyelids slanting, lips pressed together.

Glout felt sorry for me.

It took me a little while to steady myself. "It's shock," Glout said quietly. "We think of it as an emotion, but it's a biological response. That's one we managed not to get rid of."

"Yeah, I know," I finally said, finding my voice. "Instincts. I got the damn textbook."

Glout grimaced. "The book they give you in high school is a little reductionist. It doesn't really talk about all other instincts that we still have. Or explain that modern science doesn't understand them. Or that all of modern science is a social construct. Like religion. Or magic."

He was trying to talk me through it. I could hear him even though there was still a roaring in my ears. I wanted it to go away. "You must take empathy," I observed, trying to move the conversation out of my head.

His grimace faded to a gentle smile. "I should have clarified that. Even though I believe empathy is the key to affect decline, it's not what we call an 'emotion.' It's an approach to emotions. Comparable, say, to repressing or expressing emotions. A thing you *do* with emotions, not an emotion itself." He watched me carefully. "But I do take a combination of synaffs that mimics pity. It's not quite the same thing. Not the same thing at all," he admitted. "It doesn't really work to pity someone when they're angry. Or happy." He gave a little sigh.

"Can a corporation be an adoptive parent?" I asked.

Glout nodded. "It can. Same legal rights as individuals. But I misspoke. It's still easier and faster for the adopting agent to be an individual. The person in question in this case is RealCorp's chief executive officer, Tanner Philbrick. The same one who recommended I look at Cal's results."

Tanner Philbrick, I said in my head. The words didn't make much sense. I didn't understand how some person I'd never heard of had the motivation, let alone the right, to adopt Cal. How was that possible? I guess the shock was taking a little longer than I thought. I felt nauseated.

I took a deep breath and looked closely at Glout, who was watching me in turn. He looked a bit concerned, but he was concerned on my behalf; he wasn't in the least concerned about what I was going to do next. Maybe he was right.

"Can you help me?" I asked him.

Glout's concern deepened. "Yes and no. I can't hand Cal over to you. Apart from the fact that I think he's got something important going on in his brain, and we need to understand it, Cal is here legally. I'd be assisting in an abduction if I put him in your hands."

I was still feeling nauseated. I waited for Glout to tell me the "yes" part.

"But I can assure you that Cal is doing fine, and I can promise to keep you updated."

That didn't make much sense to me. "Updated on what? You won't even tell me where he is."

Glout looked apologetic. "I mean I can keep you posted on how he's doing." Something on one of the screen decals caught his eye. "Ah," he said. "I see Kathy has gotten wind of this. She's on her way now with a couple of the big guys."

I had no desire for a rematch with Kathy and her cashmere. "Can you send me a photo? A text from him? Can you tell him that I came?"

Glout's eyebrows knotted. "Here," he said, scribbling on a corner of the spiral-bound notebook. "This is my office phone. I will answer whenever I can. And I will tell you how he's doing. Promise."

It was all he would give me. A lousy phone number.

13

CALVINO

oct-11

7:05 p.m.

calvinopio:

Essay: <u>What keeps the world working in the absence of emotions?</u> By Calvino Peña

This is what is called a leading question. The answer is rules. I have answered this many times in school, Dr. Glout. Rules keep the world working. Rules are the only way adults without emotions can still get through life. Rules protect us from each other. Rules are the best. Hooray for rules.

This is true to some extent. There need to be laws against murder and theft and terrible things like that. But what you don't realize is that rules do not actually replace emotions. They are a form of emotion. It comes from an emotion to want to protect people's lives. You might call it an idea, but it is also an emotion. The idea alone would not stand a chance.

The other thing about rules is that they all come from one very overwhelming emotion which is fear. If society did not have fear then it would have no problem with everyone just being murdered left and right. It is fear of that type of world and fear of it happening to oneself that creates rules in the first place.

This is what I mean about invisible emotions. They are there, but they are so quiet that adults seem to not hear them. But they still act based on them. Imagine you were in a room and it was very noisy. You could hear traffic and people talking in the next room and the furnace clanking. It was so noisy that you did not realize that in the background was a very, very quiet music that was extremely sad. Or how about this, not music but a very, very quiet voice whispering to you. You were not aware of the voice because of the noise in the room, but it was still whispering. "Look out the window. Look out the window. Look out the window." Over and over again. After a while, for some reason, you would just want to look out the window and you would have no idea why.

That is how it works with emotions in adults. The voice is very quiet, but it is still whispering in the crowded, noisy room: "you are lonely, you are lonely, you are lonely." And that person, what do you know, doesn't want to be alone.

That's it, I don't have anything more to write, Dr. Glout. You said this would be the last one.

hglt: Last one for today! So I did. Thanks for this response, Calvino! This is a very creative way of explaining what you observe as affect. What you're describing is called "subliminal" stimulus. It's a very interesting theory.

calvinopio: It's not a theory. I have seen it.

hglt: Can you give me an example?

calvinopio: I'm really tired. Can I please come out of here for just a little while?

hglt: Maybe tomorrow. Could you give me an example of the subliminal messaging you were talking about?

calvinopio: If I do can I come out?

hglt: Sorry, I'm trying to keep things calm in there for you, and having people go in and out wouldn't help.

calvinopio: Sorry?? If you are sorry, then you would help me.

hglt: You're good at catching these. It's a figure of speech!

calvinopio: I would like to go home now.

hglt: It's important that we finish this test.

Calvino?

Hello, Calvino?

Okay. Good night, Calvino. Try to get some rest. Talk to you in the morning.

14

NATALIA

When you're a child in a world of faded grown-ups, grown-ups are confounding. Rational is not always reasonable. It might be rational to skip a kid's birthday when you barely have money for groceries, but that doesn't make it right. And to a child, most of the things grown-ups do are like that. Rational. But not right. I see it all the time in Cal's eyes, when he looks at me, at Cass and Tabby: he's waiting, wondering. *How on earth are they going to explain this one?* And I remember feeling it myself. That sense that grown-ups followed a logic that was inscrutable and often damaging. They could never be made to *see*.

When Cal was two and I was nine, Mom had pneumonia. She checked in to a hospital and didn't come home for a week. She hadn't said good-bye, and she wouldn't let us visit. It was rational, because she was contagious and too sick to take care of us. But it was also brutal. It felt like she'd abandoned us in the wilderness. I remember holding Cal in my lap at night, soothing him to sleep, waiting for his breathing to slow down so that I could cry, and cry, and cry. I would cry until my eyes were swollen and I was hiccuping and Cal was squirming against me. She was never coming back. She had turned her back on us. She had never loved us to begin with. *Why? Why? Why?* The pain was indescribable, and it was only one week.

I didn't want Cal to feel abandoned.

I wanted to spend the rest of the day trolling the corridors of RealCorp, banging on doors until I found him. I wanted to set up camp in Glout's office and hound his every move until he gave me a clue.

Despite the bad odds, I even spent some seconds debating the more extreme possibilities: knocking Glout to the floor, taking him hostage, demanding they release Cal. But the plan had a few flaws, not least of which was the legal angle Glout had explained to me. One benefit of feeling next to nothing is long-term planning, and I could see that abducting Cal, as the law would see it, could have serious drawbacks for our future together.

I settled for asking Glout very solemnly to take care of my brother. He said he would. I didn't say "I'll be back," but Glout was smart enough to figure out what my leaving without a fight really meant.

It just meant I was taking the fight elsewhere.

———

On the way home I thought about the next step, and I had a lot of ideas, most of them about as useful as the empty ID badge holder that was banging against my leg. As a measure of how distracted I was leaving RealCorp, I hadn't even thought to ask the security guards what had happened to the three Fish. That seemed like a lifetime ago.

I managed to hit rush hour. The trolley was full, the BART was full, and I walked home through downtown Oakland in my janitor's uniform with the rest of the laboring classes, tired and spent and all of us a little older than we had been that morning. Under the freeway near Lakeshore, three cops were cleaning up what looked like the remnants of a Fishing spree. They had paperwork and water hoses and sawdust. The pink water ran beside the edge of the curb, gurgling along to the storm drain.

When I got home, Joey was standing in his open doorway. He looked me over. "I tried calling you," he said.

I waved him into our apartment as I unlocked the door. I told him about Cal. Joey sat down on the tweedy sofa and stared at the casement windows. While he stared, I had time to eat three pieces of toast and take a shower. I've seen it many times, and maybe that was what had happened to me at Glout's lab: when something big happens, in the absence of emotion, you feel a long pause, like all the wind has been knocked out of you. Or maybe like you've been dropped in the ocean and you don't see land. You know it's there somewhere. But you have no idea where. And so you swim and swim, trying to find it.

I pulled on black pants and a sweater and came out of the bathroom to check on Joey. He hadn't found the shore, but he was clinging to some driftwood. When I came in, he stood up and put his arms around me. It's funny how nice that felt. Joey can be very expressive with his hugs. This one said, "What happened is beyond my comprehension but I am going to help you fix it. Starting now." He stepped back and looked at me.

"When are Cass and Tabby getting home?"

He looked at his watch. "About an hour, depending on traffic."

"Knock on my door when they get back? I need a quick shut-eye."

"Sure."

He headed out, closing the door behind him, and I pulled out the bed and fell on it facedown. The darkness of the pillow made a familiar void, and I sank forward without resistance.

———

I woke to knocking followed by footsteps on the creaky floorboards. Tabby was standing next to my bed, and the room was bright. "What time is it?" I mumbled.

"Eight. In the morning. We came in last night but you were out cold. So cold that Cass checked your vitals."

I sat up with effort and realized that Tabby was handing me a cup of coffee. Then she walked back to the doorway and hollered through it. "She's awake."

Cass and Joey filed into the room while I sipped coffee. Tabby and Cass sat on the tweed sofa, and Joey eased gingerly onto the wooden rocker—it had broken more than once before. They watched me sip. "I'm guessing you already talked to June?" I asked Cass.

June was Cass's friend who worked in downtown Oakland as an overextended and underappreciated public defender. She was the only person with any legal training the four of us knew. Cass nodded. "She called back this morning after checking the database records to say it's true. The paperwork is legitimate."

"I looked up this guy Glout," Joey said. We turned to him. "Seems to be exactly who he says he is. He did his PhD at Stanford and lectures there. He's been at RealCorp for more than thirty years. The only thing interesting I can find about him is that he was fired from another company, Emotive, before the RealCorp gig."

"Why?" I asked.

"Don't know. Also maybe of interest are some articles he's written on empathy. I sent them to you."

I waved a hand. "He gave me that spiel."

We were all silent for a moment. "You probably know what I want to do," I said, "and you probably don't like the idea, but as far as I can tell it's the only thing that would work."

Cass and Tabby looked at the coffee table and left their eyes there awhile. The coffee table didn't move, but it seemed to shine a little bit, cheered by the unexpected attention. Joey and I exchanged a glance.

"We don't know where Calvino's father is, Natalia," Cass said finally, looking up at me.

Cass and Tabby have very defined views on relationships. Those views are strictly by the book and somewhat unforgiving. In their eyes, the absence of emotion is not an excuse for the absence of commitment. On the contrary, they believe commitment is about making a plan and sticking to it. You can commit to a job without emotion. You can commit to a house. You can commit to any number of things. So commit to a person. That's what they say, anyhow. Thus their being married and even wearing rings and raising Joey and being our foster parents. Some people make exactly the same set of choices entirely for the government benefits, but I think for Cass and Tabby it's purely rational conviction. I get it, in the sense that I'm committed to them and to Cal and nothing would ever change that. But I also find the idea of it unimaginable with every adult male I've ever met, apart from Joey, and with Joey it's not like that. So while I understand their lofty view, I also understand why Mom had a couple flings and quickly moved on.

"I know," I said. "All I need is for you to tell me everything you know about him and I'll find him."

Cass and Tabby shared a long look, and finally they seemed to reach a decision. "Lila met him at the bookstore," Tabby said. That was the bookstore on Grand Avenue where Mom had worked since I was four. See? She was very capable of commitment in some areas. "She met up with him a few times and really liked him, but she didn't want him as a father for you. She said he was 'too establishment.'" Tabby smiled at the thought. "So she stopped seeing him."

That was news to me. Mom had always made it sound like Dylan was a momentary diversion who had turned boring after forty-five minutes. What Cal and I knew about him wouldn't fill a teacup. Mom had said that he was funny and gentle and had beautiful hands, which was a typical description from her—not the most helpful for tracking him down. I didn't even know his last name.

"He was a philosophy professor," Tabby continued.

"At Berkeley?"

Tabby and Cass both nodded.

"Well, that should make him easy to find."

"It should," Cass said, "but it doesn't. Lila tried to look him up a few years ago and he was gone. Dylan Hoffman hasn't been at Berkeley for at least five years."

Okay, I thought, *but Mom wasn't motivated by the need to save Cal from lab-rat purgatory.* It was a place to start, anyway. I said as much. "I'll go see what I can find about where he went after Berkeley."

"What do you want us to do?" Cass asked. I liked that she was letting me direct the show.

"Get June to prep the paperwork. Or if she can't do it, maybe she can recommend someone. Dylan will have to prove paternity and then there's probably something else he has to do to challenge the adoption claim. I don't know what that is."

Cass nodded. "Okay, yes. I can do that."

"I'm not sure if you wanted me to or not, but I called the Landmark and said you'd had an emergency," Tabby said.

I took a deep breath. "Yeah. Thanks. Let's make it a short emergency."

I insisted that Joey go to work because, like me, he didn't have any days off to spare. I promised him that I would ask for help when I needed it. I also promised him, with a silent nod, that I would tell him later about the part I hadn't mentioned to Cass and Tabby. He could sense it was there.

After they all went back across the hall, I put the unspoken part of my plan into action. I took a quick shower, ate more toast, and dressed respectably. At nine I left the house wearing a gray pantsuit, laced oxfords, and a cartwheel hat trimmed with a canary-yellow ribbon. All my necessities were nicely packed in a straw purse. I took the streetcar into downtown Oakland so I wouldn't get my suit all sweaty. Near Jack London Square, in a junky shop barely larger than a closet, I bought a nickel-sized decal that I didn't plan on using. But it gave me a hard-hitting backup plan, and I needed at least one of those. One of Raymond Chandler's lesser-known gumshoes is an amateur named Walter Gage who makes a detour mid-denouement for a roll of quarters. What for? To hold in his fist when, a few scenes later, he has to punch a guy twice his size. So. The decal was my roll of quarters. From what I'd seen, RealCorp looked more than twice my size.

With that done, I made my way to the central police station, where the officer at the desk directed me to the police gym, a block down. I had been there a couple times before, so I had no trouble finding it. It's a nice gym. Law enforcement can afford to live large. With 25 percent of the country's population in prison, no one is complaining that they don't do their jobs. I think most people would be happy to see that number become 35. Without the cops, this country would probably be run by Fish. So yeah—they can pretty much have anything they want.

The Oakland gym is a warehouse with an indoor basketball court, a prodigious assortment of free weights, cardio equipment, a matted area for mixed martial arts, and a boxing ring. I saw Officer Gao right away. He was standing beside the boxing ring, watching a man and a woman throw their gloves at each other like they were swatting at flies. His arms were crossed and he had that familiar look of thunderous disappointment, expressed by the half-millimeter lowering of his eyelids. Fortunately the look was trained on the boxers, not on me. I stood next to him quietly and waited. After a couple minutes he said wearily, "All right. Stop." The boxers stopped and looked at him, waiting for the consequences. "Take a break, please. A long one." He turned to pick up his jacket. To me he said, "Peña, how did you hurt your hip?"

He hadn't even glanced in my direction yet. I smiled. "Someone with mace in his eyes got in the way of it."

Officer Gao pulled on his jacket and looked me in the eye. "Clumsy of him."

"Very."

"Shall we walk outside?"

"Sounds good."

I followed Officer Gao back out and across the street to a curbside café that seemed an unlikely cop hangout. It had scalloped yellow awnings and window boxes filled with purple pansies. The name was stenciled in white cursive on the picture window: PANSY'S CAKES AND COFFEE. Gao sat down comfortably at one of the white bistro tables. He handed me a handwritten paper menu. "The brioche is excellent," he advised.

We ordered two coffees and two brioches from Pansy herself, an aproned, middle-aged woman who patted Gao on the shoulder with an air of faint reproof, like he was a roguish nine-year-old. Then Gao crossed his arms over his chest. "Let's negotiate," he said.

When I first met Gao I thought he was just a typical hard-ass—one of those guys who walks into the room and is immediately measuring his testosterone level against everyone else's, is immediately eager to put people down for the sake of showing he can. A guy who worships his own strength. It took me a while to realize he's not like that. He *looks* like that: only four inches taller than me and roughly twice my weight, he has the strength of a bodybuilder and the agility of a gymnast. Once I saw him disarm a six-foot man using only his left hand up to the elbow. (There was lots of quick jabbing.) Crew cut, thick neck, thin lips, and small ears. He has a cluster of scars on the left side of his jaw shaped like a pigeon's foot that he's never explained and I've never asked about.

One time early in our training, Gao had a little wrestling tournament going, and somehow this big bully in our class, Sal, ended up scrabbling with a girl named Libby who was maybe four foot five on her tiptoes. Gao watched them impassively as Sal played pretzel maker, and the rest of us watched Gao, wondering when he was going to stop them. Finally Libby, out of desperation, found an angle and shot her knee into Sal's undercarriage. Sal let out a high-pitched squeal and curled up on the mat. Libby extracted herself and stood there, looking frazzled and sorry. "She's not supposed to do that," Sal howled, when he could speak. "It's against the rules."

"Get up," Gao barked at him. He waited for Sal to drag himself up to his feet, where he stood next to Libby like a leaning skyscraper. Gao looked around at us to make sure we were all listening. "The rules are not there to be followed blindly. That is not the purpose of them. Blind rule following is for the brainless. I mean really brainless. You have been declared legally incompetent and you have to do what someone else tells you to. All the time. And last I checked, no one here was brainless. So what is the purpose of the rules?" None of us could tell him. "The rules are designed to create parity and fairness." He watched us. Libby started to look a little better, like maybe she would make it out of this alive. "This fight was not fair. It was entirely correct for Libby to break the rules."

Gao doesn't worship his own strength, and he doesn't worship the rules, either. He just uses both of them. He's not like many other cops, and that's what I was hanging my hat on.

"Okay, let's negotiate," I agreed, because if Gao didn't

want to beat around the bush, I certainly wasn't going to. "I'm trying to get an address. Tanner Philbrick. The CEO of RealCorp."

The coffee and brioches arrived. Gao thanked Pansy and did not move his arms. "Why," he said.

I knew this was an invitation to tell the long version, so I described everything from the first letter we'd received about Cal to this morning's decision to find Dylan Hoffman. Gao didn't express any phony grief over Cal's dilemma, but I could see his eyes making silent calculations, and he was clearly displeased with the numbers. "If you're going to find Hoffman, why do you need Philbrick's address?" Gao asked.

"Because I don't know if I'm going to find Hoffman. And I am not only interested in legal avenues." I looked Gao straight in the eye. "I will do anything it takes to get Cal out of RealCorp. And I'm figuring 'anything' might involve Philbrick, since he's the one in charge. If I have to hold a knife to his neck to get him to release Cal, I will do it. I'd prefer some other way, but at this point I'm not setting boundaries." Notice that I said "knife" rather than "gun," because Gao thinks guns are for idiots. Weapons for weaklings, he calls them.

Gao considered my explanation. He drank his coffee and ate brioche, and I did the same. The brioche was, in fact, excellent. When he had finished his and was tapping at the crumbs with his fingertips, he spoke up. "All right. But," he added, before I could make a move to thank him, "there are strings."

I waited.

"I give you Philbrick's address, and you agree to train with me three times a week."

I gave a long, silent, inward groan. "That is a very high price for one address."

Gao lifted his shoulder an inch. "That's what it costs. I'm breaking the law to give you an unlisted address. Three times a week."

"Okay. But," I said very seriously, "I'm in a day-to-day situation here. I don't know if I'll be in Oakland tomorrow, let alone next week for a friendly karate match."

"I don't teach karate," Gao said.

I sighed. Even though the words had not been spoken, we were veering into familiar territory. "Officer Gao, I am never going to become a cop. Now there's even less of a chance. I'll probably be running away to Canada with Cal, if I'm lucky, and we'll be settling down in some suburban tundra near Manitoba."

"I didn't say you had to become a cop. This is purely for the short term. The situation you have described to me has the potential to be very dangerous, perhaps even fatal—high stakes, people with a lot of power, and a willingness to break every rule on your part. I would be remiss if I let you go into a situation of this kind without trying to train you better, Peña."

There wasn't much I could say to that. I had known from the beginning that I would have to agree to his terms anyway. But it was nice to know he was doing it to look out for me. "Okay," I said. "Thank you."

"You're welcome." Gao drained his coffee and paid for both of us, which was considerate of him. I didn't know when I'd be seeing another paycheck. Then we walked back to the central police station, and Gao left me waiting outside while he went in to get the address. He returned with a slip of paper, which he showed me before handing it over. "Philbrick's details," he said, pointing to an address in Pacific Heights, "and the time and date of our first training. Tomorrow night at eight thirty. Eat your dinner early—you'll want your stomach very empty."

I took the costly scrap of paper from him and tucked it into my straw purse. "Thanks, Officer Gao. See you tomorrow night."

15

NATALIA
October 12—morning

Before heading across the bridge to track down Philbrick, I took the BART to Berkeley. I probably could have called, but I preferred to be there in person in case something unexpected came up. It did.

A long block of cheap eats connected the Berkeley BART to the campus entrance, marked by a grove of towering eucalyptus. Beyond the fragrant trees, with their illusory air of dusty repose, I found the sprawling, incomprehensible Humanities building, in which the office layout challenged my slim claim to numeracy. There were too many entrances and not enough signage. Floor two somehow became floor four. Or was it five? Finally I arrived at the philosophy office, not entirely lost but befuddled enough to believe I had earned my way to a straight answer after making it through the labyrinth. I put my purse firmly on the counter to draw the administrative assistant's attention.

She didn't see me. Just like most people, she had an array of screen decals streaming lives, mundane and momentous, to the dozens or hundreds or millions of suckers more interested in watching strangers go about their distant days than in going about their own. They make a low, constant din in every room, and I honestly don't get the appeal. The tackiest are the Fish streams, with their predictable and apparently irresistible bone-crunching. The admin had one of those, as evidenced by the octopus tattoo around the subject's left eye. The Fish was standing at a kitchen table, using scissors to cut what looked like a big piece of flayed skin. There was one of a diva in New York who liked to scream at people. Another one I recognized of a prison inmate in Nevada who was battling lung cancer. Not sure how either of those got so popular, but I'm apparently a luddite where streaming is concerned. I didn't recognize the other three. The admin was glued to the one she had pasted on the bottom left. From where I stood, it looked like the person in question was fixing a leaky faucet. No wonder she was mesmerized.

"Excuse me," I said loudly.

"Yes?" she asked, turning to me with obvious reluctance.

I'm the only Marlowe knockoff I know, but I'm not the only one who's had the bright idea to latch on to a character as a way to navigate the world. Lots of us witty people do it. Books and old screen dramas are like disorganized bargain stores where you hunt for an angle: someone memorable, someone to imitate, someone who gives you a usable script. Someone behaving with emotional coherence so that you can follow along, seeming both emotional and coherent without being either. I've seen more Elizabeth Bennets in my day than I can count, and the admin assistant was apparently going for one of the downtrodden minor characters at the periphery of an Austen novel. She had pale eyes, hunched shoulders, and hair permed so often it had become wayward and brittle. Her clothes were fussy and demure at the same time. There was something thin and cheap from the pharmacy working its way through her bloodstream, giving her an expression of permanent disenfranchisement. Sagging eyes. Visible pout. The tip of her nose was sunburnt.

"I'm trying to locate a professor who used to teach here, Dylan Hoffman, and I'm wondering if you might be able to help me find him. It's a personal matter of some importance."

By the way her eyes softened on "Dylan" and narrowed on "personal," I got a pretty clear picture of how well she had known Professor Hoffman while he was still at Berkeley. Good thing I was here in person. I hastened to amend my explanation. "It has to do with my brother."

This did seem to strike her as less threatening, but she still took a few seconds to come up with anything. Then she stalled. "He hasn't been back here since he left the department, and that was seven years ago in May."

Hm, very precise. No doubt the date was etched in her mind. She still looked wary, and I could see I would need to give her more. "My little brother is in a lot of trouble," I said, "and I think Professor Hoffman might be the only one who can help him."

It's tough to play on people's sympathies when they don't have any, but with the right kind of person, you can still play on what they think their sympathies ought to be. That is, you can press on their ideas of right and wrong, if they've learned them by the book and decided to follow them.

The admin assistant had. She sighed. "It was very unfortunate," she said. "Dylan—Professor Hoffman—was a very popular professor."

Uh-huh. I had already figured that out.

"But he had an experience in his final years here . . ." She trailed off and looked out the window. There were some dry leaves there on the branch of one of the eucalyptus trees, and she studied them hard. "He had what he called an awakening."

"An awakening?"

"A religious awakening."

"Oh," I said.

"He was a different person afterwards. He said that none of it made sense anymore. Philosophy, I mean."

"What did Professor Hoffman teach?"

"Ethics." She sniffed. "Moral philosophy."

"I'm impressed he managed to make that popular."

She looked at me like I had just exposed myself as an idiot by calling London the capital of China. "Moral philosophy is at the very center of every current debate about what emotions are. It's what organizes the ethical codes by which society functions. His work was absolutely vital."

"I see."

She shook her head. "And even despite that, he stopped believing in it. He said it was pointless. Even misleading. He felt like he was lying to the students."

"So he had to stop teaching."

"Yes. He said he had to follow his new calling."

"And do you have any idea where that new calling took him?"

"I heard he became a minister." She gave a hard little laugh. "That seemed strange to me. But I guess you could say lecturing in front of students isn't so different from giving a sermon to parishioners."

So he liked the sound of his own voice either way. "He was good with an audience."

"That's right," she agreed.

"You don't know where? Or what kind of place?"

She wrinkled her nose. "A church. One of those trendy ones that's a mishmash of old and new." She caught herself, and I could see her trying to figure out if I was trendy myself.

I gave her a crooked smile of reassurance. "I know the kind you mean. In Berkeley?"

"Honestly, I don't know. I don't think so. I think if he were nearby we'd hear more about him. Those types have a presence in the community, if you know what I mean."

I did. "Thank you so much . . ." I dangled, waiting for her name.

"Nora."

"Thank you so much, Nora. If I find him I'll let you know where he ended up."

She thought about saying no but instead gave a little nod. "He was a very good professor," she said, as if this explained the wish to know where the man who had left her hanging had disappeared to.

On my way to San Francisco on the BART, I wrote Joey a long message explaining what I'd learned and where I was going now. While he chewed it over I did some quick research on trendy churches, but I could tell it was one of those things I would have to do on foot. Many of them were premised on a rejection of everything contemporary, so that meant no evangelizing online and in some cases no online presence at all. This was going to be a job for the phone book and my walking shoes.

Maybe Joey would help.

He wrote back to say that I was crazy for agreeing to train with Gao. Joey didn't get along with Gao as well as I did. He doesn't like hitting things, even in self-defense, and Gao definitely believes in hitting things.

I agreed with him and asked if he would help me make a list of churches catering to disenchanted philosophers and their ilk. He said he would. He also told me that he'd deployed a trio of unemployed buddies to watch RealCorp.

I don't advise it, I typed. *They might get eaten alive.*

Don't worry, he replied. *They know what they're doing.*

If you say so.

Speaking of being eaten alive, he typed, *sorry but you have another problem.*

What?

He sent me a screenshot. It was a photo: me, glancing over my shoulder as I hurried an old lady off a subway. The white text beneath the image read 10/11, 3ASLTS; 74K BID HERE.

Uh-oh? I typed to Joey. *Should I be worried about you? Why are you browsing Fish apps?*

Not browsing. Searching.

I sighed. I'd been too occupied to think about the Fish, but Joey had gone to the trouble. It isn't hard to find the sites where the Fish troll for bait. They are free for all, open seas. It's either total coincidence or wry cunning that makes the Fish apps an exact mirror of the police listings, where bounties are posted for the most notorious sea creatures. There are plenty of people who aren't Fish but still glom on to the rise and fall of bounties, the catch and release of prey.

In case you are curious, he went on, *that means there's a 74 thousand dollar bounty on your head. And growing.*

Maybe I should take myself out? That's a lot of cash.

Dimwit, this is real.

Who has that kind of money to burn? I wondered.

Small bids. They add up. There's a related story about your heroics. You're in tenth place.

For beauty?

Highest bounties on the site.

Well. Can't be helped.

Be careful, Joey typed.

I could do that, to an extent. I kept my eyes peeled on the BART, but the trains were almost empty and there was hardly any talking, let alone uninvited solicitations with a switchblade. I got out at Montgomery and took the bus from there to Pacific Heights, with its breezy perch above the bay, its baroque beauty, its nasty secrets tucked away. Pac Heights is a starlet with rotting teeth: beautiful until she smiles.

As I climbed the hill to the address Gao had given me, I considered whether it was time to empty my meager savings account and buy a car. It would make all this back-and-forthing a lot easier. And I was probably going to need a getaway car for Cal. Then again, maybe I was going to need those meager savings to pay a 0.1 percent down payment on legal fees. At this point, anything could happen. Better to wait on the car.

The views from Philbrick's mansion were, predictably, breathtaking. Also I had just climbed a nearly vertical hill. But from the corner I could see the sparkling water and the toy boats and the low, easy hills of Marin County. The more immediate view wasn't bad, either: a stucco palace with iron balconies and rampant bougainvillea, a Tudor mansion with shuttered windows and a mysterious flag, a block of glass and cement with an integrated greenhouse and a front door that looked stolen from a Buddhist temple. I could tell this was the kind of crowd that stole stuff but didn't call it stealing. They were collectors.

Philbrick's house gave me a crystalline impression of the man's self-regard. It was a stone castle with turrets. Ivy and climbing roses covered most of the walls. The picture of medieval authenticity was a little marred by the massive windows—easily ten feet tall and just as wide—but I guess you can't blame Philbrick for wanting more than the occasional peephole from which to admire his view. Besides, if he wanted to throw burning tar from an upper story on his visitors, the big windows would work as well as little ones.

The streets were quiet. Eerie quiet. No one walking a dog. No one playing music a little too loudly. No one getting in or out of a fancy car. The only sound was the occasional whine of a leaf blower. I took out *De rerum* and leaned against a high garden wall so I wouldn't look quite so suspicious standing there on the corner staring at Philbrick's house.

Besides, while Pac Heights napped, I had more work to do. I read the articles Joey had sent me by and about Hugh Glout. He had been in the business for decades. Stanford boy twice over, with a five-hundred-page dissertation on pupil dilation. Really scintillating stuff, believe me. As for the later publications, it was like reading a book with half the words cut out. I could see that a lot of the RealCorp work was proprietary—couldn't be written about, couldn't be referenced—and yet it was there, by insinuation, signaled by the blank spots and the surrounding words. I could also see that there was a handful of scientists who would have liked to see Glout chopped up and pickled in his own juices. I think the in-house term is "scholarly dispute." As far as I could tell, this seemed to revolve around methods, not results. They thought Glout jumped to conclusions from small trials, and Glout had some indignant things to say about their ethics. He'd even gone so far as to advocate the expansion of some regulation called the "common rule" so that minors had greater protections. A lot of people didn't like that. So the articles told me that Glout was kind of an outsider, maybe even a scientific loner. Well, I had already deduced that from the long fingernails.

Time passed. The white lace in the windows of the stucco palace billowed in and out, reminding me of Marlowe's office: net curtains puckering like the lips of a toothless man sleeping. The muted wails of ship horns drifted up on the ocean breeze. A landscaping truck roared down the street, the equipment bouncing noisily in the back. More whining from the leaf blower. After an hour I came to the conclusion that gardeners were the only living people in Pac Heights.

Almost an hour after I arrived, the iron gate of Philbrick's house rolled aside on its motorized wheels, and a small car peeled out of the driveway. It was painted blue with big white bubbles, and the lettering on the sides said CRYSTAL CLEANERS. I was standing close enough to see the driver as she zoomed by, but she didn't see me. A bit older than I was, leaning forward in her seat, jaw clenched. She looked like she wanted to get out of the stone castle in a hurry. The motorized gate groaned shut. I stared at it a while longer, my own wheels turning, while the monotonous silence of Pac Heights settled in once more around me.

After a few minutes' deliberation I looked up Crystal Cleaners. Their central office was in Chinatown. I chugged down the hill a little ways and caught a bus heading east that crossed Van Ness and carried me to the edge of Chinatown. The streets were not quiet. Every other store had vegetables in crates on the curb, crowding the pedestrians. These were a lively lot. In the span of a block, I saw a heated argument in Cantonese, an attempted seduction that ended badly, and three children chasing a live chicken. There were no landscapers.

Crystal Cleaners was on the second floor above a dumpling shop. I climbed the steps, knocked on the open door, and walked into the surprisingly spacious office. There were more than twenty-five screen decals on the otherwise blank wall to my left, arranged in three tidy rows. They honked and roared and jabbered away at half volume. All but one were streaming people in China. The last was the same prison inmate in Nevada battling lung cancer. I guess he was getting to be as popular as the Fish.

Three women sat at their desks against the wall, and from the contents of their work screens I could see that they were juggling schedules, supply orders, and employee files. Another woman, tiny and round, slept upright in an armchair upholstered with red damask. The fifth woman sat facing me at the reception desk and was on the phone. She had an air of fidgety efficiency: neat hair cut short, ironed shirt, fingernails bitten down to the quick, polished shoes peeping out underneath the desk. "Yes," she was saying expressionlessly into the phone. "Yes, very well." She glanced at me. "Yes," she said again. "Good, thank you." She put the phone down, made a note on the pad of paper she was holding, swatted quickly at the screen decal pasted onto her desk blotter, and looked up.

"How can I help you?"

"I'm here about a job," I said. "I used to work at the Landmark and then I worked at RealCorp for a while, but I'm looking for a job with more flexible hours, since I'm going back to night school. Mr. Philbrick said I might ask you."

The woman looked at me with the same expressionless face she'd used on the phone. I knew I'd said something significant because the three typists, engrossed as they were in their work, turned around and stared at me. The tiny sleeping woman didn't budge. I waited for a clue. None of them were on synaffs, so I could read nothing on their faces. Only curiosity. One of the women looked me up and down a few times, as if considering what I'd look like in my underwear. That was interesting, but it didn't help me much. Then one of them muttered something in Mandarin that was uncomplimentary to Mr. Philbrick. I was familiar with the phrase thanks to Gao, who used it often and translated it, when asked, as "malignant son of a pernicious goat." I don't think that's the real translation, but I got the gist.

"Did I misunderstand his referral?" I asked innocently.

The three women slowly swiveled back to their screens, and the receptionist motioned to a chair. "Sit down," she said. I sat in the wooden chair and shimmied it across the floorboards to the edge of her desk. She tapped the tips of her nail-bitten fingers together. "This is new," she said, and I wasn't sure if she was talking to me or to herself. She scrolled through her screen decal and moved her teeth around, thinking. Experimentally, she chewed on her left pointer finger. "Philbrick recommended you to work at his house, right?"

"He didn't say exactly, but since I was a good cleaner at RealCorp, I guess that was the implication."

She chewed some more. When she was done with that finger she moved on to the next one. All the while she studied me with what she probably thought was discreetness. There was a calculating look to her appraisal, as if she was trying to figure out how I'd do in the ring against some imaginary opponent. She was having an internal argument about the odds.

Then, to my surprise, the tiny sleeping woman spoke without opening her eyes. Five or six words in Mandarin, slow but assured, like a master painter with a brush.

The receptionist looked at her and nodded. "Okay," she finally said. The argument was over. "Fine." She shook her head quickly with the air of someone who has decided to wash her hands of a sticky situation. "Can you drive?" she asked me.

"Yes, of course."

"All the cleaners use company cars. The cleaning equipment is in the car. You pick up and return to the garage off Van Ness. Absolutely no use of company cars for personal matters."

"Understood," I agreed.

"When do you want to start?"

"As soon as possible."

"Tomorrow?" she asked. Now that the decision was made, she was eager.

"That would be great."

"Good. Fill out this form, we'll run a quick background check, but assuming everything is fine, you'll be expected at the residence at nine tomorrow morning." She handed me a screen decal on a clipboard. It took me only a few minutes to fill in all my details, and I had to hope that they wouldn't actually call the Landmark. Usually employers just settle for the license and credit check—those tell them everything they care about anyway. When I was done she scrolled to another form, this one a rather daunting collection of legal disclaimers. Basically, Crystal Cleaners could send me in to clean up after an Ebola outbreak or a nuclear waste spill, and it would not be their fault if anything happened to me. I signed. Last of all, the nail-biter handed me a sheet of paper with Philbrick's address and directions to the parking garage where the cars were kept. There was a handwritten phone number at the bottom of the paper.

"Is this the Philbricks' number?"

"No. That number is for emergencies. *Real* emergencies," she said, giving me a hard look. "That is Ma Ling's number." She pointed at the tiny sleeping woman. "If something happens that is truly an emergency, you may call her. Not otherwise."

Ma Ling opened one eye to look at me sleepily. I nodded at her. "Okay," I said. It wasn't too clear to me what Ma Ling could do in an emergency of any magnitude, other than maybe sleep through it, but possibly she had hidden talents.

I looked down at the sheet again. One hundred dollars per day—not bad.It was interesting that they hadn't talked to me about a regular schedule, as if the first day was the only thing worth planning.

I didn't comment on it. "Thanks for this opportunity," I said, getting up from the wooden chair.

The receptionist looked a little uncomfortable at that. "Good luck," she said.

After I closed the door there was silence, a rapid volley of Mandarin, and grim laughter from all corners of the room.

Yeah, they had thrown me to the wolves.

What kind of wolves they were, I would have to find out for myself.

16

CALVINO

oct-12

8:30 a.m.

hglt: Good morning, Calvino. Here's your first essay for the day. I'll be back in about an hour to check on your reply. Essay: <u>What do you anticipate will be the most challenging thing about waning?</u>

calvinopio: I don't want to think about this right now, Dr. Glout. I have tried answering your questions and they are going nowhere. Am I supposed to be learning something from writing them? Or are you supposed to be learning something from my answers? Are they just to keep me busy?

    I get the feeling that the idea with these questions is not so much getting an answer as having me do something that is supposed to be "normal." But just giving me an assignment that looks like homework is not going to make things "normal."

    I don't understand why I can't leave. Are you giving

my sister my letters like you said you would? If you are, why hasn't she come to get me? Why can't I talk to her if everything is "normal"? Nat would not leave me here. Did something happen to her? Are you hiding some kind of accident or something that happened to her and Cass and Tabby? I know that you probably think I can't handle it because of how I am, but I can. You should tell me if something has happened to my sister or someone else.

You said that if I answered your questions and took the tests I could go home. When? How many questions and tests? I have already answered questions and taken tests. Is there one answer you are looking for?? What do you want me to say? How long are you going to keep me here?

hglt: Hi there, Calvino. I'm back. To answer your questions, as far as I know, your sister is fine. She's not here because this test has to be conducted in isolation.

calvinopio: You said that already, but that doesn't explain why she wouldn't reply to my letters.

hglt: It's better for the test results if you only interact with me for the time being.

calvinopio: We're not interacting.

hglt: Well, we're interacting through text.

calvinopio: It's not the same thing.

hglt: That's true, but it's better this way. It creates better conditions for testing.

calvinopio: I still don't understand what the test is.

hglt: Your answers to my questions are part of the test, and your response to being here is also important to the test.

calvinopio: Are you checking if I try to escape or something?

hglt: Nothing so dramatic.

Calvino? Are you still there?

calvinopio: Can you give me any evidence that you are real?

hglt: What do you mean, Calvino?

calvinopio: I have this feeling I am typing to another screen.

hglt: I assure you, I am very real!

calvinopio: But I've never met you, so to me it doesn't feel that way.

hglt: Hm. I can see where you're coming from. But my being "real" or not doesn't influence the outcomes here.

calvinopio: Of course it does. Because it changes how I feel.

hglt: That's an excellent point, Calvino. I really hadn't thought about it that way.

calvinopio: Can you tell me something about yourself that a program couldn't? Like what you had for breakfast? Or what you did for fun when you were my age? Or something?

hglt: Sure. Let's see . . . For breakfast, I had a spinach smoothie.

calvinopio: That sounds gross.

hglt: Ha! It was really good, actually. As for what I did for fun when I was your age . . .

Let's see. I grew up in a rural area, so I did a lot of bicycling. I used to bike along the path made by the power lines. And I had a collection of arrowheads.

calvinopio: Did you play much with other kids?

hglt: Not much. Honestly, other kids thought I was kind of strange! Ha.

calvinopio: I'm sorry, Dr. Glout. I know how that feels.

hglt: Thanks, Calvino. It's okay. Because then everything changed when I got older. When I waned.

calvinopio: Then you were all strange!

hglt: Haha. Yes—well put. You're right, of course—that's the irony of it. As a child, I never felt strange. I thought everyone else was strange. But then, after waning, I really did feel like I was the strange one.

calvinopio: You *felt* like the strange one?

hglt: You're right, of course. I used the word "feel," which is inexact. It's hard to explain, Calvino. I had this sense that something was wrong. But ALL the time. For me, it was a tremendous relief to be able to take synthetic affects, which I could fortunately afford. They made me feel functional again. I've taken them ever since.

calvinopio: I think I don't have to say this to you, because it seems you maybe are real and already get this. But now imagine what it's like for people like my sister and my mom who feel like something is wrong and can't do anything about it.

hglt: I know, Calvino. I know.

17

NATALIA

October 12—midday

My new employers might have been heartless, but they did have good taste in neighbors. I devoured a plate of perfect dumplings in the restaurant downstairs while reading Joey's message about trendy churches. The verdict: there were many of them. It was a broad category. And I didn't know enough about Dylan's awakening to predict which brand of religious folly had inspired his passion. There were at least a dozen places in San Francisco, another twenty in the East Bay, ten or so in Marin County, and toward San Jose . . . There were too many to count. I finished my dumplings and tried not to let the list crush my sense of conviction.

Looking out the window of the dumpling restaurant, I gave myself a minute to watch a girl my age fake-wrestling with her younger sister. Their mother, who presided over a mountain of fresh fish laid out on ice, was watching them impassively. Unworried, unfazed. Everything was normal. The little girl giggled uncontrollably as her sister turned her upside down and carried her off around the block.

Cal had now been missing for more than twenty-four hours.

I gave myself a stern internal talking-to. Yes, the list of churches was long. And there remained the possibility that Dylan was no longer even in the Bay Area. But it was just a task. A task with many steps. Many boring steps, and I simply needed to complete them. At the end of those steps, I would find Dylan.

Using a paper map and a pencil, I marked the locations of the San Francisco churches on Joey's list and numbered them in order of proximity. I probably wouldn't get to them all today, but I could at least try. This was going to be a lot easier with the cleaning car, I thought to myself with an inward grin. If the Crystal sisters wanted to abandon me to a terrible fate, the least they could do was give me a little free mileage. Lavishing thanks on the dumpling chef, I paid my bill and made my way outside.

The first two churches on my list were in the Tenderloin. I took a bus down to Market and then walked west. The neighborhood had pretty much managed to preserve its seediness over the decades. After a brief blip of good fortune decades earlier, when a square inch of San Francisco property cost more than most people make in a year, the Tenderloin slid comfortably back into disrepute and ruin. Now it could keep up with Oakland as a capital of hard times and vice. Food wrappers and a pair of soggy socks hung on a metal fence. The scrap of dry grass behind it smelled of urine. A water-logged paper sign hung taped to a lamppost; below a frantic MISSING!!! was the photo of some child, sweet and smiling and incongruous. On Pine Street I was greeted by two long-legged ladies wearing high heels and lingerie and very broad hats. They invited me upstairs, I complimented them on their hats, and they returned the compliment. "Never skimp on sun protection!" I said, wagging a finger at them. They giggled their agreement.

A block up I had a confusing conversation with a man who was clearly still feeling the effect of the panic he'd taken that morning. "Stop! Stop!" he said, barring my way with his hands. He had on a dirty button-down, dirtier pants, and most of one left shoe. When he waved his arms around, I got a little dizzy from the smell. "You can't go in there!" he shouted. I could see the sad little plaque for the church on the building entrance. It read LIGHTGATE above an adequate drawing of an iron gate.

"Why not?"

"Leo says the snakes have gotten bigger." He spoke in an undertone and with his eyes wide.

"Have you asked Leo to get rid of them?" I asked.

This startled him. "Get rid of them . . ." he echoed, lowering his arms.

"Leo's a big boy. He should be able to."

The smelly man looked deflated. I moved to step past him and he dashed off across the street. "Stop! Stop!" he shouted at another pedestrian. "You can't go in there!"

I opened the door of Lightgate and found myself in a dank little foyer that hadn't been cleaned in a long time. A door to the left hung open, and through the door was a tiled room with folding chairs. Its only light came through a grimy, barred window that looked onto Pine Street. There was no one in the room, but I could hear voices elsewhere. It was an unusual conversation.

"Pain."

"Yes!"

"Remorse."

"Yes!"

"Forgiveness."

"Yes!"

Then it went back to pain again. I listened to this cycle three times before venturing toward the door at the back of the room. Knocking lightly, I tried the knob and found it unlocked. Beyond the door was a tiny closet of an office with a tinier desk. The woman sitting there looked up at me. The long, straight hair, beaded headband, and halter top made it evident that she favored the 1970s. She was taking some heavy synaff that made her smile very mellow. Pupils somewhat dilated, corners of her mouth relaxed. She seemed about as sharp as a sponge.

"Hi, bienvenida," she said, with a warm, familiar tone.

"Hi." The voices were a little louder here, but I couldn't figure out where they were coming from. "I'm trying to locate a family friend that I've fallen out of touch with. His name is Dylan Hoffman."

Her brow furrowed. "Dylan Hoffman," she echoed. She shook her head. "I don't know him. But I've only been here a couple months."

"How long has Lightgate been here?"

"Two years."

"Could you ask someone else if they've heard of him?"

She blinked. "Sure." She stood up and I backed out of the office. As I followed her into the main room I realized that the halter top was practical as well as stylish; all along her shoulders and upper back, red welts were healing. Four of them new, many more old. They were about six inches long and an inch wide at the middle, scarlet at the center and crusted at the edges. One of them wasn't healing well: inflamed with white spots. I hadn't pegged her for the self-flagellating type. Very trendy indeed. She opened a flimsy door and leaned in. After a murmured conversation with an invisible person beyond the doorway, she withdrew, closing the door quietly. "Liz has been here for a year and a half and she hasn't heard of him, either."

"Thanks." I didn't have all day to spend with her. I asked her to look in her records to see if there was any mention of Hoffman and I left her my number. She agreed.

I didn't talk to anyone at the next place, Ascension. A placard on the inner door said MEDITATING. PLEASE PRE-SERVE THE SILENCE! Through the half window I could see about fifty people sprawled out on individual blankets; they made a crazy quilt of patterns and colors and bare feet. It looked to me like they were all taking a nap.

Ascension was more put together than Lightgate. Stand-alone building, big sign out front, table with brochures. The brochures said that the founder was a fellow named Milo Burrows and that he'd been the congregation's leader since its founding seven years earlier. It seemed an unlikely place for Dylan Hoffman, but I made a note on the map about possibly returning to Ascension.

I walked uphill toward the third place: Brothers of Light. I'd actually heard of this one, because they ran an orphanage. The building had once been a movie theater, before the film industry went bust, and it sat unassumingly on the corner of Van Ness, a massive box of unwashed windows. Even from the sidewalk I could see kids running up and down the stairs, chasing one another, dawdling and looking out onto the street. It was like watching an ant farm. From the looks of it, Brothers of Light was just as overcrowded as every other orphanage in the country. Sometimes the tax break isn't enough incentive, I guess. And not everyone has commitments like Cass and Tabby. And Mom.

A tired-looking Brother of Light was standing on the stoop, arms crossed, staring out at the traffic on Van Ness. He had a trim beard and deep-set eyes and a monk's robe with the hood down. Luring him into conversation was harder than I thought, since he seemed at the brink of collapse from fatigue. When I finally got him to understand that I was looking for a church that might cater to disenchanted philosophers, he brought himself into focus and told me that the Brothers of Light were old-fashioned Catholic. "New name, old faith," he said wearily, making it sound like this was the cause of his exhaustion.

"Got it," I said. I gave him a friendly pat on the shoulder. "Chin up, buddy. You're doing good work."

He looked at me with incomprehension. Then he blinked,

and a brief smile flickered across his face. "Thanks," he said, looking in my eyes for the first time. "God bless you."

When I glanced back at the next corner, the tired monk had disappeared.

The next place was in Japantown, and I had trouble finding it. After walking around in circles on Sutter Street, I finally found the door next to a sushi place that advertised its menu with dazzling neon. Beside it, the nondescript door with the sign ASHAEL'S CAVE was hard to spot. But the unlocked entry confirmed I was in the right spot. I took a well-lit flight of steps down to a door. This one was also unlocked. Beyond it was a corridor lit entirely with candles, which didn't strike me as the safest proposition in an unventilated basement, but I didn't plan to stay long. Ashael's Cave seemed more respectable than the other places I'd been to. A woman with a long white dress and a bonnet—yes, a bonnet—emerged from a closed door to meet me. "Welcome," she said. "The orientation is this way."

I thought about explaining the mistake but decided not to. I could always cut the orientation short. "Thank you," I said. I followed her down the corridor and around the bend. Another door opened onto a sunken courtyard, where an unexpected amount of sunshine poured in on a well-conceived Japanese garden. Another woman in a bonnet was speaking to three women, all in regular clothes like me, who sat on wooden stools before her. Bonnet #1 gestured to an empty stool and I took it.

Bonnet #2 gave me a nod of acknowledgment as she went on speaking. She looked to be about fifty, with wiry hair springing up at the edges of the bonnet. Her eyes had that unshakable stillness that I sometimes see in the very devout. "But in many ways, Puritan values, appropriate as they are to our time, also have to be updated. Puritans were not the most forward-thinking with respect to the rights of women," she said wryly. There were quiet laughs from her listeners. I couldn't disagree with her there. "What we've tried to do is join the best advances of our time with the best virtues of the Puritan ethic. Humility. Modesty. Hard work. An appreciation for simplicity. An awareness that all things are granted to us through the grace of God. And fear—yes, fear. Not fear of petty dangers around us, but a righteous fear of God, who is powerful in all ways."

Hm. It seemed Ashael's Cave wasn't for me. There was already enough fear in the world, thanks very much. For cheap, too. I glanced back at Bonnet #1 and was about to get up to extract myself from the orientation when I heard Bonnet #2 wrapping up. "Instead of lecturing for longer," she said, "I'd rather give you the chance to speak with me and Deliverance more informally. Please feel free to ask any question that comes to mind, and enjoy some tea." She gestured to the low table beside her, where a Japanese pot stood steaming in the sunshine.

The three women were eager to talk to Bonnet #2, so I ventured back to where Deliverance was standing next to an azalea. Did Puritans bow or shake hands or what? I wasn't sure. I put my hand out tentatively, and Deliverance shook it. "Nat Peña. I should have explained when I came in," I said to her, "I didn't know about the orientation. I'm actually here looking for a family friend. His name is Dylan Hoffman. I was told that he had become a minister in a church like this one."

Deliverance had a surprisingly pretty face beneath the bonnet. Snub nose, freckles, and long lashes. Her big blue eyes took me in as I talked. "He wouldn't be here because Ashael's Cave is only for women," she explained.

"Oh. Right."

"But the name sounds familiar."

I waited and watched her blue eyes thinking.

"We all take Puritan names when we join the church, but we keep our last names. There's a very popular minister in Marin who has his own church. It's called Mordecai's Hill and the minister goes by Mordecai Hoffman."

I wanted to pour blessings upon Deliverance's freckled face, but I settled for an energetic thanks. "That must be it. Thank you so much."

"They don't advertise," she continued. "So it's a little hard to find. We're not quite as extreme, being in the city. I'm pretty sure they don't use technology at all at the Hill. Do you want directions? I think Steadfast has been there." She gestured to Bonnet #2 as she said this.

"That would be very helpful."

Deliverance walked me over to Steadfast, who was deep in conversation with one of the three visitors. The woman seemed hooked. She was nodding emphatically as Steadfast talked. "Excuse me, Steadfast," Deliverance interrupted her, putting a hand gently on her arm. "This is Nat. I told her you knew the way to Mordecai's Hill."

Steadfast looked at me with faint suspicion. She had none of Deliverance's smoothness; she was all hard edges and zeal. But she gave me directions. "Yes," she said. "I do know the way. It's north of where the San Quentin prison complex ends. Follow the bridge to Marin County and stay on the coast route until you reach Point Reyes Station. You'll see a marker for Mordecai's Hill before you arrive in Inverness. It's a small sign, painted by hand on plywood. Very easy to miss." She said this with palpable disapproval.

"If you've been there, maybe you've met the minister? Mordecai Hoffman?"

She frowned. "I have. He is very committed, in his own way, but I have met very few men who have a genuine spirituality."

I thanked Steadfast for the directions and left the Japanese garden accompanied by Deliverance. In the candlelit corridor I thanked her again and climbed the steps to the outside world.

As I opened the door, my mind was on where I could get a car for the trip to Marin, wondering whether I could nab a Crystal Cleaners car as early as this afternoon. I had one foot on the pavement and another on the landing when I stopped.

Eight Fish. They were watching the door and clearly waiting for me: Bad Lipstick and seven others. The two boys were not among them. These were all bigger Fish, who had been around the block many more times than I wanted to count. The girl with the bad lipstick, still wearing bad lipstick; a lady bodybuilder with a crew cut and a baseball bat; another woman with a mass of braids dyed green, mermaid style, holding little tridents; three men of assorted sizes who sported square beards and automatics; two older men, one with a machete and a long mustache, the other with a whip and chaps. My eye snagged on the mermaid, who looked familiar. They were a colorful crew. It took me only a fraction of a second to do the math. I stepped backward, pulled the door closed, and threw the bolt at the top of the door frame that I'd seen out of the corner of my eye.

The bolt would probably hold for about ten seconds. I launched myself down the stairs, hollering for Deliverance. She was still standing there in the corridor, eyes wide under the bonnet. "Fish," I said. "We have to get out. Everyone." They were after me, and I knew it, but I didn't want to be responsible if the Fish decided to broaden the playing field.

Deliverance stepped past me and shut the inner door that I'd just come through, throwing the deadbolt.

"That won't be enough," I said, pulling her away from the door. "There are eight of them. Sorry," I added.

She didn't ask about the apology. "Go tell Steadfast," she said. "There's a way out through the garden. I'll get the others."

I ran down the corridor toward the garden and burst into the little oasis of azaleas and maples and gravel. Steadfast and her eager convert were both looking expectantly toward the open doorway. "Fish," I said. "Deliverance says there's a way out through the garden."

"What about—"

"She's getting the others," I interrupted.

Steadfast pointed to the rear of the garden, but all I saw

there was a bamboo screen. "There's a ladder back there," she said.

I hurried to the screen and found the ladder she was talking about. It was a rickety bamboo thing that probably wouldn't hold more than a hundred fifty pounds. I had to hope these Puritans were as abstemious as the real ones. At the top of the garden wall, at street level, was an iron fence. I couldn't tell from where I was standing, but it looked like the fence bordered a walkway between buildings. Hopefully there wouldn't be any Fish there.

I held the base of the ladder and urged Steadfast's convert to climb up. The whole thing rattled like a bundle of twigs, but it didn't break. As she was clinging to the metal fence at the top and maneuvering her way over it, Deliverance ran into the garden with four more Puritans. I looked skeptically at their dresses. Perhaps later I would suggest to Steadfast that her notions about women's emancipation extend to their choice of wardrobe.

There was a crash from inside the building that announced the demise of the deadbolt. Deliverance had the sense to close the garden door, and with another Puritan she blocked it with a stone bench. The latch, naturally, was on the other side. Steadfast was already climbing the ladder, and the other ladies followed suit. I urged them on while holding the ladder in place. Really, holding the ladder was an excuse. If the Fish made their way into the garden, the Puritans would be made into mincemeat, and then I'd be stuck there all day. As Deliverance was flinging herself over the metal fence, the stone bench toppled, and the garden door was flung open. I was already halfway up the rickety ladder. In the time it took them to cross the garden, I reached the top.

To my surprise, the three beards didn't shoot. When I swung over the metal fence I saw why. Deliverance stood at the top with a semiautomatic pointed at the Fish. Her bonnet had fallen off. She looked much prettier without it, even with the grimly pursed lips. *Weapons for weaklings indeed, Gao*, I thought. I reached through the metal fence and awkwardly pulled the bamboo ladder up after me. Then I tossed it aside. "Go," Deliverance said, glancing at me quickly.

"You're coming, too."

"In one sec," she agreed. She fired twice into the beautiful little garden, sending clusters of gravel flying. It gave us enough time to duck down the passageway toward Sutter Street. The shots they fired back bit chunks out of the neighboring building. Only seconds later, I heard the first police siren wailing.

18

NATALIA

Deliverance and I turned onto Sutter Street as the sirens neared. She pulled me into a consignment shop and closed the door behind us. The shopkeeper, a slender gentleman in a mint-green sweater who was holding two hats up to a customer, turned to us and shook his head. "Oh no you don't. Out."

That was pretty bold, considering that Deliverance was still holding her weapon. Between that and the Puritan dress she looked a little like a nun on a rampage. She ignored the shopkeeper. Without a word, she starting taking off her dress. I didn't interfere. Under the dress she had on black leggings and a button-down, and she tucked the gun into a holster. From some unseen pocket she drew out a wallet and waved it at the indignant shopkeeper. I caught a glimpse: police badge.

Well, that explained a lot.

"Give me those hats," she said to the mint sweater.

"Under no circumstances."

"Did you not see my badge?"

"You can't just take things," he protested.

"Would you rather we hide here while the eight Fish on my tail search the nearby stores?" I asked.

He handed me the hats. A purple cloche, which I passed skeptically to Deliverance, and a broad-brimmed straw hat that I balanced on my head. "Thank you," I said. I folded my own hat carefully and tucked it into my bag.

Outside, a dozen police motorcycles sat in the road like glistening cockroaches. Four store windows had been smashed to bits, either by bullets or by the muscular lady with the bat. I could hear the messy sounds of pursuit from all sides. From the amount of gunfire, it didn't sound too good for the Fish, but it didn't sound like they were making things easy for the cops, either.

Deliverance took my arm and walked me silently along Sutter Street eastward. I stayed along for the ride, curious where we were going. We'd gone a block from the clothing store when the mermaid stepped out from behind a white van. She'd been waiting. She stood on the sidewalk in front of us, holding the sai comfortably against her quads like oversized forks. Deliverance was still holding her semi-automatic, so for a few seconds we all just stood there, measuring.

The mermaid wasn't interested in the semiautomatic. She had eyes for me only. Her face was bonier than I remembered, and the dark green makeup made her look even older, like a sea witch with a few lifetimes behind her. But I had no doubt who she was.

"Hi, Coral."

Her eyes crinkled a little. "Hey there, Nat," she said quietly.

Deliverance kept her eyes on the sai, and I could feel her listening to the gunfire, occasional bursts of it, still not too near.

"It's been a while," I said affably. "What have you been up to?"

She gave me a little wink but no smile. "You know, fishing."

I nodded sagely. "Dangerous business."

"You're the one in danger, Nat." She tucked the sai into her belt abruptly and folded her arms over her chest. I guess she didn't like her chances with the semiautomatic. "Your bounty is too high," she said, her voice still quiet. "Every Fish in the Bay has your face on a screen."

Deliverance moved a few paces forward. "Step against the wall and put your hands behind your head."

Coral glanced at her with faint interest, as if she'd just noticed the cop was there. Then she gave me a small nod. Without a word she jumped, leapfrogging off the hood of the white van beside her. I didn't even hear her footsteps on the pavement. When we rounded the van, she was gone.

Deliverance muttered something under her breath that sounded like "slippery worm." To me she said, "Come on." Three blocks down she turned in to an alley, skipped down a short flight of steps, and unlocked a battered beige door onto a ground-floor apartment. The room had seen better days. Wall-to-wall carpeting, a single bed, a recliner, and a coffee table piled high with soda cans. Deliverance apparently played many parts: Puritan crusader, undercover cop, deadbeat bachelor with bad habits.

She motioned to the recliner and I perched on the very, very edge of it. The corduroy looked like it hadn't been cleaned. Ever.

Deliverance tapped a very small screen decal on her inner wrist. "This is Officer O'Rourke," she said into the decal. She listened. "That's fine by me." She listened again. "Will do." She tapped the decal and dropped her arm. "Friendly with a lot of Fish, are you?"

"Not really," I said. "I was friends with her before. Before fading. I haven't seen her since high school."

"You should report her."

I made a noncommittal noise. "So," I said amicably. "What gives?"

Officer O'Rourke sat on her bed and looked thoughtful. "We're just waiting it out."

I'd figured that much. "Why are you undercover with Ashael's Cave?"

"Oh." She nodded. "Lots of churches have cops undercover."

I nodded back. From Gao, I'd learned that religious organizations could function as fronts for prison bosses. The churches do charity in prisons, and they get to know the prisoners. Mostly it's completely innocent, and every once in a while it's anything but. "Ashael's Cave just seems kind of small-scale."

"Yeah. It does." She gave me a sideways look. "But New

Age Christian cults aren't always what they seem. I can't really say more."

"Got it," I acknowledged.

She leaned back against the wall and crossed her legs on the bed. "So why are the Fish after you?"

"I did a little dance with one of them yesterday. They were on the BART and it was unavoidable. I lost her yesterday afternoon but I guess they tracked me down."

"Not Coral, I take it. Which one?"

"The younger female. Bad lipstick."

"Yeah, I saw her." She nodded knowingly. Then she tapped on the decal affixed to her wrist for a few seconds. "What kind of info do they have on you?"

"Just a photo I think."

She tapped around some more. "Oh yeah. Here you are. Eighty-six thousand dollars. That's bad," she added helpfully.

"Thanks."

"This is one of those apps where they have a gallery of kill shots." She scrolled. "Here's a guy they got yesterday. Nice. Very nice. They favor dismemberment."

"I should think the site would be shut down."

"We have people on it twenty-four seven. They just bounce up in another location." She dropped her wrist. "Well, once we catch the Fish who originally posted the bounty, we can usually negotiate to get the listing taken down. Then you should be in the clear."

"Lucky for me you were around. I appreciate the help."

"They're vermin." She rolled her eyes. "Where Fish are concerned, I'd gladly sidestep arrests altogether. And no matter how much damage they do, there's always some crackpot trying to argue that all they need is a little counseling. More like a little lobotomizing."

Well. That was one solution.

She put her hands back behind her head. "What's your real reason for tracking down Hoffman? Not that it's any of my business."

I told her. Nothing I was doing was illegal—not yet, anyway—and she seemed well-disposed given that she'd saved me from eight carnivorous Fish. The story impressed her. "That . . ." She shook her head. "You could not have picked a bigger Goliath."

"Pretty much."

"Good luck," she said.

People were saying that to me a lot lately, and for some reason it wasn't encouraging. "It sounds quiet out there," I said, getting up.

"Yup." She got to her feet as well and pulled the purple cloche back on. Maybe she'd taken it because she liked it. "I'll walk you to the station. We'll see how many Fish they caught and you can give them a description of any who got away. Including Coral."

I stifled a groan. This was not how I wanted to spend the rest of my afternoon. "In case the whole RealCorp thing didn't make it clear, I'm kind of in a rush . . ."

Officer O'Rourke shook her head once and her tone was uncompromising. "Lo siento. We've got to do it."

I sighed. "Fine."

———

Despite the generous gunfire, they hadn't caught any of the Fish. (Guess Gao was right about guns after all.) So I had to give a description for each of them, and since most of them I'd seen only fleetingly, we spent a lot of time going around and around in circles. Japantown doesn't have as many surveillance cameras as other places, apparently, and the Ashael's Cave people didn't have one outside their door. So it was up to me to tell them about Coral, the bad lipstick, the weight lifter with the bat, the bearded gunmen, the cowboy, and the cane cutter. I felt like I was describing a failed circus act, and by the end I could tell the cop taking my descriptions was as sick of the Fish as I was.

When I was free to leave, it was evening. No time for Marin County. All I had time to do was call Glout, and he didn't answer. So much for keeping me updated. It was weighing on me that Cal had been missing for more than twenty-four hours. To him it would feel like an eternity. It *was* an eternity. A lot can happen in twenty-four hours.

As I rode the BART home I put the ticking clock aside and tried to tally my successes. I had a lead on Hoffman. I had a way into Philbrick's house. One of the two had to work out, right?

Maybe it was the exhaustion, but as we rumbled through the tunnel to the East Bay, both my leads seemed too uncertain, too flimsy, too insubstantial. It felt like I was trying to get to Cal across a high wire through the fog. I had to hope that when the fog lifted, I'd find something solid under my feet. Something real that would carry me across. Vain hopes are not hard wires.

19

CALVINO

October 12

Dear Nat,

I have told Dr. Glout that I won't answer his questions anymore. I said I would only write to you. I am writing on paper so that he can't read what I'm writing.

Dr. Glout said you came to see me. That made me feel a little better if it's true. I would like to leave this place now. I don't know what he told you, but I am not staying here because I want to. Maybe he told you something different. Dr. Glout just keeps saying one more test, one more test.

The problem is that I am not even sure who Dr. Glout is. That is the name of the person who writes to me while I'm in here but I have never met him. For a while I thought it might just be a program, but I think it is a real person. But who? The only person I have seen here is Dr. Baylor who brought me in the first place and then left and then the next thing I knew it was Dr. Glout writing to me. I feel like if

I could just see him then I might be able to figure out if he is telling the truth or not.

I thought about it and maybe the person who writes to me as Dr. Glout is not really in charge. He may not even be a doctor. He may not even be a HE. He might be a she or a them. Someone else is deciding what to do and "Dr. Glout" is just following directions. That is a scary thought.

It could even be that you are right next door but they won't tell me that you are so that the test will be more real. Maybe they are just trying to scare me on purpose. That would not be so bad. It's like you said last time at school, just a test.

I think if I had a number in mind it would be easier. How many more hours of this.

I have been planning what we will do when I am done here finally. I have a lot of time to plan.

Nat, I was thinking. If I am here for so many tests, there must be something really wrong with me. I think maybe you didn't want to make me feel bad, and that is why you never said so. I understand why you would do that. But now I'm worried that whatever is wrong with me is actually really bad. Dr. Glout keeps writing it's not, it's not bad at all, but that just doesn't make sense. If there were nothing wrong with me, I wouldn't be here. I guess I am actually scared to find out what the results of these tests are. I hope you are here with me when they come back with the test results.

I miss you.
Love,
Cal

20

NATALIA

I debated trying to squeeze in a trip to Marin before I was due at the Philbrick castle, but in the end I calculated that Philbrick was still the shorter route to Cal. Tomorrow was Saturday. Philbrick would possibly be at home while I did desultory cleaning. If I could somehow bring him around, Cal would be out. Whereas with Hoffman, even if I won him over instantly, I still had to jump through many legal hoops, and those took time.

I arranged with Cass, Tabby, and Joey to meet them at noon so we could all ride out to Marin together. Cass and Tabby's refurbished and minuscule Ford coupe was guaranteed to be less spacious than the Crystal Cleaners vehicle, but using it meant I could avoid starting off my crime spree with car theft. I still hadn't told Cass and Tabby about the Philbrick angle. Maybe a bad call, but in my defense I did tell Joey all about it so that he would know where I was if the wolves tore me to pieces.

When I drove up to the castle the next morning, it looked the same as the day before and there were no wolves in sight.

Still silent. Still eerie. I rang the bell, and the iron gate rolled open. I got back into the Crystal Cleaners car (it *was* more spacious than the coupe, but it reeked of bleach), pulled in to the driveway, and stepped out with just the cleaning bucket. The back of the car had all kinds of gadgets. I wasn't about to unpack the full arsenal unless I had to.

I rang the bell. The door was opened seconds later by a middle-aged white man who looked extremely well cared for. And content. Eyebrows neutral, eyes relaxed, mouth slightly turned up. I almost called him Mr. Philbrick and then I realized he was wearing starched cotton gloves.

The castle was so white that even the servants were white.

"Crystal Cleaners," I said. Was I supposed to shake hands with him? I wasn't sure. His easy stance at the door, the suit that I now realized was a uniform, and the sound of early-morning partying from inside the house were confusing my sense of propriety. Fortunately he knew exactly what to do.

"Come in—Natalia, right?" He smiled.

Of course. Crystal Cleaners would have told them I was coming. "That's right."

"I'm Ed," he said, reaching out with one gloved hand. He looked at my bucket. "You don't need that. We have all the cleaning supplies you might want, and Mrs. Philbrick is particular about how they smell."

"Okay, good. No problem." I went back to the car, dumped the bucket, and rounded back to the house. Ed was still at the door, still smiling. I followed him into the house and over to the edge of a spacious, sunken room that entirely defied the exterior structure of the house. High ceilings, huge windows onto an inner courtyard, a spiral staircase at either end. There was a lap pool in the courtyard and someone with bronze shoulders was doing laps. Mrs. Philbrick was sitting on the white sofa: very slim, very blonde, very young. I knew who she was because her style matched the decor. She seemed to favor the 1960s, from the look of things. Blonde beehive, blond wood; gold jewelry, gold knickknacks; teal throw pillows, teal pumps. Personally, I don't like the colors, but she seemed quite comfortable among them. Very comfortable indeed. The sounds that had surprised me from the doorway came from her—she was sitting with two other women of a similar brand, glittering away, drinking cocktails.

The sight took my breath away.

It's not just anyone who can afford the quality and quantity of synaffs that make alcohol consumption worthwhile. Old-time drugs are plenty cheap, but on most of us they do absolutely nothing. Chugging a beer is about as enjoyable and mood-altering as chugging a bottle of olive oil. Mrs. Philbrick, on the other hand, was clearly very much enjoying the bubbly liquid in the crystal glass. "And to another fantastic dress on another fantastic opening day!" she said happily, offering one of many jubilant toasts. The ladies laughed and clinked.

I tore my eyes away and looked at Ed. He was watching me with friendly amusement, as if it pleased him to introduce me to such a joyous spectacle. I raised my eyebrows at him. "This place looks pretty clean to me," I said.

He laughed indulgently. "I'll show you where to get started." He directed me away from the sunken room and down a corridor until we reached a spacious kitchen. Here the decor parted ways with the 1960s, since everyone back then chose to cook their meals in ill-lit closets lined with laminate. Glass cabinets, wood counters, wood floors, and only the barest hint of the room's intended use in the form of an ornate espresso machine. "Just the kitchen and the bathrooms on weekends," Ed said. He opened a door to a pantry stacked with neatly organized cleaning supplies. "You should be out of here in a couple hours. I'll be serving drinks in the other room, so just wave me down when you're done with the kitchen and I'll point you to the bathrooms. Help yourself to water and snacks in the refrigerator."

"Thanks."

He gave me a wave and disappeared down the corridor.

I was a little dazed. I was having trouble figuring out why this wasn't every Crystal Cleaner's favorite job. *Snacks?*

Just for kicks, I opened the refrigerator, once I located it behind a wooden panel. I didn't see a single familiar label. Every item in there looked like it had been made by hand at an artisanal kitchen in SoMa. This doesn't happen to me often, but I couldn't seem to get over the fact that I wasn't supposed to be there. It wasn't the small-batch cheeses or the espresso machine built like a Rolls-Royce. It wasn't even the reality behind them, the fact that it was raining money on the Philbrick castle. And it wasn't the fact that I'd lied my way into the job. I realized, as I stared emptily at the pantry of cleaning supplies, that it was the undercurrent of emotion swirling around the rooms. People here were feeling things, good things, all the time. Disorienting didn't even begin to describe it. For the first time since I'd faded, I had that nagging sense that I was missing something. Something big.

There was only one thing to do. I assembled my cleaning supplies and got started on the kitchen.

It took me less than half an hour, since all the surfaces were already sparkling. I made them smell a little nicer with the coriander-and-honey-scented supplies that Mrs. Philbrick favored. Then I went back down the hallway to the sunken living room. The hostess had moved her party outside, and the three ladies were sitting poolside with more drinks. I waved to Ed and in due course he came in through the open doors. "Bathrooms?" he asked cheerily.

"I'm ready," I said.

I followed him to the opposite end of the corridor, where a narrow stairwell turned twice to reach the second floor. The rooms here were off a U-shaped corridor that encircled the patio. "Four bathrooms upstairs and two downstairs," Ed said. He pointed them out one by one on the second floor, then led me back down and directed me to the ground-floor bathrooms. "Supplies are in the same pantry," he concluded.

I thanked him and put together what seemed most bathroom-worthy from the pantry. It was hard to tell. Most of the cleaning supplies were nicer than what I use on my hair. The bathrooms on the ground floor were respectively dainty and dignified: lavender and lace with cream tiles in the one, gray marble and silver-trimmed mirrors in the other. I cleaned the already-clean surfaces and futzed around. Then I went upstairs.

There was still no sign of Mr. Philbrick, but I was hoping I would run into him as I made the rounds, maybe reading the paper or getting ready to go play golf, or doing whatever it is rich pharma CEOs do on the weekends. The first bathroom was off the corridor; there was a connecting door that presumably led to a bedroom. I didn't open it. The theme here was nautical—navy and white and jute. Porcelain tub with a matelassé shower curtain, tiny blue anchors on the wallpaper. I was scrubbing the spotless tub when the bedroom door swung open and someone said, "Well, hello!"

I knew before even turning around that I'd found the wolf. It was the tone of voice. Comfortable, confident, and rapacious. As a voice it was pretty nice—warm and low, with just the slightest hint of a growl.

I turned around. The wolf wasn't bad to look at, either. He was clearly the owner of the bronze shoulders I'd seen earlier in the lap pool. Said shoulders were still bare, as were the arms, the chest, the stomach, the legs, the knees—well, actually everything that didn't fit under turquoise swim briefs the size of a folded handkerchief. He had dark wavy hair slicked back, a straight nose, expressive eyebrows, and a thin mustache. He was going for early Clark Gable and pretty much nailing it. Too young to be Philbrick Senior. I figured he was offspring and made my plan accordingly. "Hello," I said.

He took a step into the room and planted a hand on the edge of the sink. His eyebrows did the talking for a little while and I looked back at him, not letting my eyes travel at all.

"You are *gorgeous*," he said warmly. He smiled and it lit up his eyes. Those were some high-quality drops he was taking.

I didn't say anything. I watched to see how quickly he would move.

Pretty quickly. Maybe he was mixing something else with those synaffs, just like the ladies downstairs. He stepped forward and put a hand on my waist. "Just on the other side of that door," he said in a low voice, "is a room with a bed." His eyebrows darted upward. "It's unmade."

Clearly the wolf didn't have to work too hard for his meals, because his lines would not have held up well in the wild.

I looked up at him. His face was only about five inches away from mine, and the rest of him was plastered up against me. "Now I get it," I said. I took a short step back, found the edge of the tub, and tapped my chin pensively. "Option one, which I'm guessing most of my predecessors have taken, is to enjoy the top-notch euphoria on the top shelf of the medicine chest. A drop or two, with maybe a promise of the bottle as a parting gift. And that's a nice option, because even if you don't want to be happy for the rest of the month, you can sell the remainder of the bottle and pay your rent off for the rest of the year. Not bad. And all you have to do for it is roll around in that unmade bed."

The wolf's smile was frozen in place. He couldn't tell yet where I was going. "Option two is to run out of here as fast as my little legs will carry me and complain to the grown-ups downstairs. I can already see how that goes. Mom is so doped she doesn't care, or maybe she cares just enough to select the right appetizers for you through Crystal Cleaners. I'm guessing that's it," I said, watching his eyes turn hostile, "since the obvious solution is to send a two-hundred-pound straight man to do the cleaning here and they haven't done that. And option three is to say no, once or fifty times, and watch you not care. But I'm guessing again that your tastes are flexible and you might even prefer that option, since I see the scratch marks on your wrists, and the castle has no cats. Very classy," I added.

His eyes were hard now, and the smile had an edge to it. Yeah, he was flexible—no doubt about it. His fingers tightened around my waist.

"The thing you don't know," I went on, leaning into him, "is that I have a fourth option, and it involves using the lipstick I have pressed against your groin." He blinked and moved to look down, but I chopped the motion off with my other hand. I held his chin and pulled his face in toward me. "This is really special lipstick," I said quietly. "Very high voltage. I don't have man-parts, so I can't tell you from personal experience, but I'm told that it doesn't feel good. And here's the thing." I smiled. "You can't threaten my job, because I don't care if I lose it. You can't buy me off with drops, because I don't want them." I pressed the lipstick into his shiny bathing suit. "A rich rapist is still just a rapist," I said.

We stood there staring at each other, him trying to figure

out if I was bluffing and me trying not to laugh at the naked confusion in his eyes.

Someone else did it for me. There was a chuckle from the doorway to the corridor.

I didn't turn, but the wolf did. He stepped away all at once, his energy drawn back and now hurled at the figure in the doorway. "Charlie's bad day," the person standing there said, his voice heavy with condescension. He made it sound like the title of a children's book about a depressed clown.

Now I turned to look at him. He was a younger version of the wolf, aka Charlie. Same wavy dark hair, but more tousled. Same warm eyes, but less vicious. Same easy smile, but less smug. No mustache and plenty of clothes, which were both significant improvements. I liked him already.

Then I recognized him.

It was Troy. Flowers and Homer Troy. Cloak and Dagger Troy. Without the wild, red, panicked eyes, he was a different person. I blinked.

Troy was way ahead of me. He knew who I was, and he wasn't going to walk away. His eyes were trained on his brother, waiting.

For a few seconds, Charlie radiated rage like a party sparkler. Then it was gone. Someone had really fine-tuned his dosages—it was kind of amazing to watch. "Bitch doesn't want to play." He shrugged, heading back toward his bedroom.

"Actually," I said to his back, "bitch would have loved to play. You wimped out."

I saw his back muscles harden and he flung me an evil look over his shoulder. Then he shrugged again and laughed. "She's all yours, Troy."

I turned to Troy and waited to see what he would do with that. He looked back at me for what felt like minutes. In that time I noticed some things that I'd missed the first time: he had long eyelashes, a not-unpleasant sheen of sweat on his neck, and very nice arms. "Charlie is an asshole," he finally said.

"Yeah, I noticed."

Suddenly something changed in his face, and I saw that he was younger than I'd realized. Eighteen at most, probably a year less. His eyes softened, and I caught a glimpse of a child who spent a lot of time alone.

"Thanks for the interruption," I said.

He smiled. It was a lovely smile, if a bit sad. "It was entirely selfish. I don't usually get to see Charlie put in his place. I can't remember the last time."

"Maybe when the queen of England visited?" I asked.

He laughed. "She hasn't been here in ages. I miss her."

I was going to make a joke about his parents having more money than the queen, but something stopped me. For some reason I didn't feel like embarrassing him. We had an awkward pause as I didn't make the joke. "Riding?" I asked, nodding at his boots.

He looked down at them as if he'd just remembered where his feet were. He was wearing khaki riding pants and chestnut-colored boots along with a loose white shirt. All of it looked comfortably worn-in. "Yeah, over at Orli Fields."

"Right," I said, like I knew where that was.

"Is your lipstick really a stun gun?"

I held up the cylindrical pink case. "Yup. Handy, huh?"

"Very." He looked at me, considering. "Would you have used it?" I liked the way he asked—not as a dare and not with ghoulish curiosity. Just wondering.

"Definitely. You tell me if I'm wrong, but to me charming Charlie seemed totally serious about putting his cute plan into action. When they're serious, you have to be serious right back."

He crossed his arms over his chest, and something like sorrow moved across his face. "You're not wrong."

As I watched his face shift from sorrow to pain—remembered pain, it looked like—I started wondering how many times he'd heard the wolf go through his routine. What did the little brother do? Listen? Step in? Call the police? It didn't seem like there were many good options.

I decided to change the topic. "You and me and bathrooms," I commented.

He smiled. "Yes. There's no way this can be a coincidence, so I have to conclude you've been following me. I'm flattered."

"Nope. Totally a coincidence." As I said it, something sparked in my brain. Wait, *was* it a coincidence?

"Seriously?" Troy's eyebrows shot up. "No way, someone put you up to it. I'm betting that sweet lady who works with you at the Landmark. Martha?"

"Yeah, Marta. If she had her way I'd have shown up on your doorstep with a ball gown and one glass slipper."

Troy laughed. "I like her."

But Marta hadn't put me up to it. Troy was right. How could this be a coincidence? Pieces of information clanked around in my mental engine. The blonde woman downstairs. Frances Peters at the Landmark. Insults traded over the roof of a cab. Cal's letter from school. Dr. Baylor, employee of RealCorp. Tanner Philbrick, CEO of RealCorp. I could see all the parts, but I couldn't see how they fit together.

I hid the many confusions behind a single one. "I'm a bit baffled. Mrs. Philbrick downstairs isn't the woman I remember from the Landmark."

Troy shook his head. "Monica's my stepmom. She's barely thirty." He said this with faint pity.

"Got it," I said. Words failed me. I couldn't figure out how to ask him if Frances Peters had mentioned me to Tanner Philbrick. Obviously she had. Had Cal been whisked away by RealCorp because I'd insulted Frances Peters? Wait. Had *Troy* mentioned me to Tanner Philbrick? The thought silenced me.

I stared at the boy in front of me, trying to find a way out of the obvious. He smiled, still friendly and hopeful but a little embarrassed by the lull. While we both thought about what to say, a female voice, high and tinkly from champagne, called from somewhere on the ground floor. "Troy! Charles!"

Troy looked over his shoulder. "I've gotta go," he said to me. "Are we still on for the Cloak and Dagger sometime?" His eyes studied the floor, then glanced up at me with a flicker of shyness.

It didn't seem possible that he could have done anything to make Cal disappear. Not knowingly, anyway. Maybe unknowingly? I had to find out. "Sure," I said. "How about tomorrow?"

He smiled, a rush of happiness flushing his cheeks. I wondered what that felt like. "Want to say three?"

"Sounds good."

Turning away, he flashed me a grin. "Bye."

"Bye," I said. I listened to the two future Philbrick billionaires, the belle and the beast, make their way downstairs to the company of their stepmother and her intoxicated friends.

As I listened I tried to figure out where my wits were. There was a dotted line that connected me and Troy to Real-Corp and Cal, but I couldn't see it.

"Stupid," I muttered, turning back to the tub.

I was still missing something. Something big. But what?

21

NATALIA
October 13 — midday

Finishing the nautical bathroom, I decided to focus on the elusive senior Philbrick. There had to be something in the house that would tell me a thing or two about him. I cleaned my way steadily through the other two bathrooms, each shinier and more resplendent than the last, until I reached the master suite. From the tuxedo on the clotheshorse, I gathered that the CEO had a formal engagement in the evening, but I gleaned nothing else from it. The tuxedo had the look of a suit of armor for an invisible man. His presence in the house seemed dim, dialed down to the lowest possible setting. Old-school shaving supplies, sandalwood soap, a toothbrush, and a regimen of synaffs that to my eye (trained secondhand by Joey, who trained firsthand at the pharmacy) seemed to favor ascetic productivity rather than pleasure or indulgence: these were the only hints of him in the bathroom. A furtive glance through the bedroom revealed a separate walk-in closet for him, filled almost entirely with suits and black shoes. He had very little casual clothing. I was getting the impression that Philbrick lived more at the steel and glass monolith by the pier than he did at the castle.

By the end of my cleaning circuit I was beginning to feel a little dizzy from all the opulence, as if I'd been staring too long at the sun. I was used to the Landmark, where wealth was well in evidence but pretty monotonous. This was something else. It was hard to accept that it existed. Especially considering that only a few miles away across the Bay Bridge, people had trouble paying for heat, paying for groceries. The grandeur was so at ease with itself, so settled; it belonged to a different world. A fully cogent, fully functional world which I had no part of. It was like opening a dresser drawer and finding the household mice in the midst of a ball, waltzing in their tiaras and gowns. *I can't believe they live like this*, I kept thinking.

I have to admit that it changed how I looked at Troy. If I'd seen the house before calling him, I wouldn't have called.

Their voices drifted in and out as I moved from room to room, the women's high laughter, Charlie's occasional growl. I didn't hear Troy at all. In one of the bedrooms that looked out over the patio, I paused for a moment and watched. The five of them were sitting in the scant shade of a lemon tree, beside the glinting waters of the lap pool. Mrs. Philbrick reclined in a lawn chair at the far edge, smiling and drinking. One of her friends in a floppy hat was laughingly fencing with Charlie; he leaned in to whisper something and she held up a jeweled hand, pushing him away by pressing a single finger to his lips. The other friend dangled over Troy's chair like an eager marionette, all jerky pats and playful shoves. She was even thinner than the stepmother, with a platinum head of hair like Chandler's Silver-Wig. Troy smiled tightly, not looking at her. He looked about as happy as a mouse in a glue trap.

There was something wrong with the house, but I couldn't figure out what. Something no amount of polished brass and blond wood could remedy. Something to do with flirtation and coercion, with a stepmother who made herself deliriously happy and a stepson who did not. Maybe I was trying too hard. Maybe it was just as simple as the unsubtle Charlie made it look: the predatory son of a predatory man who ran a predatory company. Predation of different sorts, sure, but predation nonetheless. They all had their various victims. And the people around them—Troy, Monica, Frances Peters—were merely accessories, some abler than others, to their habits of persecution.

But maybe it was more complicated. What made the whole thing tick? What was the purpose? I didn't get it.

No answer ran into the bedroom to declare itself. Philbrick Senior didn't appear, either. Suddenly all I wanted to do was get out of there so I could ponder the problem in peace. I ran a coriander-scented rag over some surfaces, scurried back downstairs to stack the supplies, and tried to make my way out of the house as discreetly as possible.

Ed caught me on the way out. "Hey!" he said. He looked at me hopefully. "Will we see you again on Monday?"

"No schedule yet from the boss, but I'm fine to come back," I said. I didn't explain that by Monday I would have found another solution. I had to.

Ed seemed elated. It was probably the first time he'd gotten that answer. "That's great. Thanks for everything." He opened the door for me and waved cheerily as I stepped out. "Enjoy the weekend!"

I shook my head as I started the car and watched the motorized gate rolling open. The place was seriously off-kilter.

Driving down the hill toward Van Ness I began to feel a little better. By the time I parked the car in the underground garage, I was back in familiar territory. Van Ness was incurably, reliably seedy, and I relished the walk down to the bus stop. The air smelled of ocean, as it sometimes does in surprising pockets. Three crusty vagrants stood under an awning sharing a sandwich and looking for all the world like they'd stepped right out of Cannery Row. Their matted beards and bushy eyebrows disguised their faces entirely. I tipped my hat and one of the three Steinbecks decorously raised his own broken hat and swooped it downward with a gracious bow. "Bonjour, mademoiselle," he said with a perfect accent. I grinned at him.

I took a crosstown bus that left me at the far east end of Fisherman's Wharf. Walking south, I came up to RealCorp ten minutes later. The place was even quieter on a Saturday. I called Glout from outside the building and he didn't answer, so I dove into the lobby. Lucy and my friends from the previous visit were not on duty. Nevertheless, the weekend receptionists followed the same playbook. A smiling, twiggy thing with feathered bangs tried to sell me synaffs, and I fended off her advances. When I insisted she call Glout, she made a disappointed face and turned to the rotary phone. The conversation was short. She reported that Glout was in a meeting until three and could not be disturbed.

It was difficult to leave empty-handed. I found my feet dragging as I headed back to the revolving door. I reviewed and discarded for the fiftieth time the crazy schemes I had considered during the last forty-eight hours. Threatening self-immolation would be dramatic, but most likely the ladies at the counter wouldn't even flinch. Nuts, they'd probably smile and clap.

No, my two best schemes were the ones I already had cooking: Philbrick and Hoffman.

On the way to Marin, Cass told me that June had prepped all the legal paperwork and that it was sitting in a briefcase in the trunk. "She's been working nonstop on it, Natalia," Cass said.

"I'm grateful," I replied, looking out at the view of San Quentin. The state prison begins on the far side of the 580 bridge and sprawls northward, occupying thirty square miles. It's like a city, only more so. The population is larger than San Francisco's. The towers are just as high. They consume more food and utilities. And from what I hear they move just as much money around, too. It's the largest prison in the area, but only because the real estate is so valuable. If you haven't been to Nevada, you should go stand near the border and look at it with binoculars. It's 90 percent prison land.

"Did she say if it would work?" I asked.

"It's going to work," Joey affirmed quietly from the seat beside me.

Cass glanced at me in her rearview mirror. "She said that if Hoffman agrees to a paternity test and proves intent to take legal responsibility then we have an airtight approach."

"The trouble is proving intent," I said.

"Right," Cass agreed.

We rode in silence. The prison loomed to our right, the high sand-colored walls like desert cliffs. Cass and Tabby's car purred quietly. As we reached the winding roads closer to the coast, the motor shifted, expending rather than generating its store of friction. Cass slowed down. I always get queasy on curves but I was almost done explaining to Joey by way of *De rerum* what had happened at the Philbricks'. He shot me a quizzical glance when I described Troy as "solid."

For his circumstances, that is, I typed.

Joey looked skeptical. *You should have zapped older brother anyway*, he wrote.

Probably, I agreed. *Any word from your army of spies outside RealCorp?*

. . . Nope. They've gone quiet.

Meaning what? Not writing you back?

All three are MIA.

That was ominous. I refrained from pointing out to Joey

that I'd told him so. *Aren't you worried? I asked.*

More worried about you, Joey typed. *Fish bounty has climbed to 160.*

What a waste of money.

And they have added + targets.

What's that.

Dinging anyone in a quarter-mile radius also gets points.

Dumb.

Their way to deal with 100 Fish all converging in one place. Many prizes.

How do they even prove radius?

Time/location stamp on photo of kill shot.

I shook my head silently. *I can't think about this right now, J.*

Okay, he relented.

I put *De rerum* down and gave a long sigh. We'd reached the bluffs. The ocean glimmered with the promise of another kind of life—leisure and comfort and days unfolding slowly.

We used to go to the Point Reyes seashore sometimes with Mom, and Cal always loved it, rain or shine. It was never the same place. Sometimes it was quiet and pastoral, with the cows bellowing in the sunlight and the mud hardening underfoot. Sometimes it was a landscape out of legend, with the elk running graceful parabolas between the grassy hilltops. Sometimes it was unearthly, with the patches of scorched grass left by the forest fires, the disfigured, carbonized trees like silent watchers. Once when we were hiking with Cal through the drizzle, he came upon the flattened and mostly desiccated carcass of a deer. The eye was missing, the fur was eaten away, but the antlers remained a perfect, symmetrical crown. Cal crouched by the deer and stared and stared until the tears started running down his face. I wanted to console him, but I didn't know what to say. The deer had a good life? Everything dies someday? The platitudes didn't really touch the fact that something once living and vibrant was now rotted to pieces.

Mom had a good response. She was often sort of awful with the little things but then came through with the big things. Death being big, rather. "What's making you cry, Cal?" she asked, crouching down and wrapping her arm around his waist.

"It was so beautiful," Cal hiccuped.

Mom nodded. "It was beautiful."

"It's not right. It shouldn't be out like this, for people to step on."

"What would be right, do you think?"

Cal's tears started drying up as he thought about what to do. He pondered for a time. "Can we move it into the woods? Then we can cover it with branches."

Mom gamely put Cal's plan into action, and I did my part by clamping my jaw down and not saying a word about infectious diseases. We spent an hour sheltering Cal's deer with branches and he gathered a clump of wildflowers, setting them reverently at the top of the pile.

As they go, it was a gentle introduction to death.

22

CALVINO

October 13

Dear Nat,

I think there is something really wrong. I did a test a little while ago. Sort of like what they did at school but with video clips. When we were done, Dr. Glout went offline for more than three hours. He never leaves for this long except for at night.

But he wouldn't tell me what was wrong with the test. He just kept saying that we would probably have to do the test again later because the results were unusual. But he would not explain how they were unusual. That really scared me. Then I kept asking and he didn't answer. He just wrote, nothing. Nothing is wrong.

What is <u>wrong</u> with me, Nat?? I really wish you had told me before this started. Maybe you didn't know, but you are pretty good at figuring these things out *before they happen. The things you told me that would happen this year pretty much happened just like you said. But I never thought this would happen. So what is this?*

Love,
Cal

23

NATALIA

We reached Mordecai's Hill in the early afternoon. The sign was exactly as Steadfast had described: rickety plywood and spray paint. Maybe Cass would get some business out of this visit, I thought.

The winding dirt road seemed to get drier and drier as we climbed. The almond trees gave way to cypresses, their leaning trunks long and wanting. A white gate with a padlock stood open half a mile in. The air carried scraps of something pungent—tangy and mineral.

"Hot springs," Joey said, looking out through his open window.

"God, I hope they're not nudists," Cass commented.

"They're Puritans," Tabby reminded her. "I think the two are not compatible."

"If there were to be a place for Puritan nudists," I said, "this would be it."

Cass pushed the little coupe into the uphill. "Fingers crossed that it's not."

As we crested the hill, the buildings came into view. The

main house was a rambling late-Victorian structure that had never been flashy and had dwindled with time. The exterior was brown wood shingle. The spindled frieze around the wraparound porch looked chipped and broken in places. Sash windows on every wall were shuttered against the bright sun. Facing it across the dirt road stood a giant barn painted brick red and a long, low building of recent construction and uncertain purpose. On a high hill beyond all of these rose a church unlike any I'd ever seen: a Romanesque box made of thin, wooden slats. The slats were spaced evenly, so that narrow slices of blue sky appeared all through the walls and roof and steeple. It made you think of the church as a delicate wooden cage.

Cass stopped the car by the side of the dirt road, since there seemed to be no designated place to park. We all climbed out of the coupe. I felt the waves of boiled-egg air coming up from the hot springs. A stream ran past the low building, and I was willing to bet the Puritan nudists had their baths in there.

Or not nudists, as it turned out. We walked toward the main building and a woman came out to meet us wearing a version of the white dress and bonnet that Deliverance and Steadfast had been wearing at Ashael's Cave.

"Welcome," she said, stopping in the road before us. "Bienvenidos to Mordecai's Hill, New Puritan Church of God."

"Thank you," Cass said. She introduced us all one by one.

"I'm Cressens," she said, giving a slight bow. She was an older woman, and she had a courtliness about her that I thought was less Puritanness and more agedness. Her eyes were pale blue and white-lashed, her nose long and purple-veined where the nostrils flared. She held her hands folded at her waist while she spoke. "Please come refresh yourselves out of the sun," she said, gesturing toward the faded porch of the Victorian pile.

We climbed after her and sat on a mismatched assortment of wooden furniture that had clearly been repaired many times. I sat on a rocking chair with one purple arm and new webbing. Hey, they were frugal. There was nothing wrong with that.

Cass explained our visit to the New Puritan without mentioning Cal or paternity or anything potentially hair-raising. "We are trying to locate someone we knew in the past as Dylan Hoffman. We believe he now goes by Mordecai Hoffman—your minister. Is he the same person?"

Cressens blinked at us. "I couldn't say," she replied slowly. "I didn't know him before he was Reverend Hoffman."

"Could we ask him ourselves, perhaps?" Cass prompted.

"He isn't here at the moment. Reverend Hoffman and many from the community are doing their weekly educational outreach in Santa Rosa."

"Will he be back soon?"

"It's likely. They often return around three or four. Sometimes later."

Cass paused. "Could we wait here to speak with him? Or would it be better to return another time?"

"You could wait." She looked around the porch. "You're very welcome to stay here. Or inside. Or you may enjoy the grounds—many daytime visitors use the trails on the property."

I couldn't tell if she was being evasive on purpose or if she was innately vague in her thinking or if the bliss of Puritan life had made her a little weak-witted. Cass was having a hard time figuring it out, too. She glanced at us each in turn. I gave her a one-shouldered, one-inch shrug that said "Why not?"

"Thank you," she finally said to Cressens. "We'll wait here."

"Very good. I'll be indoors, and please make yourselves at home. Let me know if I can bring you anything."

Cressens disappeared through a screen door on a loose hinge. The four of us sat without speaking, listening to the silence.

"I bet there are no decals besides ours in a mile radius," Joey said in a low voice.

"I saw solar panels on the way in," Tabby offered.

"Not enough for screens."

Tabby nodded agreement. "Probably just enough to run the electric kettle."

"They don't use tech of any kind," Joey said, dropping his voice further. "Not even kettles."

"Are you sure?" Tabby scrunched up her nose. "That seems impossible."

Cass and I watched this exchange in silence. "We can ask Cressens when she gets back," Cass said.

We waited a long time. In the silence we made, lulled by

the heat and the bucolic surroundings, faint sounds reached us. Footsteps within the big house. A window closing. Splashing water. A hammer in steady bursts. We saw two more women leaving the barn carrying baskets and then, a while later, a man entering with a wheelbarrow. That was about it for forty minutes. I stood up at the end of the hour. "I'm going to go check out the church on the hill."

"I'll go with you," Joey said.

We walked down the steps and ambled along the dirt path. I had dressed for the country, with walking shoes and twill pants, but I hadn't counted on the heat. My linen shirt was damp and crumpled. Though I had a canvas hat, I would have preferred a canvas tent. The sunlight was inescapable. Joey trudged along beside me without complaint, his polished shoes dusty at once. He had dressed for church, not for a hike: well-ironed pants and a checked shirt with matching socks. "I don't think the Puritans will mind if you walk around their farm in a T-shirt," I suggested.

Joey shook his head. "First it's the shirt, then the shoes. Next thing you know I'll be wearing a bonnet and milking cows."

"Wow, I had no idea you were such a pushover. I would have tried to convert you ages ago."

"Never underestimate the Puritans," Joey said darkly. "Look what they accomplished, despite all the starvation and self-loathing."

"These aren't real Puritans," I reminded him.

"I'm not going to risk it. They might be descendants."

We had reached the base of the hill where the splintered church stood, and we climbed it slowly. Up close the structure was less poetic; it looked like scaffolding for a church, abandoned mid-project. But once we were inside, all the lyricism returned. The most impressive view was through the ceiling, which hung overhead like the rib cage of some ancient mammoth, delicate and perfectly proportioned. The blue sky lay in ribbons beyond it.

There were no pews, only rough wooden benches. By silent agreement, Joey and I lay down on one of these, head to head, staring up at the ceiling. I couldn't remember the last time I'd been in a place this quiet—probably on one of the trips to Point Reyes with Mom and Cal. It was arresting. As I watched the clouds move by in horizontal stripes, I let myself think about the future with Cal. Maybe we didn't belong in Oakland. Maybe we belonged someplace like this—not with the Puritans, but with the dry grass and blue sky. Maybe once Cal was out we should disappear for real. Convince Joey and Cass and Tabby to come with us and head to Alaska. Or Greenland. Or Tierra del Fuego. I didn't know how we'd make money, but at the moment that seemed secondary.

"I don't like this place," Joey said, his voice floating up from the bench over my head.

"You just hate peace, don't you?"

"I hate the way this seems to belittle my life. Like the only thing that matters is the big outdoor world. And it's obvious. And free. And I've been too dumb to see it."

I thought about this. "Yeah. I know what you mean. The

deep space phenomenon. Nothing matters in the grandeur of the universe and you are a meaningless speck and so on."

"It's not much, but mattering does help for wanting to stay alive."

Joey is the only person I can talk to about stuff like this. "I think because of Cal even when I am certain of being a meaningless speck, I know I am the meaningless speck Cal counts on."

He was quiet for a little while. I didn't know exactly where his mind was going, but I had a general sense that it was floating around me and him and Cal and how we all fit together. When he spoke his voice was quiet, but the silence on the hilltop made it linger in the air over our heads. "It's not just Cal who counts on you. You are eminently count-on-able. Even when things are very bad. Especially when things are very bad."

There's something different about knowing someone from before you both faded. Joey and I have been friends since we were four, and we were different as children. Not just because we felt things. We were different people. I was like a jellyfish—soft and squishy and quick to sting. It's hard to imagine, but Joey was the tough one. He used to block the door to the girls' room so I could pee without being teased. He would stand next to me at lunch while I was reading, pretending to read his own book and glaring at anyone who thought about making fun of me. He was my childhood defender. Even though we both changed completely after we faded, there is a part of us that is cumulative; every time I talk to him I see the kid who guarded the bathroom door, who held my hand when I cried even though it was covered with snot, and who made it seem like nothing I ever did was stupid. I'm sure when Joey looks at me he can still see the scared, morose little creature he looked after.

Even though he wasn't saying so, I knew that by "very bad" he was thinking of when my mom died. That night, I could tell that Joey was seeing me but picturing the little girl. It was a long night, with police and endless questions and Cal almost going crazy. Joey did not budge from my side for fourteen hours, and then only because I finally fell asleep. When I woke up he was on the tweed sofa, snoring with his head at a weird angle and his mouth open. He had cleaned the room while I slept.

That's one of the things I would want to ask Hugh Glout, if he were not my semi-mortal enemy. It's something all the explanations I've ever heard or read can't explain. Even in the absence of feelings, we put meaning into our actions. Those meanings are heavy the way emotions are heavy. They make significance. And so the past creates an accumulated weight of significant moments, and that accumulation determines what we will and won't do, what we can and cannot fathom, whom we cannot stand and whom we cannot live without. How does it do that?

I reached up over my head and Joey did the same until our hands met. There was nothing to say, so we just watched the sky for a while longer and I considered that I had never really thanked Joey for the night my mom died. I would have to tell him sometime.

The sun started setting on Mordecai's Hill, and Reverend Hoffman had still not returned. We had partaken of lemonade and olives and bread and Point Reyes blue and more lemonade, and our wizened host had unapologetically remarked more than once that the minister was out late that day. Finally Cass put the question to her directly, asking when we would be certain to find him, and Cressens told us we were welcome to attend services the next morning. Cass and Tabby were so fed up they didn't even balk at the idea of sitting through a Puritan sermon. They agreed and promised to return the next day at eleven.

We climbed back into the coupe, took the dusty road out of the hills, and drove home to a spectacular sunset in the western sky: an orange fire that waned to violet, not so much ceding to the darkness as consenting to its company. I fell asleep in the back of the car, my head on Joey's shoulder. It reminded me of old times.

24

NATALIA

I made it just in time for my training with Gao at 8:30. The night had turned cool. I wore black leggings and a racerback tank under a sweatshirt, and I brought spare shirts knowing I'd be soaked with sweat by the end of the session and wouldn't want to jog home dripping. Gao refused to hear the update on my tale of woe unless I reported while running eight-minute miles on the treadmill, so he got a somewhat abridged version. After two miles he stopped me. "You need to get back in shape before we do much else," he said. He'd had his arms crossed the entire time I was running, and he watched my heavy breathing with an expression of dour unamazement. I wanted to tell him that my cleaning schedule didn't leave time for Olympic-level training, but the panting made it tough to say anything at all.

Gao, much like the Nancy Drew novels, favors judo. Although, I doubt even George would be able to keep up with Gao's techniques, because I can barely keep up and I've been practicing them for years. Gao did not break a sweat in the hour he spent making origami with my limbs. For most of that time I was becoming intimately acquainted with the mat, getting to my feet a bit more slowly each time. Hey, we all need to practice safe falling. Finally Gao reached a hand out and helped me up—the worst possible sign. During training, Gao only helps the helpless.

"Guess I need a little more practice," I said, eyeing him.

"You were the best in your class when you graduated high school," he said.

I winced. I wasn't sure if he meant it as a measure of how much I'd deteriorated or as evidence that I could achieve a thing or two when I put my mind to it. I decided to pretend it was the latter. "I'll be here three times a week like I promised. I appreciate your taking the time," I added. "I know you have other things to spend it on."

He pulled a sweatshirt on over his tee. "Combative orphans are a good use of time."

I smiled. He wasn't giving up on me. "They can be very loyal," I agreed.

I changed out of my wet shirt in the locker room and came out feeling dry, my muscles like pounded meat. Gao was waiting for me. There were still a few cops working out late and he waved to them on the way out. "Let me see your screen decal," he said as we neared the door.

I fished *De rerum* out of my bag and gave it to him. He tapped a few things into it and then showed me. "I don't give this number to a lot of people," he said, pointing to his name, newly added to my address book, "and it's only for emergencies. I hope you don't need it. But if you do, don't hesitate. Running for—"

"Running for cover is smart when you're fast and calling for help is smart when you're stuck." I took *De rerum* back with a smile. "I haven't forgotten."

The walk home was good for my tired muscles, but by the time I arrived I felt like soup in a body-shaped bag.

It was not a good time to see Troy Philbrick on my doorstep.

He sat there looking tense, and by my estimate it wasn't just the neighborhood. "Hi," he said, standing up as I approached.

I was surprised he recognized me wearing sweats and looking, I have no doubt, like I'd just spent an hour being pummeled into a floor mat. "Hi," I replied.

"I'm sorry about the hour," he said. "And for perhaps being creepy getting your address from Crystal Cleaners."

I was going to tell him that it was nothing compared to Charlie-level creepiness, but I bit my tongue and decided to give him the benefit of the doubt. "It looks urgent," I said.

"Kind of, yes."

I lifted my chin at the building. "Come on in."

He didn't comment on the psychedelic carpet my landlord had installed in an effort to "cheer up" the corridor or on the table of goodies where tenants left items they were giving away. At the moment there was an Our Lady of Guadalupe votive candle, a box of macaroni and cheese, and two self-help books. They made a distressing group portrait.

I trudged up to the second story, opened my door, and

turned on some lights. "The living room is this way," I said, because he was lingering in the doorway, maybe wanting a more direct invitation. "I have some . . . uh, water if you'd like."

He stood awkwardly next to the tweed sofa. "Water would be great."

"Or tea," I said belatedly, as I went to the kitchen.

"Either one," he called after me.

I brought us both glasses of water and he spared me the offensive false compliments about my apartment. I had seen his home. I had a pretty good idea what he would think of mine.

"Thanks." He took a sip of water for the sake of politeness or maybe to show he wasn't afraid of being poisoned and then carefully put the glass on a coaster on the table.

He had changed out of the riding outfit, and now he wore a summer suit over a white linen shirt. His hair was combed and an undone tie in a lilac print hung over his shoulders. Running a hand through his hair, he looked down at the table, then up at me, and then down at the table again. I waited.

"I was with my mom this afternoon," he finally said. "You met her at the Landmark."

I leaned back in the rickety rocking chair. "I remember."

"It came up that I'd be seeing you tomorrow. She remembered you, too." Troy paused and rubbed a thumb on the side of the glass, clearing away some invisible stain. Or maybe visible. We don't have a dishwasher.

"Okay," I said.

"She said something that unsettled me. She asked me how you were doing."

I raised my eyebrows. "I'm touched."

"No, not like that." Troy ran a hand through his hair again, took a deep breath. Something was chewing away at him, a mean tick burrowing deep. "She asked in this way that was like she'd scored." He looked at me anxiously. "You don't understand my mom. She goes after people. Did you say something to her at the Landmark?"

Pieces began falling into place. I was right. Frances Peters was the start of my troubles. "I might have," I sniffed. "I didn't like how she treated you, and I said so."

A spasm of fear flashed across his brows, and then his face melted. "You're so sweet," he said sadly, his gaze equal parts fondness and penitence. "I'm really sorry," he went on. "But it's going to cost you. I've seen her do it before. It's like a project, upending people's lives when they piss her off. She will just find whatever angle she can. I really don't want to pry, but you have to think about what that might be. Debt? A rap sheet? A crazy uncle? She's going to find whatever weak spot she can and just go after it."

I made a decision. I leaned forward in the rocking chair and rested my elbows on my knees, looking straight at him. "I think she already has."

His eyes widened. "What's happened?"

"My brother, Calvino. He's ten, and he's a late waner. He was taken by RealCorp for testing two days ago and they won't give him back."

"Oh, God. No." He dropped his head abruptly into his

hands and held it tightly, as though at any moment his skull might burst into pieces.

I risked adding a few more combustible sentences. "I think some guy named Dr. Glout has him at the moment. But honestly I'm not even sure where they've got him. I'm trying to figure out an angle to get him back."

Troy lifted his head. "How are they keeping him? I mean legally."

"Adoption. Not Glout—your father." I saw the question in his eyes. "Cal's biological father is MIA. Our mom is dead."

"I'm sorry," he said, with a solemnity that managed to overcome the threadbare phrase. But he was still puzzled. "Why didn't you adopt him? Or did she die a long time ago?"

"I'm not of age." I grimaced. "Believe it or not, given the manifest maturity of my ways. My mom's friends, Cass and Tabby, fostered us so I could adopt Cal when I turn eighteen. She died last year," I added. I pointed to the floor beside my chair. "Right there."

He stared at me. "What happened?"

I don't tell a lot of people about Mom, but on the occasions when I do, surprisingly few people ask that. They're all curious, and yet they treat the question as off-limits. I shrugged. "I can tell you how it ended, but I can't tell you why. I never understood what she was thinking. Especially the last year. She was out of her mind."

"She was taking synaffs?"

"The cheapest, nastiest dirt you could find. Not nice stuff like you're used to."

His eyes shifted. He sat back, his body tense. "My doses are not always nice. As you've seen."

"Well, my mom didn't have a choice."

He looked wounded. "You think I do?"

That was interesting. "Are you saying you don't?"

He backed off at once, cheeks suddenly flushed, eyes guarded. "You're right, of course. We all have a choice."

"Some have more choices than others. I'm guessing you've never taken fear mixed with gasoline and chalk sold by a predatory multiple offender who also peddles underage kids to the very depraved."

"No," he said softly. "I haven't."

"Once the synaffs are adulterated they do all kinds of crazy things to you. Half the time she wouldn't even feel anything; she would just pass out from whatever poison she'd swallowed. The other times she'd be backed into a corner, crying and screaming and terrified of nothing. When I was around I could talk her through it, but I wasn't around that time." I looked at the top drawer of my dresser, the only place in the apartment with a lock on it. No jewelry in there. Just some photos, a box of trinkets, an old shirt, and a piece of evidence. "It was fourteen months ago. She shot herself right by the window. Calvino and I found her. He was only nine."

"God," he said. "Poor kid. What did you do?"

I studied the spot on the floor where Mom had been. Sure, she was out of her mind, but that hadn't stopped me trying to figure out what she'd been thinking. It wasn't about consolation. It was about getting a reason. I wanted her ghost to sit at the witness stand and account for her actions. I wanted to interrogate her, to ask her what kind of calculation made the self-indulgence of a few minutes' thrill more valuable than a lifetime with two children, both of whom relied upon her and one of whom loved her to distraction. I wanted to question her into a corner, so I could prove that she hadn't been thinking at all, that her brain was faulty, that her reasons were worse than stupid, they were not even reasons. Nothing could justify what she had done.

I was bringing Cal home from school, and he walked into the apartment first. I saw him stop. I walked up behind him and saw what he was looking at. He lunged forward, and I caught him reflexively, holding him back.

Her eyes were closed, her body relaxed. The gun, which I had never seen before, was still in her grasp. The blood was pooled on the floor, bright in the sunlight that came through the open window. It had stained the edge of the carpet. The gun wound was elaborate, looking more like the impact of a baseball bat than a bullet. But the casement window was open, and the breeze blew in, ruffling her hair, giving the illusion of life through movement. Around her head on the wooden floor, the blood was textured with pieces of brain, white and gray amid the red. I realized as I observed these things and wondered where the gun had come from that Cal was screaming.

I adjusted; my task was to stop the screaming. But I didn't know how. Cal was feeling something—immense, impenetrable, and new—and I didn't understand it. I crouched down and held him by the shoulders, putting myself at eye level, because that's what I often did when he was upset. But he just kept screaming. Every inch of his face broadcast terror: eyes wide, pupils tiny, the muscles around his jaw straining with the scream. *He probably shouldn't keep looking at this*, I thought. I tried ineffectually to block his view. "Cal?" I said. He was having difficulty breathing. What was I supposed to do? Pick him up? Get him to the window for some fresh air? "Cal?" I said again. "Tell me what I can do." His eyes suddenly met mine. He stopped screaming and his expression shifted. I didn't recognize what he was feeling. His eyes were still wide; his mouth hung open; his breathing was shaky, irregular. I knew it had to do with me, but what was it? For several seconds we both stared. Cal, feeling something. Me, trying to figure out what. It was hopeless. I might as well have been reading omens in entrails.

Abruptly Cal turned and ran from the room, and I followed him into the bedroom that he shared with Mom. His small bed was neatly made against the wall, and Mom's bed was a mess of blankets and pillows. He climbed up into her bed, nearly muffling himself in the blankets, and started wailing. *No, Mom. No, Mom. No. No. No. No. No.* I stood at the edge of the bed, incompetent.

"I called the police," I said to Troy, waving my hand around the room. "I tried to comfort Cal, but the damage was already done. Or I guess you could say the damage had already started. Because it goes on."

"I'm sure having you helped." He looked at me earnestly, wanting to hear that this was true.

Perhaps with time, Cal had felt that it was better to have me around than not. It was what I aimed for every day. Making it worthwhile for Cal to have me around. But I had not helped him that day. Not at all.

"I couldn't take the memory away. I couldn't take the pain away." I stood up and walked over to the open window. It felt suddenly overly warm in the room. "They seem so strong," I said, "because they survive unspeakable things. But children are fragile. They can break and still survive." I thought about the chasm that often seemed to separate me from Cal. It was partly the chasm that separated me from everyone, because the absence of feeling makes all people, to some extent, incomprehensible. They become a dull roar, an expressionless mass. But it was also a chasm partly made by the things that had broken inside Cal the day we found our mother dead by her own hand in our apartment. I was just trying, day by day and with limited means, to build a bridge across to him. A bridge made out of toothpicks. Slow work. Maybe hopeless.

When I looked up, Troy was standing next to me. I liked the way he stood there—somehow not imposing, not expecting, and not inserting himself into a moment of weakness. He just seemed to be holding his hand out across the void: I'm here; I'm not dull or expressionless.

I closed the two feet of distance between us. I leaned forward and kissed him. His hands fell to my waist and neck and drew me closer. I took hold of his loose tie and pulled.

He smelled like soap and hay, and the pressure of his hands was confident but gentle. More giving than demanding. For a while as we kissed, I lost sight of everything beyond the taste of his mouth and the way his eyes seemed like different eyes at that distance: clear and full of familiar meaning. I didn't have to pull away. The kisses ended on the strength of the story that had brought them about. Cal was there in the background, his grief lingering like a specter.

We drew back. Troy's smile was one of wonderment, as if he couldn't quite believe I'd really meant to grace him with kisses. That was one I hadn't seen before. He took my hand and pulled me over to the couch, putting his arm around me. We sat that way for a while as I pondered the unexpected ease I felt in his company. Normally, sitting still next to someone I'd been kissing and then wasn't would seem pointless.

"So what are we going to do about Cal?" Troy asked quietly.

That surprised me. I hadn't expected a "we." I sat up and looked at him; his arm dropped to my waist. "I've been trying to locate his biological father. Prove paternity, challenge the adoption." I paused. "Do you have ideas?"

Troy tipped his head a little and considered. "I'll start by talking to my dad."

"You think he's persuadable?" I still knew nothing about Tanner Philbrick, apart from the fact that he dripped money and adopted Cal. He could be a gold-bar bully or he could be a gilded pushover.

"Not in the usual sense," Troy said, frowning at a spot on the wall. "But there are buttons I can push."

As I thought about that, I recalled the whiff of wrongness at the Philbrick mansion, the strange inner workings of it, the tang of invisible blood. I decided to do some button-pushing myself. "So how does it work," I asked lightly, "with the mom, the stepmom, and the dad? Are they all under the same roof?"

Troy shook his head. "My mom has her own house over in Sea Cliff. My dad and Monica live at the house in Pac Heights."

"You get along with Monica?"

Now the guardedness crept into his eyes, and the arm around me tensed. "More or less. Charlie gets along with her better." He gave a dry chuckle. "Charlie gets along better with all of them."

I waited, figuring that one might unpack itself. Sure enough, it did.

"Parents all want you to be perfect. They just don't agree on what perfection is." His arm around me relaxed a little, and his thumb tapped my shoulder gently. "Charlie knows how to give each of them the perfection they're looking for. He's obedient for Mom. He's ambitious for Dad. He's beautiful for Monica."

I shifted a little so I could see his face. He was looking inward, thinking.

"I don't know how to do that," he said quietly. "No matter what drops I'm taking, I can't seem to show them the side they want to see."

I reached up and traced the line of his jaw. "You're no shape-shifter," I said. "So what? That just makes you honest."

He gave me a quick, wistful smile. "No one at my house seems to think honesty is perfection. Besides," he said, looking away again. "I'm not that honest. And I'm nowhere near perfect." Suddenly a gloom settled on his brow, heavy as a storm cloud.

I watched him. I thought about how much money his synaffs probably cost and also how much pain they probably cost him. There was some sense in the wish to balance one's emotions, so that it wasn't just endless ecstasy, but clearly balance came with consequences. I didn't understand how these fancy synaffs worked. With a regimen like his, was the sadness caused entirely by the synaff, or did the synaff simply allow for real things to upset him? If I acted sympathetic, was I pretending to sympathize with a feeling? Or a drug?

I decided on the former. "Perfect is boring anyway," I suggested.

He didn't say anything. He was lost in a dark tunnel, all noise and nightmares, and my voice didn't reach him.

I took his hand and held it tight the way I sometimes do with Cal, trying to send him some vestigial current of reassurance, lost to my brain but stored in the vessel of human skin. "Troy?" I said. "Want to tell me what's going on?"

He pulled himself out of the dark place and locked eyes with me. "No," he said. "I can't." He pressed my hand and made a visible effort to move onward. "Do you have a photograph of Calvino?" he asked.

"Sure." I got up and reached behind the bookcase for the key that hung there; then I unlocked the top drawer of the dresser and opened it. Troy had joined me, which I hadn't counted on, but there were no more secrets there anyway.

He stared down at the drawer's contents and pointed. "Is that . . ."

"Yup," I said. I don't know anything about guns, thanks to Gao and his generous disdain. All I knew about this one was that it was semiautomatic and acquired legally. The police had no difficulty concluding death by suicide, so they'd given it back. Now there it was, eating a hole in my dresser, nestled in a black velvet shirt of Mom's that I'd kept because it still had traces of her perfume. "It's surprisingly hard to get rid of a handgun," I said. "Throwing it into Lake Merritt isn't really an option, and selling it seems only slightly less stupid."

He raised his mesmerized eyes to look at me. "You don't want it for protection?"

I shook my head. "I don't believe in guns. Weapons for weaklings, says my trainer. Besides, I have lipstick, remember?"

He smiled. "Yes, I do."

I showed him the picture of Calvino that was most recent, taken on his tenth birthday. Cal grinned at the camera, his arm around my waist. He was wearing a costume crown and a vintage baseball shirt, both courtesy of Tabby, and his eyes were high on happiness and chocolate frosting. Troy studied the picture, a slow smile edging across his face. "Look how much he loves you," he said quietly. He handed the photo back to me and briefly cupped my chin in his hand.

"Not hard to see why." He smiled. "I'll do everything I can. I promise."

"Thank you." I meant it. I didn't think Troy would get far. Unless he planned to drown his dad in boyish sweetness, his odds didn't look good to me. But hey, maybe I was wrong. Maybe Troy had a very well-hidden mean streak.

"Are we still on for the bookstore?" I asked, leading the way back to the entrance. "I'm heading to Marin County in the morning. Hoping to find Cal's dad."

He followed me to the door of the apartment. "Why don't you let me know when you're on the way back?" He winked. "That way I'll have your phone number."

I smiled. "Deal."

He lifted my hand to his lips and kissed the knuckles softly, managing to make it both gallant and playful. "Bye, Natalia," he said.

I watched him pad across the psychedelic carpet to the stairs, and then I walked back to the apartment and stood in the silent living room, listening to his car door open and close, the motor starting and receding.

———

Troy had left the photo of Cal propped up against a lamp. Instead of putting it back in the closed drawer, I picked it up again and found, tucked behind it, another one. Mom was pregnant and I was seven. The day was vivid in my mind. A planned excursion to the amusement park, money saved up for rides and candy, an event anticipated for weeks. At the entrance, Mom had bought an extra ticket for a wispy pigtailed girl who was short on cash, and I could still see the way she put the ticket in her palm: firm and full of purpose. "Here it is," she said sternly, "but I'm giving it to you on one condition. You have to have *fun*. Understand? No disappointments today. Only *fun*." The girl smiled, getting the joke, and giggled. As we walked through the park I held Mom's hand and glowed with pride; she was beautiful, and generous, and funny. *My* mom. The love filled me to bursting. In the picture I had teeth missing and a radiant smile, and I was pulling Mom's face sideways into mine with passionate, possessive joy. Mom had her eyes closed and her face bunched up like I was squeezing too hard. I could recall the day but not the flame that had burned in me. Both of those people in the photo were gone.

25

NATALIA

OCTOBER 13 — NIGHT

I didn't sleep much Saturday night.

By the time I'd showered and pulled the bed out of the wall, my confidence in Troy was sagging like a year-old mattress in the Tenderloin. What kind of persuasion did he plan to offer Daddy Philbrick? I wasn't sure Troy even knew what persuasion looked like. More likely, he would find himself indignantly sticking up for the two Peña orphans, which meant Philbrick would learn way more about me and Cal than I ever wanted him to know. Then what? Any confrontation I had with Philbrick was bound to be harder, messier.

Then, as I lay in the darkness and listened to the cars on Lakeshore, I started to wonder about choice. How, exactly, could Troy not have a choice? What did that look like? I'd always thought the wealthy took synaffs recreationally, but what I didn't know about the wealthy would overflow the Philbrick mansion. Were the synaffs a prescription? Did he have some kind of condition? Was someone else making the choice for him? The dark ceiling above me had no answers.

Two cats yowled and the scent of tuberose threaded into the room. A waiting car idled just outside the window, then gunned its motor and faded into the distance. I finally fell asleep but woke again at dawn, hauled out of dreamless rest by the sound of the casement window slamming in the wind and the real problem pounding at my head: Cal. I got up to latch the window and stared out at the black trees shuddering in the wind. Cal had just spent another night out there. It's just not true that everything looks better in the morning. Sometimes it looks bleak, and in the gray light you can see the nasties that were hiding under the bed in the darkness.

———

We left Oakland at 8:30 a.m. with the idea that we might catch Hoffman before his sermon. The day before had been all sun and splendor; this one was all fog and gloom. San Quentin looked menacing in the gray mist, like a Hadrian's Wall trying to stop a horde of monsters from descending upon us.

At 9:30 a.m. we were still in the car and my phone rang. It was a San Francisco number that I didn't recognize. As I said hello, the lunatic hope that Cal had gotten to a phone buzzed at the edge of my brain.

"Miss Peña."

He was calling from his decal, not his office phone. I had no trouble recognizing Dr. Hugh Glout's voice, even though he was surrounded by noise on his end. "Dr. Glout.

Finally." There was a whooping cry in the background followed by cheers. "Quite a party this morning at RealCorp," I commented.

"I'm at a parade in North Beach."

Not where I'd imagined the skeletal Glout spending his Sunday mornings, not by a long shot.

"I'm calling with some news," he went on. His voice sounded strange because he was raising it to talk over the crowds. He was feeling something, but I couldn't tell what. Anxiety?

"Is Cal all right?"

"Cal is fine. I'd be lying if I said he looked happy, but he looks fine." That was something, at least. Assuming I could count on Glout's notion of "fine," which I wasn't entirely sure I could. "However." A trumpet blared in the background, and Glout paused. "What I have learned so far about Cal has changed his status."

"What do you mean? What have you learned?"

"He is . . ." Glout paused and I could hear him readjusting, pulling back to recast what he wanted to say. "RealCorp usually brings in twenty to thirty kids a month for additional testing. It's always informative. We test whenever kids go beyond the median waning age."

That sounded hopeful. Cal was one of many. "Yes?" I prompted him.

"There would be no way for you to know this, because it's very gradual and we have international data. But across the globe, the waning age is getting slightly younger each year. A generation ago it was 10.8. Now it's 10.1."

I wasn't sure what to do with those numbers. "Is that fast?"

He let out a short cough of surprise. "Very fast. Terrifyingly fast."

"I see." But I still didn't see how this changed Cal's status.

Glout tried again from another angle. "How much do you know about what happens in the brain when people wane?"

"Not much. Only what we see on the outside."

"Okay. Imagine that you're looking at a child's brain. It's like a network of roads going everywhere, connecting all over the place, with some main roads and lots of side roads. When waning happens, more and more of those roads go unused until eventually, all you have is one main road with deep tire grooves. In adults, those grooves are so deep you can't get the car out. You just keep going back and forth on that same road. The rest of the roads are still there, probably, in theory, but they're overgrown and abandoned. That's a scientifically inaccurate but metaphorically useful picture of how it works."

"Okay," I said.

"That is what happens to all of us, even children who wane late. Except for Cal, it seems. Cal doesn't seem to be abandoning all his side roads. On the contrary." A cymbal crashed and the trumpet sounded again, but quieter this time. It had moved along on its slow march. "He is trailblazing. He's making new roads."

I listened as the pumping music of Glout's parade tooted and a kid shrieked with delight.

"We're not sure why," Glout went on into my silence. "I'm hypothesizing that the timing of your mother's death may have something to do with it, but that's just a guess. Maybe that event, that trauma, violently engrained some of the processes that in other children start to disappear. Then again, lots of kids suffer traumas at this age and still wane, so I might be wrong."

I heard Glout's guess, and I thought about it, and I saw in my mind the evidence Glout had not seen, accumulating over the last year. Cal's inexhaustible grief, his dizzying highs and lows, his sudden tendency to fall apart at unexpected moments, his endless, imponderable questions.

The first time he asked me about Mom was about a month after her death. I'd woken up in the morning to find him sitting in front of the open closet, looking at her shoes. Sneakers, loafers, and a pair of scuffed pumps. They looked old—crooked and creased with the shape of her feet. Too old, as if they'd been stashed for twenty years, not four weeks. Cal's tearstained face looked up at me. "Why?" he asked me.

For a moment I wasn't sure what he meant. Why are her shoes still here? Why do they look so old?

He swallowed and pushed the words out. "Why did Mom shoot herself?"

Slowly, I sat down next to him on the floor. Even though I'm not that dumb, I tried the easy answer first. "She took a really bad dose. It messed her up."

He looked at me with mournful condescension. "You know that's not really why."

I considered the old soul in Cal's eyes and something

tugged at me—an awareness of something bigger than me, more profound, more discerning—in the person who was my little brother. It commanded honesty. "I don't know, Cal," I said. "I don't get it, either."

This made the tears well up in his eyes. "But you're *like* her," he whispered. "You're grown up. You're supposed to understand her."

"I know." What Cal didn't know was that I spent just about every night trying to reason myself through the same question. So far, I had no answers. Her death defied explanation. She wasn't supposed to feel. She wasn't supposed to *want* to feel. She was supposed to be impervious to the absence of emotion. She was supposed to be rational, and she was supposed to survive. "But I guess we're not alike enough," I said.

Cal suddenly started sobbing, and his hands grabbed at me with desperation. "You can't be like her," he wailed. "Please don't be like her. Please don't." He looked me in the eyes, his face close to mine, searching for proof of something. "Promise me, Nat."

I looked back at him, unflinching, willing him to see certainty. The workings of her mind, the gravitational pull of forgotten emotions, those were all a mystery to me. I had never even seen the path that led her to the edge. "I'm not like her, Cal. I promise." It wasn't enough, but it was true.

Glout was waiting for me to say something. The music near him crashed to a climax. "I am not totally surprised," I finally said. "It was evident in his behavior."

"Yes," Glout agreed. "I thought you would say that. The

problem," he went on, "is that from RealCorp's point of view, Cal's brain is an incredible opportunity. We only know of a few hundred cases like his. In the US, a couple dozen."

"Okay," I said again.

"As a consequence, RealCorp has changed Cal's profile. As of tomorrow, all seven research departments will be able to . . ." I could hear him reaching for a word that was both accurate and palatable. "They will determine independent research protocols for Cal. Independent of mine. And I can tell you from personal knowledge that they will be less delicate. Some of them much less delicate."

"What does that mean?"

Glout didn't answer right away. "Well, for starters, a standard protocol is to observe the test subject's response to undue stress."

It took me a moment to translate. "You mean torture."

Glout didn't respond. We had reached the winding roads again, and Cass was taking them slow due to the fog. For a few seconds I watched the headlights of oncoming traffic appear ten feet away, the cars materializing suddenly like machine phantoms. "Why are you telling me this?" I asked Glout.

He was walking away from the parade now. The noise of the crowd had died down, and the music was a distant, whimsical warble that floated on the air. "I feel responsible," he said. "And . . ." He hesitated. "I like him. Calvino is unlike any other kid I've met. I can't say there are many ten-year-olds who have pushed me to think differently about my work.

Self-aware but not self-involved. Vehemently interested in others. Relentlessly curious." He gave up trying to pinpoint it. "I don't want to see him get hurt. Lastly," he concluded, "you should know that I have a very long-standing enmity with more than one of these researchers. I am a little worried that their actions with Cal will more reflect the enmity with me than the importance of the research opportunity."

His comment called to mind the articles I'd read, the venom of those scholarly exchanges. So Glout hated them and they hated Glout. Which is why he felt synafftically responsible and why he was telling me in advance that Cal was likely to be turned inside out and lobotomized on Monday.

"Before you ask," he said, "officially, I can't do anything. I can't let him go for the same reasons as before. Nothing there has changed."

We turned a corner that I knew placed us on a cliff above the Pacific. Yet the ocean was nowhere to be seen. Fog lay over it all the way to the horizon, as heavy as a dream from which you cannot wake.

"But I am in charge until nine tomorrow morning," Glout said, not shouting anymore. "If you happened to be at RealCorp at an odd hour, say six fifteen in the morning, it might be possible for you to talk to Cal briefly." On his end a door opened and shut. He had walked into a smaller space— a café, by the droning sound of milk being steamed in the background. "Miss Peña?"

"Yes, Dr. Glout. Thank you." I shifted *De rerum* because

it was slipping. My hand was sweating. "I will be there at six fifteen."

"Very good." He paused. "I'm sorry I can't do more."

"See you at six fifteen," I said. I closed my book and put it in my bag. Joey and Tabby were staring at me, and Cass was shooting her eyes up at the rearview mirror every five seconds. "It was that guy Glout at RealCorp," I said unnecessarily. "He said that Cal isn't just not fading. He's, like, reverse fading. So starting tomorrow other researchers will have access to Cal, and Glout predicts it will be nasty. If I want to see Cal one last time I have to go to RealCorp at six fifteen tomorrow morning."

There was a long pause. Cass stopped looking at me. She focused on the road and her eyes narrowed.

"What are we going to do?" Joey asked.

"We're going to get Hoffman to sign these damn papers is what we're going to do," Cass said, her voice level and deadly.

I hoped that would happen. I really did. But I also knew now there was no way Cal would be in RealCorp after tomorrow morning. I would get him out if I had to burn the place down to do it.

26

CALVINO

oct-14
11:32 a.m.
calvinopio:
Essay: <u>Describe a time when your emotions were at</u>
<u>odds with your instincts. How about a time when your</u>
<u>emotions were at odds with what you knew to be rational?</u>
By Calvino Peña

Dr. Glout, thank you for calling Nat and promising to give
her my letters. I will answer your question. But I want you
to know that I am only doing this because you promised
to give Nat my letters.

I have spent a lot of time thinking about this and I
can't think of an example. The reason is that there are always emotions in both directions. What I'm saying is that
one emotion is at odds with another emotion, and my instincts fit with one or both emotions. And it's the same
for being rational. Though it may not be visible to you, the
same is true with adults.

This is an example that happened to me.

People in my grade play something called poker. It's not a card game, it's a game where you have to show no emotion. Only it's not really a game, it's more of a dare. Some people really don't feel anymore, others are only pretending not to feel. So it's a dare to see whether or not someone who has pretended to fade already really has. Maybe not so much a dare as a test. They test each other by saying things that will bring out an emotion in someone who can still feel.

So this is the example I have to explain what I mean about emotions in both directions. There is a girl in my class called Greyson and she used to be my friend before she faded. This happened at the end of last year. Some people had already faded and others were changing one day to the next. I would never know when I got to school whether Greyson would be herself or not. She was pretending that it had already happened, but I could always tell as soon as I saw her how much she could feel that day.

Greyson and I were sitting in the alley (where the dumpsters are behind the school) when Kate and Plex came around the corner and came up to us. (Plex is a nickname.) They came and sat down in front of us. Greyson was not fading that day but she made her face totally blank. I was pretty nervous.

I guess it's good that no one ever asks me to play poker because I am so bad at pretending it isn't interesting. Although they find other ways to be jerks of course.

Kate said to Greyson, Let's play poker. Fine, Greyson

said. I don't remember what Kate said first, but it was something pretty mean. Then Greyson said something about how Kate had no friends. I could tell she had no idea what to say. Kate's face didn't change at all because she of course had completely faded. Then Kate said, I heard your mom is giving you away as soon as you fade. She can't wait. She has been counting the days.

I could see that Greyson was trying really hard not to cry.

Part of me wanted to cry too. Part of me wanted to hug Greyson and tell her it was okay. Part of me wanted to hit Kate really, really hard. Part of me wanted to say something smart that would just make Kate and Plex go away. Part of me wanted to just disappear and be by myself. Some of these were instincts and some of these were rational and all of them were emotions.

This is what I mean. I don't think it makes any sense to say that the three things are separate. I know it probably makes sense to you, but I just don't think you can split them apart like that. I think that wherever there are reasons and instincts there are also emotions. I have seen this going on in adults too. The quiet voices I was saying, sometimes there is more than one and they are telling you to do opposite things. Even if you cannot hear them, their words are affecting you.

hglt: Thanks for this thoughtful reply to the question, Calvino.

calvinopio: Do you understand my example?

hglt: I think I do. The kind of ambivalence you're describing must seem like second nature to you—something that happens quite often. But however ordinary it may seem to you, it's an incredibly complex reaction that cannot really be produced by the synthetic affects we have today.

calvinopio: So are you saying that even with really expensive synaffs adults never feel contradictory emotions? Never feel ambivalent?

hglt: That's a good question. There are some synthetic affects that release simultaneously and create something _similar_ to ambivalence. But that's what's so tricky. It's not _exactly_ like ambivalence. What you described in the "poker" encounter was an interplay of emotions: each one was affecting the others. Imagine that your mind is a bowl of water and you add five drops of paint color. They would all swirl and combine—that's what you've described happening with your friend Greyson. In adults, we can't get that effect. It's more like having separate bowls of water—one green, one red, one blue—in your head at the same time.

calvinopio: Wow. Do you remember the last time you felt ambivalent for real?

hglt: There have been many times as an adult where I have experienced the situation described in the prompt: my (synthetic) emotions have been at odds with what I know to be rational. But I think the last time I truly felt ambivalent was as a teenager, when I left Fresno to go to college.

calvinopio: You still had emotions as a teenager?!

hglt: I did. So did many other kids my age. Waning didn't universally happen at age ten yet. That was many decades ago. I'm really old!

calvinopio: So you felt emotions the whole time you were a teenager.

hglt: Yup. And that adolescence really made me who I am. Honestly, I don't think I'd care as much about affect decline if I hadn't lived through adolescence with emotions.

calvinopio: Wow. Why were you ambivalent about leaving Fresno?

hglt: It's hard to explain in retrospect. You are very good at explaining your emotions, but I don't have your expert way of teasing them apart!

calvinopio: Can you try? It is helpful for me to hear it.

hglt: Sure. I both loved and hated Fresno. On the one hand, it was lonely and I felt bored a lot. On the other hand, it was safe. I knew everything about it. Moving to the city felt exciting but scary. It was also scary because my parents had just waned—before me—and I felt like I had lost them. Moving away seemed so complicated. I felt guilty and sad about leaving them, but I also felt hurt because they didn't care in the least that I was moving away.

calvinopio: Because they had waned.

hglt: Exactly. And I also felt something that I had trouble explaining to my parents: the power of unpredictability. To them, the unpredictable future had simply become a set of rational choices that would be made when they needed to be made. Not to me. The unpredictable future was combustible. Fraught. They didn't understand that unpredictability meant volatility.

calvinopio: Yeah. Adults don't get that. What happened after the move?

hglt: Well, very soon afterward I waned. And all of the things that had seemed like problems didn't anymore. I had different problems.

27

NATALIA
October 14—midday

Mordecai's Hill seemed less serene and more uncanny in the fog. The place radiated an air of neglect, and you could sense that the energy of its inhabitants was bent on something as obscure and unattainable as salvation rather than on the incremental, tedious, and material business of surviving.

After poking around the houses closest to the road, we found the New Puritans gathered in their stick-wood church, sitting silently side by side on the wooden benches. It is California, after all. Even the Puritans meditate. Cass and Tabby and Joey and I sat down quietly at the back of the church, and I prepared myself for a long wait.

The church was just as striking in the fog. It was thick enough to fill the vault, so the ceiling appeared to be made of gray cloud. Through the splintered walls, I could see the hills of the estate appearing and disappearing like great hunch-backed wanderers in search of something long lost. There wasn't much to study with the Puritans. I could see a lot of shoulders and a lot of bonnets. And then there was Hoffman. He sat on a raised wooden stool at the front of the congregation, his head slightly bent, his eyes closed. He had a blond beard, cut close, and neat blond hair. Slim shoulders under a blue denim shirt. Hands well used to work. Frayed jeans. Old but cared-for laced boots. Apparently the men and women adhered to different sartorial standards.

Close to eleven a.m. he opened his eyes and looked at his watch. He stood up and folded his hands together. After a minute he spoke. "When you're ready to join us, open your eyes."

The people before him began to stir, lifting their heads and making slight noises as they shifted on the benches.

Hoffman ran his eyes over them—considering, not critical. "Four years ago," he began, with a thoughtful air, "a former colleague from the university invited me to a concert. A famous violinist was touring the West Coast. Famous because she rose above the technical perfection expected of musicians to offer something more—something we rarely see now: a rendering of the music that conveyed emotion." Hoffman paused and looked at his silent parishioners, a slight smile playing across his face.

I'm not what you would call an expert on Puritan religious services, but it seemed to me that Hoffman was departing pretty radically from the script. Well, they were *New* Puritans. Clearly they did things differently. Also clearly, Hoffman was taking something that made him feel very, very good. He seemed relaxed and confident and buoyed by a sense of effortless well-being. I didn't think it was the hot springs.

"I went to the concert," Hoffman continued. "And the

violinist played beautifully. It was true—the music conveyed emotion, even if it could not move its listeners to feel that emotion. There was reluctance and dread, grief and despair, triumph and joy. There was a sense of indelible spirit—a sense of God's majesty." Hoffman waved his arms around like he was directing an imaginary orchestra. "And because my friend knew her personally, I was able to speak with the violinist after the performance. I complimented her on the music, and she thanked me." Hoffman gave us the slight smile again. This time it was more supercilious. "Then I told her my impression—that God moved through her music. That she was animated by grace. The violinist did not like this. She said to me, 'It's not God. It's called practice.'"

Hoffman let out a loud, hollow laugh. The congregation echoed it with a precision that made me itchy. Hoffman continued, a look of sharp glee in his eye. "I did not contradict her. I merely nodded and let the matter pass. But I thought to myself, *Pride—you are a wicked thing indeed. A wicked thing, and a dangerous thing, and sometimes, as with this musician, a dangerously beautiful thing.*

"Only four months later, my friend told me the sad news. The violinist had suffered an accident. A routine biopsy had resulted in a severed nerve, and her right hand was irreparably damaged. She would not, as far as they could see, ever play again."

Hoffman raised his arms, and with a flourish he waved them back and forth, bringing the imaginary orchestra to a crescendo, then a sudden, crashing stop. "Given. And taken. By the grace of God."

The congregation around him intoned: "Given and taken by the grace of God." It was a phrase they had said many times. They made it sound like an aphorism: a thing so true that it had become pointless in its repetition.

It was ugly. The parable of a great artist wounded and severed from her art, and here a crowd of vultures gloated over the loss. Maybe that sense of effortless well-being I saw in Hoffman's face was only partly synaffs. Maybe he was just as high on religious self-righteousness. I shifted on my seat.

It was then that Hoffman saw me.

I'm not sure why he hadn't seen me before. He was staring out at the congregation, and I thought he'd looked our way—we visibly stood out. Lack of bonnets, for one thing. Maybe he had faces he searched for among his parishioners, or maybe he was so consumed by the pithiness of his own story that he couldn't really focus on anything else until it was over. When he saw me, he stopped. The look of smugness vanished as if yanked from his face, exposing the naked expression underneath: he was startled, confused. Something like hope crept in at the edges of his eyes.

He was looking at me, but he was seeing my mother, Lila.

In the sudden silence, I got up from the bench. I walked out of the church and down the hill a ways. I waited. After a few seconds I heard the whole congregation reciting something in a dull monotone that was probably a concluding prayer. And then Hoffman came barreling out of the church into the thinning fog, looking wildly in every direction until he saw me, as if I might have been carried away by the mist.

He slowed as he neared. His gaze had become desperate

and searching, but when he stopped a few feet away from me, his expression changed. The air went out of him, and he crumpled like a sheet falling from a clothesline. "You're not Lila," he said.

"I'm her daughter. Nat." I held my hand out.

He shook it sadly. "You look so much like her," he announced. "So much. I thought—I don't know what I thought." He scrutinized my face. "But you're younger than she was."

I nodded. "By a bit. She must have been about thirty when you met her."

"Yes. More than a decade ago." His blue eyes grew remote. They were focused on that other time. "Wow, suddenly it seems like last year."

The congregation had begun to leave the church, and they walked past us downhill, many of them casting looks our way. I saw Cass and Tabby and Joey at the door, and I waved them off. Cass nodded and signaled that they'd be inside the church.

"We used to come here, you know," Hoffman said. He rubbed the blond scruff of his chin, smiling a little. "Not here, right here, but the coast. Lila liked to swim in the ocean."

"Yeah, I know."

His eyes returned to me, his short voyage to the past ended. "I read about her death in the news," he said.

I looked down at my walking shoes and then, with effort, lifted my head to face his false sympathy, his expressions of consolation, so heavy with the condescending certainty that God arranged all things for a greater good. He didn't say them. Maybe he could see the sharp bristles in my eyes.

"She was beautiful. Like you." He smiled. "And she had soul. She was like the wild elk at the Point. Graceful and sure and totally unself-conscious. Never selfish. Never cruel."

Never too smart, either, I thought. *Those elk are easy prey.* "Yup. A real free spirit," I said. "She would have been right at home in the summer of love." I could not resist just a little jab, but he seemed not to notice or not to mind.

"That's right," he said, smiling. "That's how she was. She didn't just belong in it. She *was* a summer of love. She seemed to bring warmth into the room wherever she went." He paused. "I was very hurt when I read of her passing. She meant a lot to me."

I didn't ask how he could afford either sentiment. Clearly Hoffman's brand of spirituality came with a heavy dose of emotional indulgence. This was my chance to move in. I had to drop the sarcasm and go for it. "I'm glad to hear you say that," I said. "It's why I came to find you."

His eyes refocused. He looked at me, not wary but prepared: the look of an expert salesman who knows he's about to get the pitch and knows he's too good at the game to be worried. "What's up?" he asked. He put his hands on his hips and stood with an easy slouch. The man in charge. The man people turned to for faith. For healing. For love. For favors.

I didn't try to pretend otherwise.

"It's my brother, Calvino. Your son."

Hoffman listened to my story from start to finish without interruption. His face didn't change much, except for when I mentioned how Cal and I had found Mom's body. Then he blinked like he was trying not to wince. When I explained the situation with Cass and Tabby and the looming deadline, he got very focused. He crossed his arms. I could see him thinking.

"So . . ." he finally said, into the silence I left. "You want me to take a blood test to prove I'm Cal's father. Then sign a document asserting my paternal rights and my willingness to take responsibility for Cal's parenting."

"But you don't have to actually parent him if you don't want to," I clarified, cringing at the rushed sound of my own voice. I slowed down. "Cass and Tabby and I have that covered. Cal is a happy kid, really. All he needs is to get out of that place, and this is the best way to do it."

Hoffman stroked his beard again, the thumb and forefinger running over his jaw in a practiced way. "I've never met Calvino," he said quietly. "Though I knew Lila was pregnant. She shut me out after she learned she was expecting."

There wasn't anything in that for me, as Philip Marlowe says, so I waited.

Hoffman's look grew more remote as he stared into the valley below him, where the fog was wrapping and unwrapping the buildings like Christmas ornaments in tissue paper. "Did Lila ever tell you about how we met?" he asked.

"She never told me much about you," I said frankly. "I was what—seven?" *A little young to be telling your daughter about your lover, dummy*, I thought.

"We met at the bookstore where she worked," he said. He was far away again, in that bookshop eleven years ago, where the shelves were so high you could hide for a few hours in a back corner and no one would notice. Ratty chairs with broken springs. Rugs covered with food stains. Thousands and thousands of books. It was a rat's warren. A book lover's dream. "I asked her for a philosophy collection—I don't even remember which, actually—and she got this scornful look in her eye. 'Philosophy,' she said. 'Unemotion for the unemotional.'" Hoffman laughed. "Like it was so despicable she couldn't stand it. 'It's philosophers who are responsible for the way we worship reason blindly. False idols,' she said dismissively. Then she walked me over to the philosophy section and said, 'There is only one author in this section worth reading. Don't bother with the one you're looking for. Read this. He has passion.' She handed me *Fear and Trembling* by Søren Kierkegaard."

That sounded like Mom. Not so subtle with the reading recommendations. And I'd heard the line about worshipping reason before. A few months into high school I asked her about whether the rules of moral reasoning changed with time or if they had been the same when she went to school. She looked at me with interest; something flickered in her eyes. "Of course they were different. None of these things are set in stone." I tried to wrap my head around that.

"They want you to worship reason, Talia," she said, "but only *their* reason. Why do you think that is? Though I can't persuade you that they're wrong, maybe I can try to persuade you to listen to your instincts. Do *you* think reason can solve everything? Do *you* think our instincts are so awful that they drive us to do terrible things?" I gaped at her. It was all way beyond me. "It's okay," she said with a smile, putting her palm on my cheek. "You'll figure out your own answers. I'm just asking you not to believe theirs without thinking about them yourself."

What was perplexing to me seemed sweet to Hoffman. He smiled at the memory. "I knew the book, of course. But it was different, having it handed to me by a beautiful, imperious woman who said my entire life's work, my entire field of study, was meaningless with the exception of this volume. I read it many times in the months that followed, while Lila and I were together. After she left me, I kept reading it. She could not have known the significance it would have."

Hoffman turned to look at me, and his blue eyes burned. "It's the book that brought me to God." I hadn't noticed him do it, but he had stepped nearer. He was only a couple feet away from me now. "Do you know it?"

I shook my head and resisted moving away. "Kierkegaard rings a bell."

"It's about Abraham. In the Old Testament. Who was asked by God to sacrifice his son. 'God tested Abraham and said to him, take Isaac, your only son, whom you love, and go to the land of Moriah and offer him as a burnt offering on the mountain that I shall show you.' Kierkegaard tries to fathom what Abraham must have felt, as he took the slow journey to the hilltop, agonizing the loss that awaited him. Only to find that God would not require the sacrifice of him after all. The book is about hope. And about finding faith in resignation."

I looked back at Hoffman, letting him see into me. I understood he was looking for hope, and I could hardly tell if the thing I felt would pass for hope or not. My fragile high wire through the fog, made of stretched logic and brittle persistence. I couldn't remember the feel of real hope, the hope I'd known as a child. But I could recall the effect: the way you are lifted upward with a great swell of near-dread, as if someone were holding you suspended over a cloud. Hoffman stared at me, his gaze both promising and demanding.

It was compelling. I could see why all those people in bonnets followed him around.

"I would love to be Calvino's father," Hoffman said, the intensity dropping abruptly like a wave that has finally crashed and left you standing, not drowned. He smiled. "Not just on paper. To really be his father. When Lila vanished from my life, I thought I had to give him up, the way Abraham had to give up Isaac. But now I find that God has had mercy on me."

I didn't know what to say. Part of me was imagining a torrent of events that began with dragging Hoffman down the hill to Cass and Tabby's car and ended with pulling Cal out of a padded room at RealCorp. But another part of me was wondering if in Hoffman's mind, the series of events ended with Cal here, at Mordecai's Hill, gazing at him adoringly from the front row of the pews. *It doesn't matter*, I said to myself firmly. *It really doesn't matter. New Puritans are a better fate than vivisection at RealCorp.*

"Thank you," I said aloud to Hoffman. "Thank you so much."

He basked in it for a couple seconds: my gratefulness and his sense of—what?—religiously reasoned vindication?

I was about to segue from profound gratitude to businesslike haste when something down the hill caught Hoffman's eye. Throughout our conversation, I'd been facing the splintered church and he'd been facing the valley. Now I saw his eyes narrow. "Is that smoke?" he asked. I turned.

It was hard to see them because of the fog, but then the fog shifted and they stood out clearly: slow-moving mounds of smoke, piled high like dark batting over the Victorian house. As we watched the smoke build and slowly dissipate, a long scream suddenly cut into the air. High and winding and agonized. It was not a scream of surprise. It was a scream of anticipated pain.

Hoffman stepped forward, about to burst into a run, and I stopped him. "No," I said. "No. You cannot go down there. Look." I pointed, and in a moment he saw what I saw. Behind a thin layer of mist, chasing across the footpaths and through the tall grass, dozens of Fish swam across the valley.

They had followed me.

28

NATALIA

I took out *De rerum*. First I sent Joey a message that said *Dozens fish. Hide.* Then I tapped my location on the map and sent it to Officer Gao with another message: *Need help. Fish. Estimate 30+.*

It took me about seven seconds. In that time, Hoffman remained standing with a look of paralyzed indecision. As I put *De rerum* away, another scream pealed out across the valley, piercing through the fog.

"I have to go," Hoffman said.

"Do you have a clone army? Or a tank? Because that is about the only thing that might stop them."

"I can't just let them . . ." He trailed off, not wanting to name the horrors he was imagining.

"If you go down there, you won't be able to stop them, either. You're doing as much here as you would do there." I took his arm. "We should take cover. They'll come this way at any moment." I put my hand up to his face and turned it toward me. His eyes were wide and haunted. "Dylan," I said. "I am good at calculating these kinds of odds. We don't have a chance. Please believe me—we will not make a difference."

For a moment he just stared. "I'm sorry," he whispered. "If they're all going to die I have to be there."

He pulled away from me and began running down the hill. I watched him. I watched him go like he was Cal himself, plunging downhill into a lake full of merciless Fish.

Then I ran after him. I tucked my bag against my side and put my walking shoes to work. My quads protested; they were still getting over those eight-minute miles. As I pounded down the grassy slope I considered that Hoffman had surprised me. Two acts of generosity in the span of five minutes: one probably somewhat self-interested, the other one entirely not. I had to admire him just a little. Maybe Mom wasn't such a sucker after all.

When I caught up to him, he gave me a look. "You should stay in the church," he panted. "Cal needs you."

"Cal needs *you*," I said. "I'm no use to him without you."

Hoffman didn't say anything to this. Maybe in his confused analogy to Abraham and Isaac, he'd decided God was pulling another trick on Abraham.

We reached the bottom of the hill, and I pulled Hoffman to a stop. "Behind me," I said, showing him the baton I was holding.

He nodded and stepped in beside me. We jogged along the dirt road that led to the cluster of buildings, letting our breathing settle. Now that we'd arrived, there strangely didn't seem to be anything going on. The air around us was silent. I didn't like that. As we came to a low point before the rise that led to the Victorian house, we saw a smear of blood in the dust, along with the remnants that had caused it. Two hands, cut off at the wrist, one facing up, the other palm down like it was patting the dirt.

"Good God," Hoffman said. His fingers seized my shoulder and gripped hard.

I stopped. "We can go back."

"No," Hoffman said sharply, on a quick release of breath.

I heard running footsteps behind us, but the fog obscured the runner. I drew Hoffman aside into the tall grass and pushed him down. A lone Fish came into view, probably back from the pursuit of some quarry who had fled the buildings. He was young, with a muscle shirt and camouflage pants and military boots. He carried a short sword in each fist, pumping them back and forth as he ran. When he was a foot past me, I jumped out, slamming the baton down on his neck. Before he could turn I used the lipstick, right where his kidneys would be. The soldier crumpled, the swords still clenched in his fists, and he lay in the road folded up on his knees like a warrior-monk at prayer.

Hoffman was watching with a look of glazed shock. The hands in the dust had already thrown him; nothing would make much of a difference now. "We can stay here," I offered. "Or go back to the church."

He shook his head obstinately and climbed out of the grassy rut beside the road. Silently cursing Hoffman's misguided impulse to martyrdom, I walked beside him toward the buildings. The Victorian house was burning in a slow, smoldering fashion, like damp wood in a stove. The fog kept the flames from leaping to the grass all around it, but I could see that the fire would eventually get adventurous and make the jump, and then all the hills around us would be ablaze. As we neared, another scream erupted, startling in its closeness. It came from the barn.

We came upon the building on silent footsteps, and the sounds from inside began to reach us. Sobbing. A thrashing sound, as if someone was tossing and turning in a pile of hay. A saw biting into wood. When we stood a few steps from the door, I turned and stopped Hoffman in his tracks. "We can't just walk in there," I whispered.

"I have to," he said blankly.

"Do you want to help them, or do you just want to die with them?"

He blinked at me like he was trying very hard to understand the meaning of the question. *If Glout were here he'd be telling Hoffman about the chemistry of shock*, I thought. "I want to help them," Hoffman said, his voice barely audible.

"Do you have any weapons, any explosives? Gasoline?"

Hoffman shook his head over and over. "No. Nothing." He paused. "We have candles."

I refrained from rolling my eyes. "Great," I said. "Perfect. Can you get them?"

He turned to look at the Victorian house. "They're in there."

"Okay. Let's go."

"To get the candles?" He blinked at me again.

"That's right. I have a plan. The candles are going to help."

It was a little underhanded, I reflected, as I steered Hoffman away from his intended self-sacrifice in order to pursue an utterly useless bundle of candles, but there was no way I was going to let him get chopped up into pieces. We walked over to the porch, which was still untouched by the fire; it had started at the rear of the house.

I opened the tattered screen door for Hoffman and followed him into a foyer heavy with dark wood. "Let me go first," I whispered. He nodded. "Which way?" Hoffman pointed to a corridor. I took it, and as we moved on I realized we were spared the worst of the smoke because the fire had started on an upper floor. A large dining room with more wood—wainscoting, long tables—met us halfway. Then a kitchen with wooden countertops and wooden cabinets. In the middle of the room was an island with three-inch butcher block. The fire was going to have a real blast when it discovered the first floor.

"They're in the pantry," Hoffman whispered, pointing. Past the kitchen island, where someone had been chopping scallions, stood an open door to a room with white shelves and neatly stacked jars. I took a step toward it.

That's when the kitchen screen door opened. Bad Lipstick and two buddies: the cowboy and the cane cutter, both of whom had seemingly not changed a fragment of their attire since our rendezvous in Japantown. This time, I noticed, Bad Lipstick was playing it safe. In addition to her usual little switchblade, she carried a handgun.

I pushed Hoffman down toward the floor so that the kitchen island stood between him and the Fish. "Hey," I said to the girl.

She smiled. Both the gun and the blade hung by her sides, relaxed. "Hey," she replied.

"Nice of you guys to show up," I said.

"Wouldn't miss it for the world."

I considered her easy posture. Her two sidekicks seemed to have no interest in talking, but they were eyeing me and the kitchen island like a pair of cats drooling at the canary cage. "I've gotta hand it to you," I said to her. "You really know how to hold a grudge."

"I'm only in it for the cash," she said pertly. "You're worth a lot more than my last kill, only five thou."

"Oh, was that someone else who managed to leave you scrambling on the subway?"

She didn't bite. Her smile widened. "I'm just glad I was the one to find you," she said. "Everyone else is scoring low in the barn."

"Yeah, we heard," I said, looking past her at the door. "But they're still looking to score high."

This time she did bite. She glanced over her shoulder at the screen door and I threw the knife I'd taken from the counter. It hit her in the ribs. She flailed as she fell, shooting the automatic with no aim at all. The two men stepped forward, but I had already swung onto the island and caught the cowboy in the neck with the full force of my right foot. The cane cutter had more lead time and he used it. He raised the machete and brought it down toward me hard, and I rolled away, letting it thwack into the wooden butcher block. I swear I felt the breeze on my back.

I dropped to the floor while he was struggling to get the

machete out of the countertop. Then my lipstick made the acquaintance of his bare navel. One second, two, three, and he sank to the floor with the machete still embedded inch-deep in wood. But by then the cowboy had recovered. Before I realized how, his whip wrapped itself around my waist. I went limp. It was enough to throw him just a little off balance. Then I reached out and yanked the whip from his hands. He wasn't prepared for that, either, and the momentum brought him toward me fast. I put my feet up like a bug to try to catch him and fling him off, but my legs were sore and I wasn't quick enough. He landed on my bent knees just as two shots rang out from the girl's gun. I held his neck and he wrestled against me for a moment and then abruptly stopped. When I pushed him off I realized why. Bad Lipstick had shot him twice in the back.

She held me at gunpoint, her other hand pressed against her bleeding side. I was panting.

"Remind me not to become friends with you," I said to her. "So tempting but high fatality rate."

She didn't smile at that. I'd finally managed to get under her skin.

"What?" a feeble voice said.

"Not you," I said to Hoffman. "Stay where you are."

Something about the way I said it betrayed me. Not emotion, but maybe speed. Bad Lipstick suddenly had her smile back. "He matters to you," she said, getting carefully to her feet.

"Yup. I know—it's weird. I have this quirk, you might have noticed. I like people when they're alive."

She was standing now, and she began stepping slowly toward the island. "Him especially." From where I sat I couldn't block her shot to Hoffman, and I wouldn't be able to dive in front of her in time. I didn't have any great ideas. The only thing I could do was draw her fire. I threw myself to the side toward the cowboy and she fired twice, and when I came up again I flung the whip toward her. It caught her in the face. I stood up and lunged at her, throwing us both down and smacking her onto the tile floor. Her head hit the ground hard, and her body was suddenly soft beneath me. Soft and warm, and there was blood from her gashed head in my hair.

Up close, her face was pimply. Reddened eyes painted black at the edges. Her skin was caked white with powder.

I pushed myself up and turned to Hoffman. He was sitting where I'd left him, his hands on his worn jeans. The two bullets had made red blooms on his work shirt, and his face had a look of startled sadness, as if he'd realized that something he had counted on to be there, always, had never been there at all.

29

NATALIA

I'm not sure how long I stood watching Hoffman's blood, and with it my chance of saving Cal, oozing onto the tile floor. I heard gunfire, and I could tell by the rapid report and the instant response that the police had arrived. Then I looked at my watch. It had taken them twelve minutes. Twelve minutes was not a lot of time. Only long enough for a few bonneted Puritans to lose their hands. Only long enough for Hoffman to lose his life.

I walked out of the house and past the barn, swarming with cops, and headed uphill to where I had to hope Cass and Tabby and Joey were still hidden. They were. I told them what had happened and we sat outside the church and waited for the police to process every inch of the site. Tabby put her arm around my shoulders, Joey took my hand, and Cass stood in front of us with her arms crossed, frowning at the officers who climbed toward us up Mordecai's Hill. It was so useless it was sweet. Like making a warm padded box for a detonated bomb.

Gao showed up, which was nice of him, because it was quite a drive. I was telling an Officer Petri the story for the third time when Gao hiked up the hill and tapped Petri on the shoulder. "I got this," he said.

Petri, who seemed overburdened by the task placed before him, did not complain. "Thanks, man," he said, wheeling away.

Gao sat down next to me and looked out over the valley. The fog had cleared. Fire trucks had extinguished the flames at the Victorian house, and it stood in the yellow grass like a charred dollhouse, burnt by some spoilt child who didn't know the meaning of restraint. Beyond it, the hills were pale orange. As Marlowe said once, I had the feeling that I'd written a very good poem and lost it and would never remember it again.

"Thank you," I said.

"You're welcome." He considered me briefly. "You don't look well."

"Yeah. Somehow I don't think I got the worst of it."

He nodded in acknowledgment. "Eleven dead. Eight others have serious injuries from mutilations."

"Mutilations," I echoed.

"Hands, ears, and noses."

"How . . . precise."

"It seems you stumbled onto a crew that calls itself the Conquistadors."

This was news to me. I tried to think of something funny to say about that, just to let Gao know I was okay, but nothing came to mind. Gao and I stared at the hills and listened to Cass, some distance away, giving her statement in a quiet, even voice.

"Sometimes when the Fish bounties get really high, a site administrator starts what's called a game. Wherever the target is becomes the center of the game."

I could feel Gao glance at me. "So they called a game on my location."

"Right."

"You got lucky, though."

I disagreed. "Oh yeah. Way lucky."

"Someone else called another game at the same time in Santa Rosa." He tapped at his screen decal and showed me a map with two dozen red dots. "Drew more than half the crowd away." He looked at me sideways. "Quite a coincidence, don't you think?"

I shrugged.

He tapped the screen again and held it up to me.

"That's who called the game in Santa Rosa?"

Gao nodded. "Recognize her?"

I did, of course, as did Gao. The Fish's profile photo showed a sea witch with dark pools for eyes and a pile of green mermaid hair. Coral.

For some reason, I found this the most problematic of all. More problematic than severed hands and conquistadors. More problematic than eleven deaths. It was problematic because she'd done something for me, and if she could do something for me, how could she also disembowel people with oversized forks? It made no sense.

I thought about what Glout had told me, his theory that

Fish were desperate to feel something. Was this Coral trying to act on other instincts? "I don't understand why she would help me."

"Fish aren't logical."

No, they weren't. Coral or no Coral, the costs had been high all around. "I caused those deaths," I said. "I caused all of them."

Gao did not look at me. "There's nothing I can say to change that."

"I know."

"You caused it by saving a woman's life. By my rules, by our rules, you did the right thing."

"The rules don't seem to add up to the right result in this case."

Gao pondered. "There are two Fish in custody down the hill—one with a mustache and another in chaps. I'm betting you know them." I nodded. "I heard their statements."

"Okay," I said.

"You did what you could with the odds, Nat." He paused. "You did good."

"I don't know." The hills looked damp and faintly silvery, as if the fog had left its cast-off garments on their undulating sides.

Gao shifted. "Peña, I know what you're really worried about, so I'll just say it. Yes, you can keep training with me."

I smiled. I resisted the desire to keel over. My bones felt tired. I wanted to sink back onto the dry grass and be swallowed up by the earth. I wanted to forget everything that had happened that day, and then I wanted to forget everything that had happened before it, and forget who I was, and forget every circumstance familiar enough to remind me.

Very deliberately, I thought about Cal. I imagined his dark, untidy hair. His pointy teeth when he was laughing. His wide eyes in rapt suspense while I was reading to him. The feel of his arms wrapped around my neck with an outburst of tears, his face sticky and hot, and then the rhythm of his heartbeat slowing to a steady calm, saying to me like it always did, *I trust you, I believe in you, I love you.*

I pushed myself up with Gao's shoulder. "I need to leave," I said.

In the end it was more than three hours before I got out of there. The cops gave us sandwiches and coffee. I almost did the Fish a favor and chewed my fingers off waiting. I could see the minutes disappearing. They let us go, finally, at four in the afternoon. Gao saw us to the car and told me not to be late to training on Monday evening. I nodded, as if that would happen—as if Monday evening existed.

On the drive back to Oakland, Cass and Tabby talked continuously with June on speaker about the other legal options that she had been preparing as alternatives, should the approach with Hoffman not come through. They all sounded like long shots. I didn't say anything. I let them think I was still lost in the morning fog, still wandering through the memories of what had happened to Hoffman. I opened *De rerum* and sent Troy a note telling him it was too late for the bookstore, asking if he'd had any luck with his dad. As I was writing, Joey's message appeared and I did not have the temerity to ignore it. *What are you planning?* Joey asked.

Going to SF to see Philbrick, I replied.

Can I come.

Absolutely not.

Why.

I might outfish the Fish.

Joey paused in the conversation. He did not look at me. He stared out the window. *You cannot disappear without us,* he typed.

I promise I won't.

I did mean it. I had every intention of telling Joey where we were if, by some miracle, Cal and I were still alive at 6:30 in the morning.

By the time we got back to Oakland, Troy still hadn't responded. It surprised me a little. All it meant was that I had to make my own plan, just like I intended to all along. Cass and Tabby wanted to go straight to June's office, but I insisted they drop me off at home. They left Joey looking after me and sped off. While Joey waited on the tweed sofa, I showered and changed into my best clothes, a twill suit with a double row of horn buttons. I wore the pearl brooch Mom gave me, heeled oxfords, and a sculpted hat of hunter-green felt. When I walked back into the living room, I found Joey, showered and dressed as if to match. I glanced over his combed hair and neatly ironed shirt. "Where do you think you're going?"

"You've kept me out of this every step of the way. I will only half believe it when you say it's to protect me. It's also because you don't want anyone interfering with your methods."

"It's both."

He plowed on like I hadn't spoken. "I know you think I'm useless in a fight, but not everything is about fighting. I'm coming with you."

I wanted to hug him and throw a shoe at him. I settled for a sigh. "Fine."

He stood, waiting.

"And I apologize for keeping you out."

He nodded. He swung his jacket over his shoulder. "Okay. Apology accepted. Let's go."

———

We took the bus to the BART and rode in silence. The train into the city was quiet at six p.m. on a Sunday. As the doors opened and passengers rolled in and out, I had to admit that having Joey along seemed like a good idea. Some part of me was still wired, even though Gao promised that the bounty posting had been taken down; I expected Fish to pop out of every open doorway. Besides, when our long journey by public transportation concluded in Pac Heights, it looked much better to stroll around holding hands with Joey than to stroll around on my own. There was still no word from Troy.

As we climbed the sidewalk steps to the corner with the view of the bay, I saw another couple walking downhill across the street. At first I didn't recognize her, because I hadn't expected her to be there and because she looked different on the street, not surrounded by friends and easy laughter. I saw a woman small and thin, with the artificial delicacy of someone who has starved herself for many years. Bleached blonde hair, coiffed to Kim Novak circa 1963, and a white dress with silver sequins. A thirty-five-year-old face carefully pruned to look twenty, almost believably so. On it was an expression of deliberate neutrality, a willful containment of troubling synafftic emotions. I realized it was Mrs. Philbrick.

The man beside her was either Tanner Philbrick or a very confident interloper. He was tall and heavy. Thick blond eyebrows, thick nose, thick neck. Costly suit and shoes. From the look on his tanned face, he didn't take many troubling emotions or bother much with anyone else's. I could see both his sons in Philbrick Senior. The attentiveness with which he held his wife's arm was all Troy. The roving eye looking my way at the moment was all Charlie.

I lifted my chin and kept climbing. A few steps later I squeezed Joey's hand and stopped. "That was him," I said.

Joey looked over his shoulder. "He's huge."

"Come on," I said.

"What's the approach?"

"We'll just watch them for now."

We followed at a short distance as they walked down a few blocks and then east toward Fillmore. The Philbricks, with unwitting irony, stopped at a restaurant called the Steakout and took seats outside. One glance at the clothing of the hostess told me we wouldn't be able to afford it, but almost every spot on Fillmore had outdoor seating. The café next door with Parisian bistro chairs had three empty tables. "Let's have some coffee," I said to Joey.

Joey smiled, pulled out my chair, and gave me a peck on the cheek as I sat down. "You are glaring," he said, in a sing-song voice by my ear, "and it makes you look like an angry rabbit. If you cannot pretend to be out on a happy date with your happy boyfriend, let me sit facing them."

I smiled up at him. "Thank you," I said sweetly.

"That's better," he replied, also smiling, and took his seat. "What would you like?"

"I would like pancakes," I said. "But I doubt they serve them."

The waitress came up and batted her eyelashes at Joey. She tossed her long hair over her shoulder and drew the note-pad from her scalloped apron. Somehow, she made it look like these were preludes to flinging her clothes off. "How can I help you?" she said to Joey. She ignored me.

"Do you have pancakes?" Joey asked.

She pouted. "Oh, lo siento. We don't."

"It will have to be tea and macarons, then. Two pots of tea, six of the best macarons."

She giggled like this was a witticism. "What kind of tea? We have a menu." She dipped forward to point out the list.

While Joey was fending off the waitress, I was watching Tanner and his wife. Separated by the width of a table, the illusion that they belonged together fell apart. She was skittish and vulnerable and brittle, he was two hundred fifty pounds of sangfroid. They looked like a poodle and a gorilla out on a date. Only the money they shared made it seem like they were from the same world.

Their table was less than ten feet away, but with the street noise and the chatter, it was too far to hear anything. She had already ordered a cocktail, and he was drinking sparkling water. Philbrick took a sip. Then he glanced my way and did a slight double take. He was remembering me from the street, wondering if it was coincidence that we were sitting nearby or if I'd sought out his proximity on purpose. I regarded him noncommittally and then let my eyes drift back to Joey.

The waitress had finally retreated to plan her next assault. Joey looked around, taking in the other café diners, a man on the sidewalk walking a collie, and two women in heels who trotted daintily past, arm in arm. "Nice neighborhood," he said quietly.

"I like Oakland better."

"Oakland does have more . . ." He rubbed his thumb against two fingers pensively. "What's the word I'm looking for? Sweat? Dirt? Grime?"

"Character. And taste."

He raised his eyebrows. "I don't know. I don't mind French cafés and steak houses."

I glanced over at Philbrick and found that he was looking directly at me. So was his wife. I blinked once at each of them and then turned to Joey with my best imitation of adoring. "This might proceed very quickly," I said, smiling tenderly. "It appears I have sparked someone's interest and someone else's jealousy."

Joey leaned over the table and took my hand. "That doesn't surprise me." He lifted his other hand and tucked a stray hair behind my ear. "I'm going to murmur nonsense and you can focus on watching them." He started off on one of our favorite topics of conversation when things were normal, fantasy time-travel destinations.

I glanced back at the Philbricks. They were staring hard at their menus. Mrs. Philbrick had a frozen look on her face, and I could see from the immobility of her eyes that she wasn't reading. Words and thoughts were going through her mind. Mr. Philbrick was tracing a thick finger over the wine list. He put it down and folded his hands together. She imitated him reflexively, placing the menu on the table and taking the folded napkin in her bony fingers. Saying something quietly, she opened the napkin and placed it on her lap. Then a sudden silence around us—a lull in several conversations, a pause in the street traffic—conspired to lift Tanner Philbrick's voice above the other noise, so that his casual words rang out clearly. "That was before you got fat." He calmly took a drink of his sparkling water. I watched Mrs. Philbrick accommodate to this. She flinched and her body tightened; she stared at the potted plant next to her. Then she looked down at her lap and put herself back together. It took only a few seconds. A familiar cruelty, then. One she could prepare for, even if she could never entirely protect herself from it. I thought about Troy and Mrs. Frances Peters. These rich people had a lot of practice cutting each other to pieces, I thought. Not so different from the Fish.

Joey had paused in his wandering monologue about Renaissance Italy. He had heard Philbrick's words as well, and we looked at each other for a moment. "Wow," Joey mouthed. Then he continued. "Even if I couldn't actually talk to Michelangelo, maybe watch from a distance while he worked . . ."

The waitress appeared at his elbow with the sweets and tea. She placed a plate with seven macarons of different colors directly in front of him. "The seventh is on me," she said to him, with a little wink. "Red velvet." The two pots of tea were purposely mismatched Wedgwood; the cups, too. There was a silver pitcher with milk and a silver pot with sugar cubes and a tiny pair of tongs. As she went to work converting her instructions for how to steep the tea into the next phase of Joey's seduction, I saw Philbrick rise from his chair. He glanced at me as he did so, but his wife was staring at her hands and didn't see it. Then he drifted into the restaurant.

I pushed my chair back. "I'll be right back, dulce," I said to Joey, interrupting the waitress. She shot me a surprised look.

I left my hat on my chair. I walked over to the Steakout, where the hostess was thankfully engaged seating a rowdy party of bankers who were roaring and high-fiving on the crest of some hedonistic synaff that would wear off quickly, leaving them somber and deadened by two in the morning. Heading into the restaurant like I knew where I was going, I walked along the bar and toward the rear. The bathrooms were off a wood-paneled corridor, dimly lit. There was a door with a high-heeled shoe and a door with a mustache.

Me and the Philbrick men and bathrooms, I thought to myself. I opened the door with the mustache.

The men's room of the Steakout reminded me of the Landmark. Shiny tiles the color of onyx, two black bowls with silver faucets, heavy gilt mirrors on the cream-papered walls, and white orchids. There were no urinals, only two stalls of pale wood. Below one of the closed doors, Philbrick's pricey shoes gleamed. I opened my bag and took out my lipstick and the nickel-sized decal I'd bought near Jack London Square on the morning I had brioche with Gao. It was light as a sticker. I peeled off the paper and tucked it carefully into my right palm, superglue side up. I walked to the mirror and held my lipstick up as if trying to decide where to use it.

Philbrick flushed the toilet and a second later he opened the stall door. He stood in the doorway and looked at me, his face unsurprised and only mildly satisfied, as if the first course he'd been served was fortunately adequate.

The next step would be easy. All I had to do was turn around, close the five feet of distance between us, and put my hand with the nickel-sized decal on the back of his neck. He wouldn't stop my embrace, but even if he tried to, I had the lipstick in the other hand. Then Cal was as good as mine. The decal could detonate by remote at any distance. I would just inform Philbrick of the particulars and talk him through the steps like a toy robot. Toy gorilla robot.

I watched Philbrick watching me. I thought about his easy brutality to his wife, his comfortable castle, his grotesque treatment of my brother. I thought about him refusing to follow my instructions. Stubborn. Arrogant. Immovable. Refusing to let Cal go, forcing me to open *De rerum* and trigger the little decal, the circuits inside the plastic working to rip all two hundred fifty pounds of him into tiny pieces, bits of red flesh all over the inside of the steak house bathroom.

I could do this.

I *would* do this if he refused to free Cal.

Then, without wanting to, I thought about the Fish. I saw two hands severed in the road, and I heard long screams and groans of agony. Deliberate pain, intentional damage. Not for self-protection, but for gain. The calculated harm of a defenseless human being. I saw fog and rolling hills and Hoffman's face, startled and bereaved. I saw again what Hoffman's story had provoked, the memory of Mom talking to me about instinct and reason. Her face serious and beautiful and laced with the undercurrent of pain that always throbbed about her like an extra pulse. *Though I can't persuade you that they're wrong, maybe I can try to persuade you to listen to your instincts. Do you think reason can solve everything? Do you think our instincts are so awful that they drive us to do terrible things?*

I hadn't understood what she was getting at. Now I did. She meant that instincts are not five neatly labeled urges that course through us like electrical currents, switching on and off to get us through the day. Instincts are as varied and subtle as shades of color. They could make a scene from a window look gray, even if the sky was cloudless. They could make a person's eyes look like dark, bottomless pits, regardless of their hue. They could make a room look like it had been splattered red, even if there wasn't a drop of blood in sight. Instincts were too complex and too unrecognized.

They were feelings. And I'd been ignoring them.

Maybe Mom wasn't an easygoing airhead after all. Maybe she was too smart, and the strictures of our world made her seem all futility and waywardness. I'd imagine brilliance would look that way in a world made of dead ends.

Philbrick shifted, like he was trying to decide which fork to use. My eyes in the mirror drifted away from him to my own face. Slight nose, serious mouth. Good choice of lipstick. Ears slightly too large, but the wavy brown hair did its best to conceal them. The brown eyes were cold. Cold like a Fish's eyes. But these were the same eyes that looked in on Cal to make sure he was sleeping. That watched him sing while he made a sandwich. They had watched him do these things and thousands of other things for more than a decade. I stared into them, trying to figure out if the two things could exist together.

Staring. Being stared at. A spasm of something moved through my stomach, hot and violent. I felt sick. The sight of my own face made me sick. And suddenly I remembered someone else staring at me this hard, trying to figure out what lay behind my cold eyes. Cal, in the moments after we found Mom. At the time, I hadn't understood what he was feeling, but now, as I looked at myself and the rational intention planned in my face, I understood, because I *felt* it. It was revulsion. After seeing our mother broken, strewn across the floor like a *thing*, the destruction obliterating any trace of familiarity, Cal had looked at me and seen this. These eyes.

Apathy.

Indifference, at the sight of a shattered face, at the prospect of an exploded body. What I had seen and what I would do were the same. A sensation moved across my skull, like a trickle of ice-cold water. I shuddered. I was still looking at my face in the mirror, and it was hideous. I wanted to break the glass to pieces.

I gasped.

Philbrick cocked his head, confused. I tore my eyes away from the monster in the mirror and turned to face him. He blinked, wondering and shifting to wariness, but the moment had passed: Philbrick was safe. I understood that I could no longer do it.

Mom was right. I had not been listening to my instincts. Now I would.

Four steps took me to the door, and then I was out again in the wood-paneled corridor, tapping the decal gently back onto its wrapper while I walked toward the dining area. I tossed the lipstick into my bag and wove past a waiter with a giant tray. Outside, I stopped briefly at Mrs. Philbrick's table. "He's a beast. You should leave him," I said. She looked up at me, astonished, her eyes following me as I walked away.

Joey was sitting very still, his fingers templed before him. I took my hat from the chair and sat down. He reached across and took my hand. "You okay?"

"I'm fine," I said.

"What happened?"

"Nothing. Nothing happened." I waved for the check unsteadily. "I just stared at myself in the mirror."

30

CALVINO

October 14

Dear Nat,

Dr. Glout says that today was my last day of testing with him and that tomorrow I will be in a new lab. I am so glad because I am really sick of this room!! He said the tests in the other lab would not last very long, which is good. He didn't know what the tests were like because other doctors are running the tests. It will probably be like Dr. Baylor again, which is not great, but as long as it is a real live person I don't care. I would even be happy to see Dr. Baylor at this point. Can you believe it!

I decided I would tell you my surprise plan for what to do when I am done with testing this week! It might be too expensive, which I understand if it is. But if it is not too expensive what I wanted to do was go on a boat. Any kind of boat! Even a ferry. Doesn't it seem strange that we live right next to the water and have never been on a boat? I was reading about boats these last few days, especially houseboats. There are no canals here but I would love to live on a boat in a canal and just float along from one place to another! Maybe we could have cats! I think almost all our furniture would fit on the houseboat, except for your foldout bed—ha!

Well that is my idea. See you soon after these last tests.

Love,
Cal

31

NATALIA

The trip home was mostly silent. Me because I was retooling Plan C. Joey because he was busy radiating approval. Somehow, he managed not to make it seem self-righteous. I didn't bother pointing out to him that my brief flirtation with nonviolence would possibly cost Cal his life. I didn't want to ruin his moment.

We got home at nine and found that Cass and Tabby were still out with June. Joey called and talked to them for a while. He reported that they were coming up with emergency filings and would probably be with June for a few more hours. Then he made peanut butter and jelly sandwiches while I explained Plan C. It was nothing fancy. Once at RealCorp, I would use the decal I'd been too spineless to use on Philbrick as a distraction. Hopefully it would buy me enough time to get Cal out of the building. I was about 78 percent certain that Glout could be persuaded to sit, tied to a chair, while Cal's maniac sister executed a rescue. If his empathy didn't stretch that far, or if he'd skipped his dose, I'd knock him over with an envelope and tie him up anyway. Then I had to hope that most of the security guards were still distracted. "It really has the potential to get very messy," I said to Joey. "And I don't expect you to come, but I won't refuse your company, either."

"That's terribly kind," Joey said, taking the plates to the sink.

"Come on, Joey," I said. "This can end very badly. It would be good to know that you're safe."

"I know," he said, coming back to the table. "I'm sorry." He slid the sheet of paper I was using to sketch Plan C toward him. "But I want to come. The point here is for Cal to be safe. Explain the details to me and tell me what I can do."

For the next half hour I told him the particulars and we added a few fixes. Joey surprised me with some good ideas and we drew them in. Then while he took a catnap on the sofa, I added as much as I could to the building plan. Most of RealCorp I hadn't seen, but where there were exits and corridors that I remembered, I penciled them in.

At 10:17 my doorbell rang. Joey sat up groggily on the sofa. "Who is that?"

"I have no idea." The front door wasn't visible from the apartment windows. I walked down to the ground floor and peered out toward the glass door to the street. Troy Philbrick's silhouette loomed darkly. A night angel, resting wearily on the stoop.

I opened the door. The lightbulb on the doorstep was busted, and I saw the side of his face in the blue glow of the streetlight. It was damp with tears. He looked at me solemnly, not stepping forward. Then he lifted his right hand, showing me something black and metallic, only just larger than his outstretched fingers. "I shouldn't have taken this," he said hoarsely. "I'm sorry."

It was my mother's handgun. It took me several seconds to figure out how it had gotten there. Lifted the night before from the dresser drawer, carried in a waistband or a jacket pocket across the bay, now carried back and balanced on a trembling palm.

I finally took the handgun and stepped back. "You'd better come in," I said.

He followed me up the steps and into the apartment. I tried to give Joey a two-second warning of what lay ahead by showing him the weapon. I opened the drawer and placed it inside just as Troy paced woodenly into the living room. "Troy, this is my best friend, Joey. Joey, Troy." Joey stood up and said nothing.

Troy looked at him and then at me. He crumpled onto the floor slowly, like his bones had suddenly turned to sand. Then he wrapped his arms around his knees and started sobbing, hard and then harder, the spasms shaking his back. Joey and I exchanged a glance.

I got down on my knees next to Troy and put my arm around his shoulder. His arms flung out and seized me and he held me like a drowning man, the sobs so violent I had to push against him to keep from falling. It lasted several minutes, and then the shuddering sobs started to slow. Finally he lay almost limp in my arms, his face buried against my shoulder.

He sat back with effort and looked at us, dazed, like he

wasn't sure what had just happened. Joey handed him one of my old-school handkerchiefs, white with embroidered edges, taken from my dresser. "Thanks, man," Troy choked out. His voice was scraped raw. He wiped his face and then folded the handkerchief and stared at it. We were both still sitting on the floor. I got up and offered him my hand. He took it, got to his feet with effort, and let me lead him over to the sofa.

Joey brought a glass of water from the kitchen and put it in front of him on the table. Troy folded the handkerchief into the tiniest possible packet, and then he clasped it in his fist and squeezed. We waited.

"My parents and stepmom," Troy finally said. "Mom and Dad and Monica. They change my drops. They have since I faded. Usually they give me a normal regimen, but sometimes I get rewards . . . And sometimes I get punishments." His face flushed. He pressed the handkerchief to his forehead. "Rewards are nice—short highs." He paused. "The punishments are not so nice. Once I tried to leave. I stayed with a friend for a couple weeks. But my drops ran out and I was like a zombie." He reached out with a shaking hand and took a long drink of water. He put the glass down and sighed. "When I went home the drops changed and made me depressed for a month. It was the worst month of my life. I couldn't do anything, I didn't want to get out of bed, I thought about killing myself. I felt constant pain, just from nothing. Just pain at existing. Pain with no escape because it came from inside me. That was the first time. Other times it's been for longer." He stared off into the distance.

"So when I met you at the Landmark . . ." I started to ask.

"Yeah." He met my eyes briefly. "That was a punishment. I hadn't done something Monica wanted. Mom didn't know about it when we went out for lunch. I didn't know either, so it caught us both by surprise."

I didn't say anything. He opened his hand and stared down at the crumpled handkerchief for a full minute. "I talked to my dad this morning about Calvino. He told me straight out that Mom had mentioned your name and that he'd looked you both up. They could find nothing for leverage other than Calvino, his test results. So that's what they used. I asked him to let Calvino go. Annul the adoption, whatever. He said that if it were up to him, every ten-year-old in the country would be in his lab. Can you believe it?" He squeezed the handkerchief again. "Of course he thinks that. Of course he does." He shook his head. "Later on in the morning I found that him or Monica had swapped my regimen. No label. No doubt something nasty, probably like a month of self-recrimination. Or worse. A month of mindless obedience. I spent the rest of the day trying to get normal drops and I couldn't."

He looked up at us, his expression suddenly cleared, as if he'd figured out something important. "I couldn't take it anymore. I just couldn't take it. I had no idea what was real. What I was feeling. Was it just something they'd changed in my dose? Was it normal? How long would it last? Was I afraid because they'd made me afraid, or was I just afraid?" He shook his head. "When they came home from dinner today I confronted Dad and Monica." He stared at his glass of water, and then he gave a little chuckle. "Can you believe they tried to say I was only angry because of the synaffs? That I didn't actually have a reason to be angry?" He looked up at me. "That's what they didn't get. I wasn't. I wasn't angry. I was hurt. They'd been hurting me over and over and over for almost ten years." He stared at me intently, willing me to understand.

I held his gaze. "I can see that," I said.

He sat back against the sofa, relieved, his arms limp at his sides. The bundled handkerchief fell out of his hand and opened like a flower. He looked up at the bookcase and then back down at the floor. "I just left them there on the floor in the kitchen. I haven't called the police. My mom is in Paris. Charlie is in Tahoe." He glanced up at me. "I'm sorry; I didn't know where else to go, Natalia."

I spoke carefully, as if uttering the words might make something break. "Troy. Did you use my mom's gun?"

He blinked. "Of course."

Of course. Of course he had. What else does one do with a gun? It did for Troy what it did for my mom. Shoot bullets. "Are they alive or dead?"

"Totally dead." Troy took a deep breath, letting the air push him back onto the couch. "No more drops. No more highs, no more lows. Probably. I haven't thought about what will happen when my mom gets home. I don't really care." He looked up at me, his face abruptly childish and hopeful. "At least you get Calvino back now, don't you?"

I stared at him. His words made sense, but for some reason I couldn't follow them. I was stuck on an image that wasn't real, an image of two beautifully dressed people smeared on the beautiful floor of a beautiful castle. I knew enough about the house and the protagonists to wonder about the details. Had they seen what was coming? Had they felt some instinct of self-preservation? Had they run? Was their blood on the blond wood cabinets?

But what I really wondered was how I could feel nothing for the life I'd deliberately, only hours earlier, decided to spare. For a short time, while I contemplated my own face in the mirror, destroying Philbrick had seemed monstrous. Now it simply seemed like a thing that had happened. Unexpected. Unpredictable in its consequences. But no longer monstrous. I imagined them side by side, near an open window, the breeze ruffling their hair. Monica a crumpled sparrow, too-thin arms flung wide. Tanner a frozen rock, eyes open and unrelenting. It was an image that meant nothing, in the sense that it had no moorings in the real world. And it meant nothing because when I thought about it I felt nothing. Nothing at all.

I looked up at Joey, and I could see my own thoughts reflected in his eyes. I pulled myself away from that imagined room in Pac Heights, back into the Oakland apartment. "I think we should get some legal help," I said aloud, looking at Joey.

"Yes," Joey said.

Troy seemed uninterested. He stared at the bookcases. He was emerging from the hurricane and starting to feel exhausted. Now that it was over, nothing would seem to matter. It would be a while before he realized that there were events and consequences he still cared about. "I have a lawyer," he said. He gave a hiccuped laugh. "At least, my dad does. I haven't called him yet, either."

I considered. "First lawyer, then cops. Do you know the name?"

Troy reached into his pocket, took out a silver cigarette case, popped the lid, and tapped at the decal inside it. He was slow and a little clumsy, as if the outburst had frayed the finer points of his movements. "Here," he said, handing it to me.

The decal showed the contact information for Lester Bloom of Reminsky & Bloom. "This guy is going to have a bad night," I said, looking at the decal.

"I'll call him," Troy said wearily, reaching up for the cigarette case.

"Before you do, I want to send this to Joey so he can send it to Cass and Tabby. They're working with a lawyer who will contact Bloom about your dad's will and the terms of adoption." I watched his red-rimmed eyes attempting to keep up. "Is that okay?"

"Sure, fine." He had no idea what I'd just said, or no idea what it signified.

I sent lucky Lester Bloom's info to Joey, who nodded as it arrived and stepped quietly toward the doorway to call Cass and Tabby. I gave the cigarette case back to Troy.

It was almost eleven, but Lester Bloom answered on the second ring.

"Hi, Lester," Troy said sedately. "This is Troy Philbrick."

He paused. "Yes, it is. Dad and Monica are dead." Another short pause. "Mom's in Paris and Charlie is skiing in Tahoe." A longer pause. "Yes. My friend can call. But we can't meet at the house." He nodded thoughtfully. "Okay. I have my car. I can drive there, no problem. Thank you, Lester." Something the lawyer said made him smile, and he hung up. I was impressed by the man on the other end of the line. Word economy is hard to come by in the law. Consideration nearly impossible.

"Lester's in Napa," Troy reported, putting the cigarette case away. "His place is like a mile from our house in Yountville."

"You're going to drive there?"

"He said to call the cops and then drive up to Napa to meet him." He blinked. "Can you call them?" The weariness was starting to overwhelm him.

"I can. But you need some coffee," I said to him, "or you'll end up driving off a curve."

He nodded mutely.

I went into the kitchen and put the kettle on, set a cone filter over a cup. While I waited for the water to boil I took out *De rerum* and sent Gao a message. *Tanner Philbrick dead in his home. Looking into adoption fallout. Will need to verify death. Help please?* I added Joey's phone number.

His response arrived in seconds. *Are you making scarce?*

No, I typed back. *Wasn't me.*

Good. Will do.

Thank you.

Twice in one day. Do not make habit.

I smiled and tucked the phone away. My smile faded as I padded back into the living room with a cup of coffee and rejoined Troy. I sat next to him and took his hand. "Before we talk about what you're going to say to Lester, I want to say something first."

He looked at me, his eyes clearly straining to focus. "Yes."

"I want to say that what your parents did was unforgivable. I think almost anyone who hears a description of it will agree with me."

His eyes were heavy, tears welling in them briefly. "But you don't believe in guns."

"No, I don't."

"Weapons for weaklings."

I shook my head. "No one wants to be weak. But some people are made weak by others. What would the world be like if we blamed people for their own powerlessness?"

"Are you saying I was justified?"

There was no right answer to that. My choices were being wrong or being a hypocrite. I dropped my eyes. "I don't think it's right. But I find it completely understandable." I struggled for the sense of clarity that I'd found that evening in the unlikely setting of a steak house bathroom. "I think asking if it's justified is the wrong question."

When I looked back up at him, his awareness had shifted. He was looking inward now, reflecting. "I am weak," he said, his voice stony. "I'm not like you. You would have run away from them. You would have toughed it out with no drops. That's what you do every day. I couldn't even do two weeks."

"I can tough it out because I have for years. And because

I don't know what the alternative feels like. I guess I have my mom's minimum wage to thank for that. In your situation . . . Who knows? I might have become exactly like you."

He stared into the row of books across from him. "I have no idea who I am," he said.

I considered his neatly trimmed hair, his smooth skin. The white shirt, slightly unbuttoned. The costly watch, hanging loosely on his tanned wrist. A physical person, put together by money and care and food and exercise and more money. What was he made of without all that careful cultivation? What was he, but a body? A body I had pressed up against for warmth. A body that had taken the life of two other bodies. The brain beneath the well-shaped skull was an even greater mystery. That place nourished and poisoned and nourished again by liquid chemicals. What would it be like when Troy's drops ran out and the deforested landscape of his mind once again fell silent?

I had no idea, either.

"Hey," I said, squeezing his hand. "Let's figure out what you're going to say to Lester."

He nodded. "Okay."

32

NATALIA

By midnight, Troy had left for a caffeinated drive to Napa. Joey had passed the grenade to Cass and Tabby, who had passed it to June, who had verified the Philbricks' death with the San Francisco Police Department. Then June had contacted lucky Lester, who turned out to be one half of a boutique law firm specializing in family values. He broke the law and proved himself a total fairy godmother twice over by spilling the terms of his client's will.

I don't know what I'd expected. Maybe something like manumission? Instead it was something like a hornet's nest. "Yeah," June was saying on the other end of the line. "So basically half of everything goes to Charles Philbrick, the older son, and half goes to Troy Philbrick, though it remains to be seen whether that goes through if Troy is charged with homicide. And there's a specific codicil that pertains to adoptions and makes Charles the custodian."

"*Charlie?*" I could see him as the head of RealCorp, because his nastiness was all of a piece with theirs, but I couldn't see him as an adoptive father. Even Daddy Philbrick must have known that Charlie and parenting belonged together like marshmallows and hot sauce.

"Yes. But there is an angle, Nat," June said.

"What?"

"In such cases where the custodian of a child dies and a new custodian is designated, the court has some say in the suitability of the new custodian. I mean, Charlie's suitability can be contested. We could try to prove that he is not a suitable. Though I'm not sure how."

I heard a steady drumbeat in my ear, a pulse of certainty, maybe adrenaline. "I can do that," I said. "I can prove he's not suitable."

June paused. "Really? Apart from his just being young?"

"Yes, really."

"Well . . . do you think you could do it in a couple hours? Maybe three, at the most? Whatever we've got I want to put in front of Judge Horn at four a.m."

I thought about it. "I don't know. I'll get back to you."

I hung up with June and didn't bother to explain to Joey as I tapped through *De rerum*, looking for the number Crystal Cleaners had handwritten at the bottom of their invitation to the Philbrick mousetrap. There she was: Ma Ling.

Joey watched me as I dialed and waited. Ma Ling was not Lester Bloom. The first time it went to voicemail, a grouchy message in Mandarin that I hung up on. But the second time she picked up on the fourth ring. "Wei?" she answered groggily. I guess Ma Ling slept daytime and nighttime both.

"Hi, Ma Ling," I said, going for polite tinged with urgent. "This is Natalia Peña. I was in your office a couple days ago when Crystal Cleaners hired me to housekeep for Tanner Philbrick."

There was a pause. "Are you there now?" she asked. She was no longer groggy.

"No, I was there on Saturday. I have a different kind of emergency."

She gave it a beat or two. "What is it?"

I laid the problem out for her. I was murky about the chronology, trying not to shine a bright light on how I'd used Crystal Cleaners as my cover for spying on Philbrick. She didn't seem to much care about that. But she did care about Charlie Philbrick. "That snake has cost me three good cleaners," she announced. "Another six I had to give vacations."

This was good news, at least for me. I told her about my own run-in with charming Charlie and she gave a sly laugh. I could picture her on the other end of the line: sitting in bed with her flowered nightgown, eyes closed, hair like a tumbleweed, chuckling in the dark. It took some convincing, mainly because she was no dummy and could see the liability for Crystal Cleaners. But in the end, the calculations tipped in my favor. By the time we'd hung up I had ten names with phone numbers and addresses.

———

Four didn't answer. Two didn't see the point in talking to a stranger about past grievances. One lived in Daly City. The other three lived in the East Bay and ranged from amenable to zealous. I made tightly spaced appointments in Fruitvale, Alameda, and Pill Hill.

Joey had jogged to June's office downtown and picked up the coupe. By the time I finished my cold calls he was standing on the curb, bouncing the keys. "Ready to go?" he asked me.

I held up a duffel bag that held the supplies for three different contingency plans and a dozen possible outcomes. An explosive plastic decal, a change of clothes for Cal, a microphone, a pen, a file folder with blank paper, our passports, a baton, a tube of lipstick, and a coil of rope. The handgun wasn't in there.

"Ready," I said.

As we got into the coupe, he asked, "Do they all have to fit in this car? Because that might be tough."

I shook my head. "Signed statements."

"Smart," Joey said, pulling away from the curb.

I gave him the address in Fruitvale, and Joey drove alongside the lake in silence. We didn't have much to say. The air outside was cool, redolent with night flowers, deceptive with calm. I watched the minutes go by on my watch. When we reached Fruitvale, Joey said he would stay outside with the coupe and I agreed. I rang the buzzer of the townhouse and a girl in her early twenties opened the door wearing a blue bathrobe.

"Felicity?"

"Yup." She waved me into a narrow hallway and I followed her all the way down past the blank walls to a kitchen lit by a bare bulb. White cabinets, brown linoleum, and a dining table with the surface area of a magazine cover. She motioned to one of the two folding chairs at the miniature table. I sat down across from her. Felicity had bubblegum-pink nails and brown hair with natural corkscrews. Slender nose, dimpled chin, and green eyes. Quite cute. Foul-mouthed and relaxed, like a longshoreman on holiday.

"Here it is," she said, pointing to a handwritten page of yellow lined paper. "I want that fucking bastard to go down."

I glanced at the paper. "This won't do that, you know."

"It's a start. Read it," she ordered. "Let me know if it's okay."

I read. It was energetically colorful, but it was also very detailed and included dates. She had signed at the bottom. "This is great," I said. "Revolting, first and foremost—the guy belongs in jail. But also great. Hey," I added amiably. "You should press charges. Why didn't you then?"

She rolled her eyes. "My ass clown boyfriend at the time didn't want me to. Fuck knows why I listened to him."

"There's a few of us, you know. We'd have a good case."

She sniffed. "Yeah, maybe. Can't really afford a lawyer, you know? My wages barely cover the rent for this palace of shit." She gestured with two pink nails at the kitchen around us.

I smiled. "If you like I can keep you in the loop. We could share costs. No commitment, of course."

"Sure." She gave me a surprisingly sweet smile as she stood up. "I hope you get your brother back."

"Thanks."

We parted ways at the door and Felicity waited while I got in the coupe. She gave me a sisterly wave as we pulled out. Silhouetted in the light of the corridor, all the hardness vanished; she became a soft, girlish figure, ushering me out into the dead of night. I waved back, sticking my hand out the coupe window as we peeled out.

"Next stop, Alameda," I said to Joey. "We're making good time."

———

The house in Alameda was white stucco with an open front porch illuminated by string lights. Ruby was sitting on the porch at a bistro table. "Come on up," she called. On the bistro table was a coffee service with two cups and some sheets of printed paper. "Hi, Nat," Ruby said. "I thought you might want some coffee."

"You're a saint," I said, dropping into the metal chair beside her.

Ruby smiled as she poured me coffee. She was one of those women whose features seem poached from a different era. Her hair was in old-fashioned curlers. She had a smooth brow, a wide mouth, dark brown eyes with layers of unaffected calm. Without even trying, she looked like Billie Holiday at home of an evening.

"Help yourself to cream and sugar," she said, handing me the cup.

I did and drank the coffee scalding hot. She watched me as she took a sip.

"I'm glad you're doing this," she said evenly. "At the time I hadn't the wits or means to do a thing about it. Now I'm on better footing."

"Not cleaning anymore?" I guessed.

She shook her head. "I've got a secretarial job in the city. The pay is better and the work sure is better." She eyed me without judgment. "You still cleaning?"

"I actually clean at the Landmark Hotel. Crystal Cleaners was kind of a one-off. I can't pretend it's good work, but you know what it's like. Hard to find other work when all you've done is scrub toilets."

"I know. It took me seven years to get an admin degree at night school."

I whistled.

Ruby picked up the printed sheets of paper and handed them to me. "My job is at a law firm, so I have some idea what this is supposed to look like."

"Mind if I read it?"

"Please," she said, picking up her coffee cup.

I read through the statement, two typed pages of clinical precision that could not entirely expunge the brutality of their content. "I'm sorry I had to ask you to recall this," I said, putting the pages down.

She lifted a shoulder. "I didn't think I'd felt it. Only later did I realize that you can not feel a thing and still have it leave scars. You know?"

I thought about it. I thought about Mom's hair ruffled by the breeze that came in through the casement window beside her broken head. How many times had I pictured it? Five hundred times? Five thousand? The thoughts built up like grains of sand and now I carried their weight around, day and night. "Yes, I do."

"It's good to have it on real paper. I've learned that much at the firm."

I'd finished my coffee and put the cup down on her tray. "Thanks a million. And for the coffee."

Ruby stood up as I pushed back my chair. "Let me know how it goes, will you?"

"I will."

The last stop in Pill Hill was of a different category. The apartment building was little more than a brown box with cutout windows, and half the buzzers at the entrance were broken. Nicole's wasn't. She came down to the door in sweats and opened the glass door a foot wide.

"Nicole? I'm Nat Peña."

She wasn't interested in pleasantries. "I'm having second thoughts about this," she said, looking past me at the street. She had dirty-blonde hair that hung around her face like seaweed, a face tight with deprivation, shifty eyes.

"Okay," I said. "I don't want to push you. No problem if you don't feel like giving a statement."

"Is he going to read it?"

"Charles Philbrick?"

"Yeah."

"It's possible. But he might not. The first person who's going to read it is a lawyer who represents me, and then she's going to show it to a judge. My guess is that then Charlie's lawyer will read it. But after that, who knows." I shrugged. "He's got a lot on his plate right now, like his father's death and half an inheritance." I left out the part about a homicidal brother.

She continued staring at the street for a few seconds, some unexpressed indecision playing at the edges of her eyes. Then abruptly she reached into the pocket of her sweatshirt and drew out a piece of paper folded in four. "Okay, here it is. I don't remember a lot. I wrote what I could."

"Thank you, Nicole," I said, taking the paper. I held it up. "This is a lifesaver. So thank you, really." She looked me straight in the eye then, and I saw a familiar weariness: the loop of fear and exhaustion, fear and exhaustion, fear and exhaustion.

She nodded at me. "Good luck to you." She shut the glass door and shuffled off in her sweats and slippers toward the elevator.

For a few seconds I watched her go, and I thought about the scars Ruby had talked about. I knew that when I read Nicole's statement, it would recount an event in the not-too-distant past, described dispassionately in broad strokes, with areas of stark precision and areas of stark omission. The wound had been ugly, but possible to ignore; it was the scars that hurt.

33

NATALIA
OCTOBER 15–4:30 A.M.

It was past four in the morning when we left Pill Hill and headed to the address June had given us in Piedmont. In silence, Joey drove up the winding roads, past the dark houses and the blooming gardens. Sprinklers shushed their precious store of water over the grass, camellias, and roses.

The judge's house, a spacious bungalow with peach trim, was all alight. A maid answered the door and led us down a corridor with wisteria-themed wallpaper. She opened the door to the study, a square room lined with bookshelves and filled with pale furniture. A white sofa, two white armchairs, a white desk. The curtains and pillows were dotted with poppies. There were no books on the bookshelves, only curio pieces gathered from every corner of the world. A Chinese vase. A Swiss clock. An African mask.

Cass, Tabby, June, and Gao hovered by the desk around an older lady with bifocals. Judge Horn. Her black hair was a bowl cut that looked lacquered. She wore a velvet dressing gown, and her sharp nails were painted lilac. June had her reading a pile of papers a foot high. "I've seen this before," the judge grumbled, setting it aside. She looked up at me and Joey as we approached the desk.

"Ah. The evidence has just walked in," she said, baring something between a grin and a snarl. "You're Natalia?"

I reached out across the desk to shake her knobby hand. "Natalia Peña, Judge Horn. Thank you for doing this, Your Honor."

"I haven't done anything yet," she said. "It depends on what you've got in that little paw of yours."

Wordlessly, I gave her the file folder with the three statements in it.

Judge Horn slapped it down on the table like an unruly animal and wrestled it open. Then she bent over the pages and murmured to herself as she read. Every now and then, a word emerged clearly from the constant stream. "Gutless . . . prison . . . fine time . . . cheek." She fell abruptly silent as she read Nicole's statement. She held up the rather crumpled piece of paper before her eyes, frowning fiercely. The fingers were bent and bony, but there was not even a whisper of a tremor. She put the paper down and looked at me over the bifocals. "You have met this person? Charles Philbrick?"

"I have, Your Honor."

"And did you have a similar experience?"

"I did. Different outcome, but only by chance."

She tapped a lilac fingernail against the papers and looked me over skeptically. "Something tells me it wasn't chance."

"I am perhaps more inclined to aggression than the usual house cleaner," I conceded. "But with respect, what happened to me is not the point. There are at least seven other women with similar stories who weren't available to give statements on such short notice. I hope even these three demonstrate a pattern."

For a few seconds Judge Horn pondered, frowning at me over the bifocals. Then she slammed the folder shut again with the same air of combative unrest. "Damned right they do." She scrabbled at the pile of papers that June had prepared. "You all understand that I can only challenge custody, I can't alter it."

June nodded. "We understand." She glanced at me, at Cass and Tabby. "Your challenge will still need to be presented in court in San Francisco."

Judge Horn was looking at me. "The judge in San Francisco will decide, ultimately, whether Charles is fit or not."

I'd wanted more, but it would have to do. "I understand," I said.

"Give me a pen so I can start signing and get back to bed."

While June obligingly handed her a pen, the rest of us glanced at one another silently. Cass wasn't counting her chickens yet, but Tabby allowed herself a smile of victory. Gao raised his eyebrows a fraction of an inch to celebrate the moment.

For several minutes the only voice was June's, briefly introducing each document that she placed in front of Judge Horn. June looked tired. The tiny knots of hair close to her skull were as tidy as ever. She wore a suit and heels and light makeup. But I could see by the weight of her shoulders that she'd hardly slept in days. She was exhausted. "Sorry," June said. "Next line." She rubbed her temples briefly.

Tabby put her arm on her friend's shoulder.

"We're almost done," June said, as much to herself as to the judge. "This is the affidavit that Cassandra and Tabitha Lawson have already signed."

"Notarized?" the judge queried.

"Yes, of course."

"Who'd you get to do that? Russell?"

"Polochenko."

The judge cackled. "Ha. Bet he was happy to be dragged out of bed."

"Russell is out of town for a training."

"Hm, she'll be sad she missed this fun."

June lifted her eyebrows and sighed. "There was no better alternative."

"Bring Polo a chocolate crepe tomorrow morning and he'll forget all about it."

"Thanks for the tip, Your Honor."

The judge signed with a flourish and handed the sheet to June. "Is that it?"

"That's it."

Judge Horn pushed her chair back and rose creakily to her feet. She surveyed the room, looking at each of us in turn. Then she came over to me and patted my shoulder. "Good work, Peña."

"Thank you again, Your Honor," I said.

She shook her head. "I'm no magician. You've still got a few hurdles to jump."

"I realize that."

She studied me for a moment longer. "Go on, then," she said. "See what you can do with that piece of paper."

———

Once when Cal was three, I lost him. We were at the library. Mom was upstairs in nonfiction, and Cal and I were downstairs in children's. The librarians had a glass cabinet filled with elephant miniatures, and Cal liked to stand in front of it gazing at their mismatched plenitude. Porcelain elephant with eyebrows. Purple elephant with gold earrings. Goofy elephant with too-small legs. There were easily a couple hundred of them. Cal stared and I sat on the floor near him, reading. Except when I looked up after what I thought was just a minute, he was gone. I stood up, not panicked yet, and looked for him. No Cal. I started to feel a winch of anxiety winding in my stomach. Anxiety and I were on good terms then. A near-constant companion, a hovering friend, a little too persistent. I walked over to the picture book section, calling, "Cal?" No Cal. Then I started getting frantic. I called his name, running down the short aisles and looking at the other kids wildly, not really seeing them because all I could see was *not Cal*, and in this frenzy of calling and running, Mom appeared at the end of the aisle.

"What's going on?"

"Cal is gone," I said, the words bursting out of me, choking me on their way out. I was crying.

"Hm," Mom said thoughtfully. Unfazed, she walked to the

circulation desk. I followed her, tripping over myself. Mom explained to the librarian that a three-year-old was missing, and the librarian made an announcement that crackled over the speakers like a line in an ancient radio play. *Calvino Peña, a three-year-old boy, is missing. If you see an unaccompanied child near you, please bring him to circulation downstairs.* We stood and waited. In those minutes, my mind flung out a web of terrifying futures: police, mysterious phone calls, Cal kidnapped, Cal dead, me weeping inconsolably by the side of a grave. They shuffled and reshuffled, all incoherent and all certain of the doom that lay ahead. I turned to look over my shoulder at the elephant cabinet, wondering if I would forever think of that spot as the last place I'd ever seen him, and there he was. Standing just as he had been, with his nose pressed to the glass. He was only lost for a few minutes, but it had felt like an eternity.

———

Rather than pile like clowns into Cass's car, Joey and I rode with Gao, and June rode with Cass and Tabby. There was no traffic on the bridge. Inside Gao's car, we were mostly silent. I could feel Gao wanting to ask about Philbrick, but he seemed to have decided not to say anything until we knew what was happening with Cal.

I trusted June, and I knew she'd use the legal challenge for all it was worth. But it still seemed like a thousand things could go wrong. I had the nickel-sized decal in my bag, just in case.

34

NATALIA

October 15 – 5:37 a.m.

We left the coupe and the police car in the deserted street and walked through the damp air to the shimmering RealCorp building, all one hundred decals on the windows lighting up the night with their beautiful blonde woman and her eight-second catharsis. On the ground floor, the lobby was bright.

The first thing to go wrong was the reception. Glout wasn't there. Nor were the friendly models. Instead, we found a rugby player in a security uniform staring at the doorway, trying not to move his arms so his muscles wouldn't burst the seams of his sleeves. I told him I was there to see Hugh Glout and he said, by way of nonanswer, "You're expected in the boardroom."

He turned and walked toward the elevators, and we, after exchanging glances, followed. The elevator ride was silent. A minute later we were walking down a wide corridor on the top floor; it seemed more art gallery than pharmaceutical company. I'm pretty sure I recognized a Rothko. And maybe a Lichtenstein. The heavy carpet swallowed up our footsteps. Halfway down, the walls turned to glass.

Opening a door to the left, the rugby player ushered us into a glass-walled sitting room with leather sofas the color of butter. Another security guard with a crooked nose and lidded eyes stood by, protecting the furniture. Beyond the sitting room, behind yet another glass wall, was the boardroom: long, with dark wood and a gorgeous view of San Francisco at night. Twelve men, four women, and three unassuming secretaries sat around the table, reading silently, poised to take notes, or clumped in pairs, conferring. One of the men was Glout.

Only Glout looked up as we reached the sitting room, and he gave me a look I couldn't read. Knotted eyebrows, tight lips. His papery skin was blotchy; his arms rested unnaturally on the table as if he had to hold himself in place. After we'd waited silently for two minutes in the buttery sitting room, a man with peppered hair and a pale blue button-down glanced up at us, spoke to the secretary beside him, and returned to the perusal of documents. The secretary got up from the table and came out to meet us.

As she opened the door, I caught a whiff of the stillness in the boardroom. No conversation. No scribbling or typing. Only tension. And concentration. The secretary wore a silk tie-neck blouse and a pinstripe skirt. She closed the glass door behind her and looked us over, blinking a few times. I couldn't really blame her. Gao the prizefighter, arms crossed; Cass and Tabby, who happened to be both wearing black, so they looked like vengeful mimes; and Joey and I still dressed for a night out at the speakeasy. We did look a little ridiculous. Fortunately we had June, who was perfectly suited to the occasion. She stepped forward, the delegate for the clown crew.

"June Johnson, attorney for Cassandra and Tabitha Lawson. I am here to present the RealCorp board with papers signed by Judge Merle Horn of Alameda County. We are challenging the custodianship of Calvino Peña, whom Judge Horn advises be returned to the Lawsons." She held out a fat stack of papers. "I think you'll find that the materials demonstrating Charles Philbrick's unsuitability as a custodian are incontestable and potentially quite damaging, should it be necessary to rely upon them for proceedings beyond these. We could avoid a more public process in San Francisco if Judge Horn's recommendations were taken now."

The secretary pressed her lips together, polite demurral stopping just short of disdain. "Ms. Johnson, if you would follow me." She looked sideways and over our heads, as if trying to spare her eyeballs any further unpleasantness. "The rest of you may wait here."

June swept into the force field of the boardroom, and the rest of us stood around like jilted teenagers until we drifted, one by one, onto the buttery sofas.

I can't read lips. So I just watched June hand over the papers to the man with the peppered hair. He passed them without a glance to the silk tie-neck. June was still talking, her hand motions polite, explanatory, concise. She tilted her head slightly for a final nod. Old Pepper leaned back in his chair and spoke slowly. Extending a hand in explanation, he gestured to Glout, still sitting rigidly at his end of the table. June glanced at Glout. Her eyes lingered, then shifted back to Old Pepper. He finished what he was saying. June asked a question.

"This isn't going as planned," Gao said. I looked over at him. He was leaning forward, elbows on knees, staring down the boardroom as if burning a hole through the glass.

"What's wrong?" Tabby asked quickly.

"I'm not sure," Gao replied.

"They must want to take it to court," Cass said.

I glanced up at the two security guards, who stood at either side of the glass door that led to the corridor. There was a deliberate looseness to how they stood. Too deliberate.

When I looked back into the boardroom, June was looking down at Old Pepper with her chin lifted. What was that? Defiance? I didn't have a chance to speculate further, because Silk Tie-Neck stood up and gestured to the door. June didn't argue. As she came out into the sitting room, she met my eye, but I didn't understand a thing.

"Miss Natalia Peña?" the secretary asked, holding the door open as she looked at me.

I stood up. "Yes."

"Dr. Hugh Glout would like a word with you."

I followed her, conscious of the silence behind me, of June not speaking and the rest of them waiting. Waiting for the door to close.

It clicked closed behind me. The room smelled of clashing aftershaves and printer ink. Silk Tie-Neck padded around to her seat and sank into her chair. I looked at Glout, who was staring at the dark wood table, an oversized coffin with beveled brass at the edges. I looked at Old Pepper, who was reading something. He put the paper down and raised his eyes, his face expressionless. "Miss Peña, before you leave, Dr. Glout wanted to pass on some of the test results." He glanced at Glout. "I'm not sure why, but that's his prerogative."

"Let's try this again," I said, taking a few steps forward so I was a little too close to the table. A few of the people sitting around it looked up at me. "My name is Natalia Peña. What's yours?"

Old Pepper raised an eyebrow. No supercilious smile, just the eyebrow. "I'm afraid I don't have time for lengthy introductions. We're facing considerable time constraints this morning, Miss Peña."

"Not lengthy. Just a name will do. Unlike you, I don't have the benefit of omniscience."

Before he could answer, Glout cleared his throat noisily and stood up. Now I could see what it was. The blotchy skin, the tight lips. He was nervous. "Nat, this is Ellis Ayles, one of RealCorp's senior board members."

"Thank you," I said, giving Ayles a pointed look. He missed it, because he was already looking down at his fat stack of papers.

Glout cleared his throat again. "Nat, I wanted to tell you a few things about Calvino's test results." He was holding something in his hand. A scrap of gray cloth, something cheap made of jersey, and he kneaded it with his bony fingers. As he spoke, his breathing caught and he swallowed. Glout was not just nervous. He was near panic.

I felt a dim awareness at the far edge of my brain. Gao's warning about plans derailed, June's chin lifted in defiance, Glout's shaking nerves. Something was very wrong. I couldn't see what it was yet. But I felt it, like a high-pitched whine that you suddenly notice, realizing it's been going on now for a while.

"What about Cal's results?" I asked carefully, holding my eyes firm on Glout.

"I wanted you to know that in the last test he did in my lab he scored 1012." His eyes dove down to the table for a moment and his whole face flushed red. "A perfect score."

I wasn't following. He was saying something important but I just didn't understand what it was. "What does that mean? Perfect how?"

Glout took a deep breath. "If he'd had the key," he said, "he couldn't have scored any better."

"Okay," I said. It still meant nothing to me. I glanced at Ayles, who was reading again. No answers there.

"It's a test I designed myself," Glout went on, a little more steadily. "A test that scores empathy. Cal was, you could say, a perfect empath."

Something about the sentence jarred me. For a few seconds, I didn't realize why. Then I realized. Was. Cal *was* a perfect empath. "What do you mean, *was*?"

"Is that all you wanted to tell Miss Peña?" Ayles asked, his attention returning to our conversation.

"Almost." Glout pushed his chair back awkwardly and walked around the table to me. "I just wanted her to have his shirt. The T-shirt he was wearing." He held out the gray jersey and I looked at it dumbly.

"So sentimental, Glout," Ayles commented amiably. "I can't decide if it's endearing or irritating."

"I really couldn't do my job without it, Mr. Ayles," Glout replied. He pressed the T-shirt into my open palms. I took it. My hands were shaking. Glout squeezed them hard. Really hard. "It's shock," he said to me, his voice quiet and level. "Remember, it's just shock. It goes away."

"What happened?" I asked. I couldn't be sure I'd really spoken, but it seems I had because Ayles replied.

"As your lawyer will explain, there was an accident after the transfer out of Glout's lab. Something about the new space must have triggered him."

I looked at Glout, whose brow was knotted. "I don't understand," I said. "Triggered him?"

Ayles prattled on. "His records indicate that suicide runs in the family. Actually it's not that uncommon, in children who feel too much. As Glout can tell you, it's a liability." Ayles's tanned face and white teeth formed the words so they sounded pedestrian. "Your lawyer has the details." He looked at me a moment longer, as if to ensure the receipt of his dismissal, and then he turned back to the work before him.

"No," I said. "Cal wouldn't do that. Cal would never do that."

Ayles didn't answer. He'd moved on. Glout was still standing in front of me, and he may have said something more, but I didn't hear it. The high-pitched whine in the distance had grown louder, and now it filled my brain. I looked at Glout's face, which came close to mine for a moment as he pressed my hand again. Then I found myself walking through the glass door into the sitting room. Someone closed the door behind me.

The room was empty of everyone but the rugby player, who opened the door to the corridor. He was opening it for me—he must have been, because there was no one else in the room. I looked around dumbly for a few seconds before walking across the carpet, past the yellow sofa I'd been sitting on a few minutes earlier, back when the world was different. He followed me out into the corridor and then took a couple long paces to walk ahead. My footsteps disappeared into the carpeted hallway, as if I were invisible. A ghost haunting the corridors, leaving no trace. I didn't speak.

He pressed the button for the elevator and we waited. The whine in my head persisted. There was nothing else in there. No thoughts, no nothing. Just the whine. A noise broke the whine abruptly—the ding of the elevator—and as we stepped into the cold metal box, something shifted. I could trace the whining sound to its faraway origin: a fast, impossibly fast whirring; a churning mechanism that flew through one image after another, imagined and discarded, imagined and discarded again. I closed my eyes. My mind rapidly conjectured, destroying the conjecture a moment afterward and making another. His slim form, hanging from a rope; strapped to a gurney; recoiling from an electric current; running desperately through hallways; shattering a window, jumping through the jagged opening, landing broken on the pavement. Illogically, nonsensically, I saw him lying on the floor of the Oakland apartment, skull destroyed, gun lying by, just like Mom. *What* had happened?

I needed to see him. No matter what it looked like, I needed to see Cal. Opening my eyes, I realized that we were still in the elevator; we had hardly moved. My eyes drifted to the gray jersey shirt. I was holding it so tightly my knuckles had turned white. Without thinking, I loosened my grip and unfolded the shirt. It was a child's T-shirt. Across the front, in unapologetic crimson, it read STANFORD.

This was not Cal's T-shirt.

Suddenly the whining in my head stopped. I could hear the whirring of the elevator. I could hear my own breathing. I felt my blood pumping, a rhythmic pulse that felt as urgent as a ticking clock. The rugby player beside me was silent and motionless. Glancing his way, I observed that he was a good six inches taller than me and had nicked himself shaving that morning. The elevator was still dropping slowly, as it had been seemingly for the last half hour.

It was impossible that Cal was dead. This wasn't a thought. It was an instinct. He could not be dead because he didn't *feel* dead. I would know.

I would know.

I was still holding the Stanford T-shirt and staring at it like a dummy. The rugby player followed my eyes discreetly. We both examined the shirt. "I think it's a little small for me, don't you?" I said.

He shrugged noncommittally. "Maybe."

"But it might fit you," I said brightly.

He looked at me. I smiled. A moment too late, he saw what I was going to do. I lifted the shirt over his head and yanked down, the little collar catching on the crown of his head. His arms, halfway to his gun, reached up instinctively. I kneed him in the gut and as he doubled over, I tied the shirt around his neck like a plastic bag. My foot kicked out and hit the elevator panel. The rugby player wrestled with his face mask as the elevator stopped and the doors opened. He reached for his gun. I kicked him, hard, toward the open doors, and as he fell backward, he pointed, looking like a clumsy bank robber. The shots went off into the closing doors.

I was lucky. We still hadn't hit the twelfth floor. I reached into my bag as the elevator floated down two more floors and took out *De rerum*. Joey had sent me twenty-six messages. I replied without reading them: *Need that distraction now.*

The doors opened on twelve.

No one was there to meet me. Yet. I remembered the way to Glout's office just fine, and now I ran, following the maze of corridors to the office with old-school equipment.

I burst in, chest heaving, and looked around. Glout had clearly said "the last test he did *in my lab*." There had to be something in the office that told me the location of the lab.

Maybe the lab was next door. I went back out to the corridor and tried the other three doors I could see. Locked.

Back to the office. I seized on the spiral-bound notebook

Glout had left on the desk. Spidery blue writing that was hard to read. Shorthand. I couldn't read shorthand. I flipped through it, shaking my head at the illegible writing. It had nothing for me.

I gave up on the notebook and looked around the room for another clue. Seven screen decals. An old filing cabinet. The old-timey keyboard with beige wires. The old-timey monitor in the wall. Two office chairs. No doors, no whiteboards with convenient directions to the lab, no keys dangling from a peg.

Thirty feet away, the elevator dinged. I heard boots on the hard floor of the hallways.

I reached into my bag for my lipstick.

35

NATALIA
October 15 — 6:12 a.m.

A few seconds later, the boots arrived. They belonged to the rugby player. He stood in the doorway, gun drawn, and looked me over.

I held my lipstick inside my closed left fist. With my right hand, I snapped the baton open. The rugby player glanced at it. Then he smiled and put his gun down on the file cabinet that stood beside the door. As he took off his jacket, he drew a butterfly knife from the pocket. One hand opened the knife, making it twirl kaleidoscopically over his knuckles. The other hand loosened the knot of his cheap tie and unbuttoned the top button of his shirt.

"I'd love to do this in birthday suits," I said to him, "but I'm wearing a corset and unlacing it takes forever."

He didn't say anything. The knife danced silver cartwheels across his hands. Then I saw what he wanted me to see. In the gully of his neck, below the Adam's apple: a one-inch tattoo of a catfish.

Great. Just great.

The knife stopped abruptly, now closed and clenched

in his fist. He dove toward me like an Olympic swimmer, arms outstretched, and caught me around the waist. Good thing I'd perfected those backward falls on the Oakland PD gym mat. I fell back against the floor, my head missing the metal desk behind me. The knife hung in the air over my face. His fist came down, bringing the knife with it, and I jerked right. It missed my neck but pinned my collar to the carpet. I hissed.

Before he could pull the knife free, I brought my right arm up and slammed the base of the baton into the soft spot below his shoulder blade. He groaned, crunched, but didn't let go. My left arm was stuck. I brought the baton down again on the back of his neck at the top of his spine. He grunted, recoiled just enough for me to free my right leg and kick over the chair beside us, which landed on his backside, accomplishing nothing.

He curled himself up, pressing me down onto the floor, crushing my chest with his left hand. The knife was free again, skipping across the knuckles of his right hand. He kneeled on my groin and let his weight drop. Hard. I grunted, feeling like a squashed bug. The knife stopped again. He held it like a letter opener, blade beneath his thumb, and brought it toward my neck. I swung my right hand with the baton toward him and he caught it with his left hand, grinning.

I grinned back. My left arm was free and I had the tube of lipstick on his gut. I zapped.

The rugby player collapsed onto me, all two hundred–odd pounds, hitting his head on the floor past my right shoulder.

I gasped, tried to push him off. He was harder to fight unconscious than conscious. Finally I got out from under him, tearing my hose in the process. "Nuts," I said.

For a minute I stood there in Glout's half-destroyed office. We'd managed to pull down a desk and a few of the screen decals, which lay facedown like fallen kites. I let my eyes travel back to the open door. Somewhere in the building, many floors away, an alarm was ringing. I had to hope that was Joey's distraction.

I took a deep breath and tried to think. Glout had given me a T-shirt that wasn't Cal's. He knew it wasn't Cal's. He knew I knew it wasn't Cal's. He had gone to all the trouble of making up some baloney sandwich about a shirt in order to tell me something. What was he trying to tell me? I thought about Glout's face, nervous and splotchy, his eyes diving down to the table. His face had flushed bright red when he'd told me Cal's score.

Cal's score. Now I remembered what he'd said. I was an idiot. He'd said that Cal's score couldn't have been more perfect if he'd had a key.

For a moment I couldn't breathe, thinking I wouldn't be able to remember the test score. And then I had it.

The rugby player groaned, shifted. "Lo siento, little catfish," I murmured. "You'll feel better by Friday." On the way out of the room, I grabbed his gun. I ran down the corridor toward the stairs. I tossed the gun into an open office, lights off, to my left. The distant alarm was still ringing, but the commotion sounded closer. When I opened the door to the stairwell I could hear the echoes of voices, hard-edged, rapid but calm. My feet flitted down the steps to the tenth floor and I threw the door open.

1012. I was looking for room 1012.

I found it.

And along with it I found two security guards who made the rugby player look like junior varsity. They eyed me as I slowed my steps, still twenty feet down the corridor. I put my lipstick away and rested my hand against the wall for a minute, catching my breath. Then I resumed my slow walk toward 1012. When I was ten feet away I stopped.

"Hey," I said to the guards.

One of them turned his head slightly to the right, listening to something through an earpiece. This one had a blond crew cut and a neck wider than his head. Green crocodile eyes. A Frankenstein scar with needle points on his left temple. A tiny gold stud in his right ear. The other one was all shoulders with a long, horsey face. Heavy eyebrows. Black hair in a topknot. It was clear to me that either one of them could easily fold me up like a napkin and tuck me away in a back pocket.

That meant I had to talk to them.

"How are you guys doing?"

They stared at me.

"Could I see what's in that room?" Always worth a try to ask politely.

Topknot turned his head slightly, receiving some communication, and nodded in reply for the benefit of the ubiquitous cameras. He took a step toward me, the massive shoulders lurching into motion.

I took a step back. I wasn't ready for this yet. "My brother's in there," I said, pointing to the room behind them. "And I know you're going to be shocked to hear this, but the lovely board members of RealCorp lied and told me he was dead."

Topknot scowled, swiped an arm out ineffectually as I took another step back. The crocodile watched impassively.

"Can you believe they would do that? Maybe you can. Maybe they do that all the time. Lie. I mean, it would be ironic. RealCorp, faking a death. Get it? *Real* corp, *fake* death?" I chuckled, taking another step backward. "I guess that's not so different from how things usually are. Fake, I mean. Maybe the board members just have a really quirky sense of humor. But hey, look on the bright side. This is your chance to do the right thing." I gave them a winning smile.

Now the crocodile took a step forward as well, which took him a few paces away from the door. That was good, but not good enough.

"Are you guys actually unable to talk, or are you just not supposed to?" Topknot took two decisive steps forward. The crocodile followed suit. I tripped backward a few more feet, pushing myself up against the wall and away from the door of 1012, but the timing was starting to nag at me. I had only about eight seconds, and I'd run out of witty monologue.

So I did the weirdest thing I could think of. I started laughing hysterically. I kept walking backward against the wall. Topknot and the crocodile frowned at the unhinged lady with the baton and moved forward.

I stopped, my loopy laugh slowing down like a top. I let

them get close. Then I rocketed forward, off the opposite wall like a billiard ball, and down toward 1012. The nickel-sized decal I'd stuck to the wall when I was catching my breath blew up, shattering the side of the corridor. I reached the door of 1012 and as I did, I heard the stairwell door open. *Nuts.* I didn't mean to stop but I looked up anyway. The guards were recovering, the one sitting against the wall, the other already standing. In the open doorway to the stairwell was Gao. Behind him, uniformed officers.

I let out a breath. Gao raised his hand and tipped it forward, urging me onward.

I nodded. I pressed on the door handle of 1012.

It was unlocked.

———

Beyond the door was a corridor, dimly lit, with no windows. There were five doors on each side, all of them closed. I reached for the closest door.

The lock clicked, releasing. As the door swung open, lights flickered on over my head: bright, fluorescent. The room was a windowless cell. No doorknob on the inside. Cement walls, no carpet. Desk with a screen decal, chair, toilet, sink, narrow bed. In the twin bed a figure raised an arm to block the bright light. She had brown hair and a pinched face, and her squinting eyes already spoke of fear.

"Hey," I said quietly.

The girl swallowed; surprise, then hope, suddenly dawned in her eyes. "Are you here to get me out?"

There was only one right answer to that. "Yes," I said.

She started scrambling out of bed, slipping thin feet into socks, as I turned back to the corridor. I reached for the door across from hers. Identical room in mirror opposite. Slender boy, sitting up in bed, hugging his knees. He was staring at me wide-eyed, taking in the sight of the girl behind me. "Come on out of there," I said to him.

I opened one door after another. It was the same with all ten rooms. Ten little cells. Ten little children. They stood around me, silent and waiting, adjusting to the unexpected, glancing up at me in acquiescent anticipation. None of them was Cal.

Was this what Glout had wanted me to find? Could it really be that his message with the test score and the tee meant nothing about Calvino at all? Was he saying, "It's too late for Cal but it's not too late for these kids"?

Maybe so. Probably so.

But the feeling I'd had in the elevator still hung around my shoulders, a nagging sense that if I turned around fast enough, Cal would be there, looking back at me. I had to believe that feeling. Just because he wasn't behind door 1012 didn't mean he wasn't somewhere else.

The pack of sleepy children followed me out to the corridor, where Gao was standing with his hands on his hips while medics treated Topknot and the crocodile. "Hey, Gao," I called.

He turned to look at me and stood still for a moment, taking in the sight. Then he tapped the medic closest to him and they came down the corridor toward me.

"They were in locked rooms," I said.

Gao eyed them as the medic went to work, crouched down, talking to the children in a gentle voice. "We'll check every room," he said to me, "but it'll take a while."

"I have one more idea," I said to him.

He shook his head. "You can't wander off. The building isn't secure."

Which meant I might encounter more crocodiles. "I can't wait."

He pondered for a moment. "Fine. I'll come with you."

He left another uniform in charge of the floor and followed me back up two flights of stairs to twelve. He didn't ask me where we were going.

As we climbed stairs, I started to hear the high-pitched whine again; muted and distant, like a tornado siren. It screamed something unintelligible about time passing, about catastrophes looming, about lost chances.

I led the way to Glout's office. The rugby player was gone, but the room was still a mess. We looked around. "What's your idea?" Gao asked.

"Glout has a lab, his own lab, but I can't figure out where it is. He said to me on the phone once that Cal *looked* fine. He had to be watching him."

Gao nodded. "On a screen. Makes sense." He stooped to pick up one of the fallen screen decals, placing it on the desk.

I walked past him toward the old-timey monitor embedded in the wall. "Maybe not a screen but a window."

Gao joined me. We looked around the whole frame for a power button. Nothing. In the middle of the wall, thirty inches left of the monitor, was a light switch. I tried it.

"Oh," Gao said.

Beyond the monitor frame, a room had been dimly illuminated. It was better-looking than the cells two floors down. Larger, more bedroom and less dungeon. In the yellow glow of a nightlight, we saw a little bookshelf, a round carpet, a wooden desk, a twin bed. On the bed was a bundle of blankets that could have been just a bundle of blankets. Or it could have been a boy.

The room had an open door to the right that probably led to a bathroom and a closed door on the far side, straight ahead of us.

"It's off a corridor parallel to this one," Gao said.

We walked quickly out of the room, left down the hallway, left again and again. The third door had no number and was standing ajar. It opened onto a narrow corridor. At the other end was a door with no handle. I felt it unlock as I pushed.

The little bedroom seemed dark, coming from the hallway. The window I had looked through was a one-way mirror, reflecting my shadowy shape and the doorway's rectangle of light. I stepped forward, letting my eyes adjust, until I stood over the little bed, staring down at the knotted bundle of blankets.

A dark head of hair. An impish nose. The eyes of the old soul closed. Almost motionless, but for the near-imperceptible rise and fall of his breathing. Calvino. Alive and sleeping peacefully.

The pillow was pushed to the side and his head rested on his hand. I reached out to touch his face. He twitched a little. "Cal," I said quietly. "Cal?"

He squirmed, pressing his face downward.

"Cal," I said. "I'm here to take you home."

His eyes fluttered open. For a moment he was too groggy to understand, and then his eyes flung open. "Nat!" he said. He threw his arms around my neck. "Nat," he said again, squeezing harder.

"I'm here, Cal. I'm here." As I held tight to the bundle of pajamas and ribs and tousled hair, I felt something strange. It seemed as though something was expanding in my chest, taking up all the room so that I couldn't breathe. Any moment now I would burst into pieces. But at the same time, I had the sense that I'd been falling down a long, long tunnel into darkness, and now I'd landed on something soft, and steady, and sure. My face hurt.

Cal pulled back and stared at me, his eyes wide. "Nat, you're crying," he said. He was only surprised for a second. Then, with the ease he always has for ignoring the unimportant things, he smiled. He leaned forward and kissed my eyebrows, first one, then the other. "Don't cry, Nat. We're together now."

36

NATALIA
October 15–17

Joey told me afterward that he and Tabby had put their marvelous acting to work, staging a screaming match in the lobby while Gao called the SFPD. I didn't have any regrets, not really, but I would have paid good money to see that show.

I assumed the blown-up wall would be a problem, but lucky for me RealCorp had bigger problems. The police took a dim view of Ayles's little parlor game, especially in light of the fact that he'd played it before. There were seventeen "adoptees" at RealCorp that night, and the game wasn't new. The Bay Area has never been short on orphans. I could tell from the way Gao described it that the investigation would take a while.

I didn't go back to work right away. I figured if they were going to forgive me at all, they would forgive me two days more. On Monday, Cal slept until lunchtime and I sat in the armchair next to his bed, watching him. Once he woke up he wanted to tell me, in as much detail as he could remember, everything that had happened to him from the minute Dr.

Baylor took him out of class to the moment I woke him up at RealCorp. He talked and I listened all the way to dinnertime, when Tabby, Cass, and Joey joined us. Tabby made pizza. Cal was so giddy he hardly ate, and it felt like a celebration, even though I still had this tightness in the back of my head that told me it wasn't a celebration, it was a reprieve.

On Tuesday, Cass loaned me the car, and Cal and I drove to Point Reyes. We hadn't been there together since Mom died. It was one of the glorious days of October with shining waves and cloudless skies. The tall grass rustled in the wind, obscuring the sound of the ocean, so when we arrived at the sandy beach, the sea took us by surprise. Cal ran along the cool sand back and forth, never farther than twenty feet from where I sat, as if bound to me by an invisible tether. When he finally dropped down next to me, he was pink-cheeked and breathless. I waited for a while and then I told him about Mordecai's Hill, and how I'd gone there looking for his father, Dylan Hoffman. I told him the truth about all of it, I just left out some of the details that would give him nightmares. "He really wanted to be a part of your life," I said, looking down at where he lay in the sand, his eyes wide and solemn.

"Why hadn't he before?"

"I don't know for sure. It seems like while Mom was alive she didn't want him around, and then once she was gone . . . Well, it was probably hard to jump in like that. Would you have wanted him to show up on the doorstep right when Mom died?"

He shook his head slowly. After a while, he asked, "What was he like?"

"He was pretty likable. He was earnest. Most people care about nothing, but things really mattered to him, you could tell. And when he realized all his Puritans were in danger, he wanted to be there with them. Not a lot of people would."

"So he was brave. Like you," Cal said.

"It's easy to throw your fists around when you're not afraid of anything. Sometimes it's too easy—sometimes it's just stupid. But Dylan made an intentional decision that he knew would probably result in his death. A choice. It's different—you know?"

Cal sat up and nodded, very serious. "Do you think he did the right thing? Is that what you would do?" He swallowed. "I mean, do you think it's right to give up your life like that?"

He had never asked it that way before. I pushed my feet deeper into the sand and looked out at the waves, so seductive in their timelessness. A view unchanged for hundreds of years. One could easily imagine slipping through the ligatures that kept us in place, turning back to the mainland and finding that we'd traveled to another time.

I didn't want the burden of offering a verdict on Hoffman—or a verdict on Mom's suicide, which was really at the bottom of Cal's question. But the burden was mine. This was Cal, with all his anxieties and his never-ending pain from the past and his justified fears about the future. And things looked different to me now. I still couldn't see the path Mom had taken, but I did understand that she had followed her instincts there, and I understood that instincts cannot be ignored. "That's hard to answer, Cal. To be honest, I can think of situations in which I would give up my own life.

And once you can think of one situation, it's hard to judge someone else for choosing another." I looked at him. "What do you think?"

He dropped his head slowly against my shoulder. "I think I would never do that as long as you were alive. But otherwise I could think of situations in which it would make sense. Even though I would be too afraid to do it probably."

I put my arm around him. "Yeah. Good answer."

———

On the way home I called my supervisor at the Landmark, Elsa Muir, to beg for my job. She was mostly silent as I explained, minus the key details of who and why, that my brother had been abducted, and then she surprised me by saying I was the third-best cleaner on her staff and that she would count the days I'd been gone as short-term disability. I overcame my surprise and thanked her. Someone else had whispered in her ear, I suspected, but I couldn't tell who—maybe Gao. Whoever it was, I owed them.

I showed up to work on Wednesday on time and with Cal in tow. We hadn't really thought through the arrangement, but we both knew that he couldn't go back to school and neither one of us wanted the other one out of sight. I knew it wasn't sustainable. I just decided to postpone the problem. Marta gave Cal a massive hug and then set him to work sorting all the toiletries on my cart and hers. I vacuumed. I made beds. I put hair dryers away and scrubbed toilets. I glanced up at Cal at least once every minute, as if he would vanish if I looked away for too long.

Close to lunchtime, Elsa called me to say that there was someone in the atrium who knew me and wanted to invite me to lunch. I stared at *De rerum*, trying to decide if this was the moment when I had to bundle Cal into a stolen getaway car. "Who is it?"

"Madeleine Porter." When I was silent, she added, "It's the third time she's come asking for you. An older woman. Looks very respectable."

I searched my memory, but nothing came to mind. "Okay, thanks." I did a quick search for her on *De rerum* but found nothing—or, rather, a tennis player and a news anchor, but neither was familiar.

"Cal, we're going to the atrium to meet someone for lunch."

His head popped up from behind the cleaning cart. He was reading on the job again. "Who?"

"Someone named Madeleine Porter. I don't know her— does her name ring a bell?"

He shook his head.

"Okay, well. We'll go, and if it turns out to be someone we don't want to have lunch with, we'll just leave."

He looked concerned. "Do we have a way out?"

I smiled. "We always have a way out."

Cal nodded, believing me. He tucked his book into his backpack as I parked my cleaning cart, and then we made our way downstairs into the atrium. We stood there at the edge of the glittering crowd, me with my maid's uniform and my overprotectiveness, and Cal with his oversized backpack and wide-eyed wariness, looking for all the world like two desperate orphans on the lam.

I saw a hand waving at me. She sat a few tables to my right—a woman on the far side of seventy, with very neat, short hair and a periwinkle cardigan. It was the tough old bird from the subway. She smiled.

"It's okay," I said to Cal.

He nodded, relieved, and followed me to her table. She stood up as we approached and put out her hand. "Natalia, I'm Madeleine Porter," she said, shaking my hand. "Please excuse what might seem like an impertinence—I mean in tracking you down to your workplace. Do you mind?"

I liked the way she said it, genuinely asking if I would excuse it rather than assuming I would. "Not at all. I'm glad to see you're well. This is my brother, Cal."

Cal put out his hand. "Calvino Peña," he said.

Madeleine shook it. "Very good to meet you. Would you both like to join me for lunch?"

I accepted. Cal put his giant backpack down and I ignored the outraged glances I was getting for sitting at an atrium table in a maid's uniform. Madeleine ignored them, too. After we ordered, she treated Cal to an Alexandre Dumas version of our subway debacle, casting me as a swashbuckling heroine and herself as a damsel in distress. I resisted the impulse to correct her because Cal was mesmerized. Then, thanks to Cal's book of maps, we got on the subject of travel, and the two of them had an animated conversation about India, Peru, Ireland, and British Columbia, all of which Madeleine had been to. She'd been a teacher for decades, which went a long way toward explaining her easy rapport with Cal, and after retiring she'd dedicated herself entirely to "indulging helpless wanderlust," as she put it. Cal swooned at this phrase with all the reverence of a novitiate. By the time we got to dessert, he had made a new friend and was looking more himself than I'd seen him since Monday.

"Well," Madeleine said, sipping her coffee with a satisfied air. She glanced at Cal, who had been momentarily silenced by a towering ice cream sundae. "I have an ulterior motive for inviting you to lunch, and I hope you'll bear with me as I explain." This was directed to me, and I nodded. "After your kindness to me last week, I did my best to find you." She smiled. "It took a little effort, but my request with the transit police apparently made its way eventually to an Officer Edward Gao of the Oakland police."

"Yes," I said. "Gao was my trainer in high school."

"Gao called me in order to understand why I wanted to locate you, and when I explained, he told me a little more about your situation. He warned me that you would be very displeased at our meddling, but between us we thought of a proposal."

I didn't say anything. I flipped through a dozen speculative possibilities, coming up with nothing, and watched Madeleine's bright eyes dancing with anticipation. "Officer Gao explained to me, and I quite agreed, that Calvino would not do well in a traditional high school. Those programs are designed entirely for waned adolescents, and are not suitable for young people such as Calvino."

She said it like he was a member of a privileged group, rather than a freakish rarity, and I could see Cal's shoulders lifting with a sense of importance as she spoke. "I first became a teacher when I was twenty-two years old. And that was many, many years ago. Before waning was consistent. Before high school became a place where police officers taught teenagers to defend themselves and the rules that make society function. Before they stopped teaching poetry." She smiled. "So I know what it means to teach adolescents who have all of Calvino's remarkable capabilities." She glanced at Cal but put the proposal to me. "It would be a great privilege to be a part of Cal's education. If both of you are amenable to it."

I looked at Cal and saw the pleading in his eyes. I swallowed. "I think we are both amenable. But perhaps not well financed—"

"No," she said, cutting me off. "I'm sorry, I should have clarified. I mean that it would be my privilege to tutor Calvino without remuneration. Or, more accurately put, still being alive, thanks to you, is remuneration enough."

37

NATALIA

I decided to talk it over with Gao that evening at our training session. After skipping on Monday, I had received a terse message on Tuesday that said *No more days off*, and I decided it would be a good idea to stay on Gao's good side. Cal and I showed up at 8:30 p.m. and Gao pointed Cal to a leather armchair near the boxing ring where I'd seen an overweight retired cop who everyone called Daisy parking himself during the day. "You can read over there," he said.

Cal threw his arms around Gao's waist and said, "Thank you for helping my sister even when she refuses help. And thank you for finding me a teacher. We love you." Then he curled up in Daisy's chair and pulled out his book.

Gao was momentarily speechless. Then he said, "Isn't he a little young to be reading Edith Wharton?"

I shrugged. "He's precocious."

He considered it for a moment longer. "All right." He turned and pointed to the mats where I had been pummeled to pieces the week before. "Let's do some planking."

Resigning myself to my fate, I took my water out and padded over to the mats.

"One minute hold, ten toe taps, then repeat," he said.

I stifled a groan and got facedown on the floor. Gao sat down in a folding chair. As I propped myself up on my elbows and toes, I asked him, "What do you think of Madeleine Porter? Honestly."

"I checked her out. She is exactly what she says she is. Won several teaching awards before high schools were transferred to the academies. I'd take her up on it. Cal has no place in a regular program."

The one-minute timer beeped. I started my toe taps. "I guess it's the best offer on the table. Cal already loves her."

"I thought he would." He watched my toe taps critically. "What did you think of her?"

"She's wealthy enough to eat at the Landmark and pay for synaffs. Those are two strikes against her."

Gao pulled his mouth into a grimace. "That's your prejudice talking. Sounded to me like she was taking a very moderate dose, just enough to enjoy her old age. Besides, it will make her a better teacher for Cal."

I was still toe tapping. "If I'd met her before high school," I breathed, "I probably would have loved her, too."

Gao nodded. "Yeah." Ten seconds into the third plank he changed the subject. "We made an arrest today in the Philbrick homicides. SFPD, not Oakland. The younger son, Troy Philbrick, had been at the family vineyard in Napa. He drove down and made a confession."

I didn't say anything. I waited the minute out and started the toe taps. "Okay," I said.

"He explained that he killed his parents for messing with his dosages. I haven't questioned him, because he'll be processed in SF, but I suspect the GPS on his phone will be used as evidence. Depends on how his defense handles the case, of course."

I thought about this while I moved on to the fourth minute-long plank. "He was at my house for several hours," I said, my voice strained.

"Yes," Gao replied. "I figured. So, we'll see how he pleads."

"Why wasn't I brought in for questioning?"

"There was footage of you on BART leaving well before the Philbricks were shot. Whereas the bridge cameras show Troy leaving San Francisco just afterward."

I dropped to the mat and turned on my side to face him. "You have to understand, I wouldn't testify against him in court. If he asked me to, I'd lie." I was panting. It made me sound desperate when I wasn't.

Gao's eyes narrowed and looked dangerous. "Whatever happened between you, that kind of sentiment is out of your price range, Nat."

"It's not sentiment. It's reason. Cal is sitting over there in Daisy's recliner because of what Troy did."

"Because of what *you* did. It was you who collected the statements that persuaded Judge Horn. It was you who found Cal after the board said he was dead."

"I wouldn't have had the chance to do either of those things if Troy hadn't shot his father."

"That's giving him too much credit."

I was still panting like a cornered rabbit. I took a few deep breaths. "Too much credit? Officer Gao. Let me tell you how I see it. I set out to find two white guys: Philbrick and Hoffman. The bad guy and the good guy. Well, kind of good guy. And both of them end up riddled with bullet holes. Not by me, but *because* of me. Is that the kind of credit you're talking about?"

Gao looked at me intently. "No. I'm not talking about a domino effect. I'm talking about choice."

"And what I'm talking about is how choice becomes meaningless. Explain to me why choice matters when a well-placed bullet can make all my choices irrelevant. Like, completely irrelevant. What's a choice? A decision to do something because of the intended outcome. But if you're robbed of the outcome, it's not a choice, it's just an action. One action in a chain of actions redirected to someone else's purpose. It can end in anything. It can end in Hoffman and a dozen other people dead." I wasn't shouting at him, but I had gotten a little loud. Cal was staring at me over the top of his book.

Gao thought about it for a moment. "Do you want to hear my grandmother's story about the two emperors?"

I raised my eyebrows. "You had a grandmother?"

"Yeah. Many of us have two."

"That you *knew*," I clarified.

"My grandmother raised me."

An interesting morsel of background on Gao. "Sure, tell me the story."

"Okay." Gao sat back and put his hands on his knees. "Once there were two emperors in neighboring kingdoms. The emperor of the southern kingdom was benevolent, and the emperor of the northern kingdom was cruel. On the border of their kingdoms lived Monkey, an immortal who had lived there long before the kingdoms ever existed. No matter what the two emperors did, Monkey bestowed upon them the same good fortune. The southern emperor fed and protected his people; he upheld the laws; he gave from the royal treasury when families faced hard times. The northern emperor exploited his people; he killed and imprisoned those who opposed him; he grew rich at the expense of his subjects. Monkey gave the people of both kingdoms plentiful harvests, favorable weather, and long lives.

"After many years, Monkey grew tired of dispensing good fortune. He destroyed both kingdoms with an earthquake, and he exiled the two emperors to a mountaintop. There, the two emperors shared their stories with each other. The northern emperor laughed and laughed when he heard about his neighbor's generosity. 'All your good deeds, and look how fate rewards you,' he said, still laughing. 'You must feel very foolish indeed.' The southern emperor smiled. 'Not at all. I am happy that after all these years, I can still call myself an emperor.' The northern emperor was baffled. 'So am I.' 'Begging your pardon,' said the southern emperor, 'but from what you tell me, you are a murderer, an extortionist, and a thief who happens to rule a kingdom. It isn't the same thing.'"

I waited, but that was the ending. "I think you just made that up," I said.

"Nope. Although my grandmother did tell it with more beheadings."

"So the moral of the story is that we shouldn't worry about our choices because the feckless gods are going to ruin us all anyway." I grinned at him. "That's helpful."

"You're thinking about choice the wrong way. You can never choose the consequences of your actions. You can only choose the action."

"I get it, Officer Gao. You are how you act."

"People do good things all the time that end in nothing. Or that end badly. That would be a stupid reason to stop doing good things."

I sighed. "I guess that makes sense."

Gao was motionless. "Okay. Good." He leaned forward. "You're not done with your planks."

———

Starting the following Monday, Cal took the train into San Francisco with me and then caught a bus up to Noe Valley, where Madeleine Porter resuscitated her antique lesson plans to teach him literature and history. Then she made a call to an old friend who had taught biology with her back in the day, and then *she* called a math teacher. There were musicians and chemists. Sculptors and physicists. It seemed to me that Cal was accruing a lot of educational debt, until I visited Madeleine's house in early December and I realized it was the other way around.

When I arrived at the door I could hear laughter and conversation, a little party under way. Madeleine opened the door with the traces of laughter still around her eyes. "Come in, come in!" She ushered me into the bungalow, as tidy and elegant as she was, with its Deco-era furniture and walls covered with photographs of the places she'd been. Nine white-haired teachers and one jubilant eleven-year-old were milling around the dining room, drinking tea and lemonade and waiting for me so the cake could be cut.

"Nat," Cal said, seizing my hand. "Come meet Frederick!" He introduced me to a stooped old man who shook my hand gravely and said he had rediscovered geometry puzzles thanks to Cal. Then I met Celia the pianist, who said she was once again playing Chopin thanks to Cal. And Beatriz the botanist, who had returned to her abandoned manuscript about ferns thanks to Cal. You get the idea. They were like the nine muses, with inspiration in reverse.

Madeleine called everyone to attention, tapping a fork on a glass of lemonade. We fell into silence, and she made her toast. "We are here to celebrate the eleventh birthday of our extraordinary friend and beloved student, Calvino Peña. Cal," she said, lifting her lemonade glass toward him, "working with you these last few weeks has changed my life—has changed our lives," she amended, to murmurs of agreement.

"We want to thank you for making us young again in spirit, with your boundless enthusiasm, your deep curiosity, your wonderful ability to see the world and feel the world as it really is. And we want to celebrate with you these eleven years, wishing you joy and health and many happy returns." They cheered, and Cal had tears in his eyes, and then they sang for him and watched him blow out the candles.

As they cut the cake and chatted contentedly about the things that filled their days together, I sat in the window seat with my cup of tea and admired what my brother had managed to do—bring together old friends, bring new purpose to their lives, bring hope to a pursuit they had considered lost. He made it look easy. Cal was happy.

38

NATALIA

November 14

I was not asked to testify at Troy's trial. But the proceedings were open to the public, and I went to the courthouse on the day he was scheduled to give evidence. I wore a black dress and a pillbox hat with a short veil, thinking it would be better if he didn't recognize me.

There were more people than I expected at the courthouse. Most of them seemed to be reporters, which I guess wasn't too surprising. All I could see of Troy at the start were his shoulders and the back of his head. His defense attorney was not Lester Bloom, master of wills, trusts, and subterfuge, but rather one Gordon Selvedge, a tall stork of a man with graying hair, sharp eyes, and a disdain for modern technology. He wrote all his notes longhand and used a pocket watch. I was pretty sure, from the quick glance I got when he turned around, that he was wearing a cravat. For a few minutes I was a little worried that Troy had hired the Scarlet Pimpernel as his defense attorney, a choice that seemed appropriate but destined for tragedy, given the historical record.

And then I heard him speak. He was concluding the cross-examination of a witness for the prosecution from the day before, some lady from a neighboring estate in Napa who had seen Troy arriving in the early morning the day after the murders. After a gentle introduction that seemed to repeat familiar ground, he asked her a series of quick questions that intimated, without proving, that she had unsuccessfully made a bid for Troy's attentions and was testifying against him out of spite. She was easily twice his age. The jury looked on with expressions of (sexist) distaste, and the stork concluded his cross-examination with breezy self-satisfaction.

Then there was a brief recess, and when the judge returned, Troy took the stand.

He was unrecognizable. His clothes were the same good clothes, and though he'd lost a bit of the tan, his face was the same handsome face. But it was empty. Not empty like a house where the people just stepped out for a minute, but empty like a still lake at dusk, where no one will go near the water and its ominous silence. He watched the stork closely, waiting for his cues. When prompted to give an explanation in his own words of the reasons for his actions, he began a well-edited and well-rehearsed description of his adolescence that included a lot of details meant to signal emotion but contained no actual emotion at all.

I found myself remembering the Troy who had blubbered into my shoulder, wondering where he had gone. Wondering if he'd ever been there, or if I had simply found myself drawn to a chemical concoction prepared by sadists and dressed in boys' clothing. And I thought about the question he had asked that night, the question of who he was. I couldn't accept the notion that there was nothing essential about him—nothing to carry through when the drops weren't there. But I had to admit that when he spoke about riding lessons and a bully of an older brother and emotional deprivation, all in a crafted stage voice, I didn't see even a filament of the Troy I knew.

The judge called a break at the end of the hour. I lifted my veil and looked at Troy, willing him to see me. He did at once. He held my gaze for a long time, and I could sense him doing the same thing I had just done: searching and searching for some shadow of the thing that had flickered between us, bright and warm and unexpected. Or maybe he wasn't looking for the thing that had appeared between us—maybe I had no idea what he was thinking.

I winked at him. He smiled. A little ripple chased across the lake, disturbing the surface but not the air of deadly calm. Then the waters were still again. His eyes hadn't changed. They drifted away to watch the jury returning to their seats.

He reminded me of someone, I realized. As he sat, expressionless and waiting, his eyes trained on the people who would determine his fate, I recalled waking up and seeing my mom sitting in bed, the sheets a scrunched knot around her. She sat staring at Calv's tidy desk. Hair rumpled, mouth set in a line. Her face was empty. No hunger or weariness or animating instinct of any kind.

No reasoning sense that the day lay before her, and that she had things to do in it and purposes to accomplish. No awareness that two people near her relied on her to be a steward, a fixed point of certainty, an answer to the question of why things mattered. I had first woken to see her that way years earlier, but in the last few months it had happened more and more often. Her thoughts were as clear as if she'd written them on her face: *There is no point. There is no point to any of this.*

This was the answer I'd been looking for, the answer eluding me and Cal for so long, the answer to *why*. Some people, like me, and Joey, and Cass, and Tabby, and Gao—most people, actually—manage to put something together for themselves in the absence of emotion that makes a bundle of fixed points, a cluster of principles and thoughts and habits that feels like a self. Gao has his moral compass. Cass and Tabby have the commitment to us and each other. Joey has a commitment to the idea of people mattering. I have Cal. But there are some people, like Troy and Mom, who, without the emotion, cannot make anything. There is nothing to tie together. They grasp at things ineffectually, like ghosts reaching for the belongings of the living, and their hands come up empty. They cannot hold on to anything.

Troy's eyes flickered as the judge returned to her seat, and I stood up to leave. I blew him a kiss when I got to the door, but I don't think he saw me.

The stork apparently did a masterful job. The trial took two weeks and Troy was acquitted—not, as I had thought, because his actions were construed as self-defense but, rather, because he was judged to have been out of his right mind, thanks to the drops, when the murders occurred. For a few days after his acquittal I half expected to find him on my doorstep—funds restored, emotions restored, relying on a regimen now of his own choosing. But that was a fantasy, and not just because he didn't show. It was a fantasy to think that once he'd encountered the emptiness he would be able to return to the places he'd once been, the places he'd wanted to be when he was that other Troy. He had been to the emotionless void. He was someone different now.

39

NATALIA

The lawyers took RealCorp apart piece by piece, and the process took much longer than Troy's trial. Most of the fragments probably ended up the way Glout did: broken edges sanded down, neatly placed in another corporation. His online profile told me he'd made head of R&D at PSA, Pearl Synthetic Affects, a quarter of a mile down the road from what had been RealCorp. I finally made myself go back to see him on the first of February. Cal was staying late with the Muses for a music lesson, and I had two hours free before meeting him. It was raining, the kind of rain that alternates showers and mist, showers and mist for days until everything smells of mildew. At least it wouldn't be a drought year. My long trench coat was pearled with water, and in the street beside the trolley rails, someone had set a paper boat to drift in a puddle.

Glout was expecting me. The receptionist sent me up to his office, and as I strolled down the corridor, his nearly bald head popped out of the doorway. "Natalia!" he said, as if waving me down in a crowded theater.

"Yup," I said, waving back. "I see you."

He was grinning like a bookie on payday when I reached his door. "Hi."

"Afternoon. I was wondering how you'd handled the shake-up. Looks like you landed on your feet."

His grin vanished. "It was pretty ugly, actually. I just happened to be on the winning side of it."

"How nice for you." I looked him in the eye. "I haven't had the chance to thank you in person for what you did. If you hadn't helped me, I wouldn't have found Cal. You saved his life. Thank you."

Glout blinked. "I'm not a rule breaker by nature. So it's hard when I'm given a rule and the rule is clearly wrong." He looked rueful. "I didn't feel good about any of it. The other kids, Calvino, the board. I'm sorry it took me so long to help you."

"You're good. Though if we ever have to do something like that again, we should work out some different codes."

He grinned again. "How's Cal? How are you?"

"Cal has found a coterie of retired teachers who dote on him."

"Ha! Excellent!"

"He feels as much as ever."

"That's very good to hear. And you?"

"I've got my job, and I have Cal. Everything's fine."

He nodded sagely. "Yes. Yes, I see," he said, like I'd explained something of importance.

We were silent.

"Has it happened again?" Glout asked me quietly.

I peered at his skeletal face, but there seemed to be nothing malicious or covetous there—only earnest interest. Still, I hesitated.

"I assume that's why you're here," Glout said. "Because of what happened when you woke Cal up."

I nodded. "I didn't think anyone knew about that other than me and Cal."

"The room has cameras."

"Of course."

"There was an inexplicable error that deleted the footage of those few minutes, in case you are wondering. So I'm afraid the significance of that encounter has been lost."

I looked at him. "Thank you," I said quietly.

His grin was back. "Well, out with it, Natalia."

I took a deep breath. "I had tears. I felt something—I'm sure it was real."

"I'm sure it was real as well."

"How is that possible? Is it . . . Is Cal . . . Is he contagious or something?"

Glout's grin widened. "Contagious. That's funny." Then he got very serious. "Can I do a little lecturing?"

"Sure."

"The early modern model of disease maintained that we were individual bodies in which cells interacted with one another and with the world, and that while we were porous, we were also discrete."

"Like gumdrops in a bowl. Or pills in a bottle."

"Sort of. More like a crowd of mushrooms growing on a forest floor."

"Okay. Yes, that makes sense."

"That paradigm has remained in place for a long time, but there are some, myself included, who think it is a faulty paradigm. They—we—think that, instead, the body is more like a cell than it is like a body."

"Uh . . ." I said.

"So, what I mean is that you know how things happening in your hand affect things in your brain, even though the two are not contiguous. When you touch something hot with your hand, your brain knows."

"Oh, I see."

"Yes—so people are connected by processes and systems that are not entirely perceptible to us. Some of them are perceptible. Some are not. And when changes occur in one place, there are effects elsewhere, too. We should think of ourselves not as separate organisms in a given place, but as belonging to a single organism. That is, all of us together make up one organism."

"Wow."

He smiled. "Neat, right?"

"I was going to say creepy."

"So the change Cal manifests is not contagious, but the change is likely both caused by change somewhere else and effecting change somewhere else. For all we know, you are the catalyst and Cal is the effect. Or it could be someone in Tibet. This is all still theoretical."

I nodded. "Okay," I said, after a while. "Can I ask for something?"

His eyes widened. "You want me to take a look?"

"If the results can maybe suffer the same kind of accident that your camera footage suffered."

He nodded eagerly. "Absolutely." He jumped up from his chair. Then he grabbed a few things from his desk and shooed me out the door. "This way," he said, pointing down the corridor. I walked beside him past two metal doors and then he unlocked the third on the right-hand side. We came into a small room with a white dome that looked like crystallized mosquito netting. Beneath it was a bed with a white sheet. One wall had screen decals, the other had a long, framed series of old punch cards from the early days of computing.

Glout pressed a button beside the screen decals that made the dome tilt like an opening clam shell. "Go ahead and lie on the bed," he said. "You can close your eyes and relax. You can even take a nap if you like."

"No thanks." I climbed onto the bed in my damp trench coat. The white dome slid back into place. From the inside, it was opaque. It was like looking up into the heavens in the Sierras: black night and hundreds of stars.

I heard Glout's voice from behind the dome. "This will take about half an hour."

"Okay," I said. "Are you going to make me imagine awful things? I'm not very good at imagining."

"Nope," he said cheerily. "Just watch the stars."

I did as he suggested. I watched the stars on the inside of Glout's dome, and I tried to relax. I thought about Cal at his music lesson. I thought about meeting him and Madeleine afterward and having tea. Then Cal and I would ride the bus back to Market Street and the train back to Oakland. Maybe we'd have dinner with Cass and Tabby and Joey. Maybe we'd read after dinner and I'd fall asleep in the armchair while Cal read until midnight with his flashlight. It would be a nice evening.

The dome whirred quietly and started lifting. "That's it?" I said.

"It was half an hour."

"Passed by quickly."

Glout was dancing from foot to foot like an antsy skeleton doing a jig.

"What is it?" I asked.

"Okay—well, you remember how I said once that the brain was like a network of roads, and a faded brain has lost its side roads?"

"I remember. Driving in a rut."

Glout grinned and took my hand. His bony grip was surprisingly strong, animated by excitement. "You're making new roads, Natalia. Little side roads. Not too many yet. They're narrow, but you can use them."

———

When I got to Madeleine's house, I waited outside for a little while. The rain had shifted to mist, and the bungalow before me looked like the warm woodcutter's cottage in a fairy tale, with smoke pouring from the chimney and fiddle music pouring out through the open door. Inside I could see yellow light, a short corridor painted blue, and, briefly, Madeleine's upright shoulders as she walked past with a cup in her hand. Then the music stopped, and I heard a peal of delighted laughter—Cal and his irrepressible, invincible joy, filling the house in the music's wake.

ACKNOWLEDGMENTS

I began this book in the summer of 2015, just before things got complicated. As I was starting the draft, I managed to slice off two fingertips. I typed with bandages the size of bratwurst for a while. In retrospect, that was the easy part. From what followed, I have a new sense of what it means to count on people, really count on people, and I'm tremendously grateful for the help of all shapes and sizes that allowed me to get through this period and, along the way, write this book.

Thank you to Dorian Karchmar for incisive reading, for the big picture, and for support far above and beyond the crafting of a book. I have felt your steady presence through every step of this. Thank you to Kathleen Nishimoto for insight and passion on multiple drafts; I felt most confidence in this book whenever I talked to you about it.

I feel very lucky that this book has benefitted from the talent and sensitivity of my editor, Kendra Levin. Thank you, among many other things, for your ability to envision a book on its own terms. I am grateful to Ken Wright, Maggie Rosenthal, Laura Stiers, Abigail Powers, and Krista Ahlberg for readings generous and precise. Thank you to

Nancy Brennan, Elaine Demasco, and Lindsey Andrews for designing a beautiful book that made me think about the content in new ways.

Several people gave me comments on all or part of the manuscript. Alex, Ben, Ed, John, Laya, Mark, and Tui of the Newton Writers Group offered encouragement and welcome critiques on the first few chapters. Pablo and Simon waded through complete (but very rough) drafts.

So many friends and colleagues helped to keep me going during these tough times. Sometimes an understanding word at the right moment made all the difference. My heartfelt thanks to all of you, and especially to Tina, Natalie, Bill, Karen, Kirsten, Arianne, Kevin, Franziska, Ginny, Sarah, Prasannan, Zack, Deborah, and Christina.

My parents, Martha Julia and Steve, not only read the draft, they continue to cheer, genuinely and invincibly, at the slightest piece of good news. Tom, thank you for the boundless enthusiasm. Alton, thank you for believing unconditionally. Rowan, thank you for your bright light in the darkness.

This book is dedicated to my brother, Oliver. The least of it is that you read this book multiple times and gave invaluable comments. Thank you for being the most steadfast, generous, and wise best friend.